An Ear for Murder

A Sara Baron Tuned In Mystery

by

Diane Weiner

For information, email Cozy Cat Press, cozycatpress@aol.com or visit our website at: www.cozycatpress.com

COZY CAT
PRESS

ISBN: 978-1-946063-99-1
Printed in the United States of America
Cover design by Paula Ellenberger
www.paulaellenberger.com

10 9 8 7 6 5 4 3 2 1

This book is dedicated to Laura Grigull for all her help, support and enthusiasm.

Chapter 1

Sara Baron's head ached from the stuffy heat inside the rental car and the thought of lying to her parents. Hoping the night air might ease the throbbing, she searched for the automatic window button while paying more attention to the road than she felt she should have to. *Did I pack aspirin in my purse*? It didn't matter. Her Coach bag had toppled over in a heap under the dashboard, out of her reach.

She exited the New York Thruway and snaked up the icy mountain road, creeping past road signs warning of deer and falling rocks. Her stomach growled, still set to San Francisco time.

The car slipped as if driving across a hockey rink. The frigid night air wasn't helping her headache as she'd hoped. As she raised the window, blinding headlights headed straight toward her.

She screeched on the brakes, forgetting that was not the thing to do when driving on ice. The car went into a skid. She felt the seat belt yank her back against the seat. Glass shattered. Metal scraped metal. Her heart thumped against her chest.

Time moved like newly tapped maple syrup as she unclenched her fingers one by one from their death grip around the steering wheel. *Breathe in through the nose, out through the mouth. In and out. You're safe now. What just happened? That truck slammed right into me!*

She stared at the truck in front of her windshield. She stormed out of the car, pulse throbbing like a metronome, as a man in a puffy parka and bright ski cap exited the cab and strode toward her.

"Why didn't you watch where you were going! You weren't even in your own lane!"

Sara's anger welled like magma. "Me? It was your fault. You hit me!"

"What were you doing? Putting on mascara? Texting? Checking Instagram?"

"Are you kidding me? I'm calling the police."

"Don't bother. I already did. You broke my headlight." He pointed to shards of glass on the ground.

She pointed to her rental. "Headlight? Half my front bumper looks like an accordion."

"Rental car, huh?" He kicked the front wheel. "No snow tires. You should've taken an airport shuttle."

"And you should go back to the cave you came out of." Her anger was about to erupt when... *Whoa*! From around the bend, a car whizzed by, avoiding the vehicles but aiming right at Sara. She felt a strong arm yank her out of the car's path. "Where's the fire?" she shouted after the driver, who by now had disappeared around the curve of the mountain. She regained her breath and heart rate for the second time that evening.

"You okay?" asked Parka man.

"I'm fine. Just a bit shaken." His expressive brown eyes momentarily softened.

Momentarily. For half a second.

"He's a worse driver than you are. I wish I'd gotten the plate number, or at least a decent description."

"It was a dark blue, Buick Le Sabre. Late model. I can write down the plate number. Oh, and I think he's got a hole in his radiator."

"You saw a hole? In the radiator? In the dark?"

"Heard, not saw. You didn't hear the high pitched whine as the car approached us?"

He shook his head. She knew he'd underestimated her. Jerk.

He walked around his truck, then bent down and inspected her bumper. "We don't have to go through insurance. There's a body shop in town..."

"Right next to the Greek diner. I know." She knew because it was the only one in town. "I grew up here." The thought of her insurance premiums rising made her stomach churn. She was already stressed about covering her bills. "Yeah, okay. We can go over in the morning." She headed back to her car.

"Where do you think you're going?"

Dark road. Girl alone with a stranger, crippled car. She'd seen enough crime shows to where her neck hairs stood on end.

She swallowed, then stood up tall. "The police will be here any minute."

"No, I didn't really call them."

"I've got a gun in my pocket," she lied.

"Sure you do. I need your name and contact info. In case you're a no show tomorrow." He retrieved a pad and pen from his truck.

"Sara Baron." She scribbled down her info and demanded the same from him. He shoved a business card into her hand. *Travis Jennings, Physical Therapist.* "If you're a no show, I'm calling the police and my insurance company." She got back in the car, praying it would start up. It did. She pulled away first, shaking her head.

Putting on mascara. Who does that in the car? Instagram? Do I look like I'm twelve? Jerk.

She passed the diner, the mom and pop bookstore, and the hardware store that gave the Home Depot the next town over a run for its money.

Stay awake, Sara. With the adrenaline rush gone, her eyes felt like lead curtains. She opened the window an inch. *Almost home.*

Her phone vibrated.

"Mom? I'll be there soon. I'm fine, just a bit of traffic. No, I'm not angry. Ten minutes max. Start the coffee. Yes, I'm alone. I've got to go; my phone is dying." *Patience, Sara. Breathe in, breathe out.*

Did I stuff the Excedrin in there? She felt for the black case next to her, glad she'd secured it with the passenger seatbelt. Recalling the mascara comment, she stopped herself from pawing through it with one hand while steering with the other. She continued down the familiar road and soon arrived at the brick split-level in which she'd been raised.

The hand-painted mailbox at the end of the driveway read *Patty and Bob Baron.* The front door flung open before she could turn off the engine. Her mother, in shirtsleeves, ran down the driveway.

"Sara, honey! I'm so glad you're home."

Sara heard the excitement in her mom's voice, saw the sparkle in her sea-blue eyes, and smelled the faint scent of Ivory soap as her mom embraced her with a bear hug. She'd needed this many times in the past months.

"Mom, what are you doing out here without a coat? Go back inside. You're going to get sick."

Her mother stepped back and looked at the rental. "Sara, what happened? What happened to the car?"

"It's nothing. Just a fender bender."

"Are you hurt? I'm going to bring you to the emergency room."

"No, I'm okay. You should see the other guy." Her attempt at humor fell flat.

Sara's father, a few pounds heavier than the last time she was home, caught up to them. He bent down to examine the car. "What happened to your bumper?"

"Fender bender." It didn't look as bad as she'd initially thought. "Let's go inside. You have any food? I'm starving."

Bob Baron pushed up his bifocals and circled the car. Seeming satisfied, he said, "I'll grab your bags. Pop, open the trunk." She gave him a kiss, getting a whiff of Old Spice.

"Leave them. It's freezing out here. Let's get inside." She hugged the black case beneath her jacket and grabbed her purse from the car floor. Home, sweet home.

The afghan-covered floral sofa and worn leather recliner were exactly where they were the last time she'd visited, the magazine rack still stuffed with old issues of *Reader's Digest*. A log crackled in the fireplace.

"I smell cookies." She'd eat cardboard about now just to soak up the gurgling acid in her stomach.

"Your favorite. Gingerbread. Come, grab a plate," said her mom. "I'll pour you some milk."

"So, how's work?" asked her dad. "I heard your orchestra play Mahler's *Fourth* on the radio the other day. You sounded good."

"I had a couple of good reeds. Had. Past tense. This cold weather will be the death of them. While I'm home, can you replace my sticky octave key?"

"Of course, but you know how to do it."

"Where's Grandpa?"

"He turned in early."

"Does he have any clue we're planning his birthday party?"

"I don't think so. Don't go letting it slip."

"I came across the country for this. My lips are sealed."

Sara's mom put a second plate of cookies on the table. Like Sara, she was girl-next-door pretty, with honey-brown hair and a wide smile.

"I ran into Jessie the other day. He's put on some muscle. He's not the skinny kid he was back in high school and he's making good money as a plumber."

"Is there such a thing as making bad money? Mom, I haven't talked to him since the senior prom. How's your new job?"

Her father cleared his throat. "Your mom got *Employee of the Month*."

"Wow! Congratulations."

"That police station would be upside down without me managing it." Her eyes twinkled. "Such a sweet group of boys. And that Detective Lambert …easy on the eyes. Smart too. You'd like him."

"I'm glad it's working out. If anyone knows a thing or two about being organized, it's you. Have you heard from Scott?"

"He's not loving being stationed in the middle of a desert. Who would? I hope his tour goes by quickly, that's all I can say."

"I miss him."

"We all do." Her dad stood up. "I'll go get your bags."

"Wait, Dad."

"I put a new quilt on the bed, and if you need an extra blanket, there's one on the closet shelf. Oh, and I bought a new down comforter at the church craft fair last week." Her mom started for the stairs. "We've been meaning to replace the faded pink wallpaper in your room. Maybe after Christmas."

"Mom, I'm not staying here."

Her mother stopped in her tracks. "Why not?"

"I'm house-sitting for Ellie. She left for London yesterday and asked me to babysit her cat. I thought I told you on the phone."

"But, we were looking forward to you staying here." Her mom sounded like a whiny toddler.

Her dad cleared his throat. "You can bring the cat here."

"With Grandpa's allergies? I can't do that to him. I'll be right around the corner. You'll see plenty of me."

"You'll only be here for a few weeks."

She put her arm around her mother's shoulder. "We can go do some shopping tomorrow. Have you bought the decorations yet?"

She folded her arms across her chest. "I have to work."

"Then over the weekend. I'd better go. I'm so tired I could fall asleep standing up about now. I'll come by the shop in the morning, Dad. And, Mom, are you making lasagna anytime soon?"

She smiled. "Got the ingredients waiting for you. Come by for dinner tomorrow."

Sara kissed them goodbye. "See you tomorrow."

Thankfully, Ellie's house was only five minutes away. Sara wanted nothing more than to crawl into bed under a fluffy warm comforter. She pulled her car into a driveway lightly glazed with recent ice. In her headlights, she could see how much the yellow aluminum siding had faded since she'd last visited. The street was dark, with the exception of a light in the window of the house next door.

She grabbed her bags and trudged up the porch steps, her back and neck aching from the long plane ride and hours spent driving. Her hand was acting up. Gripping the bag was an effort. She bent down and picked up the tattered welcome mat and retrieved the key. Fumbling with her gloved fingers, she inserted it into the lock, but the door pushed open with a gentle jiggle of the knob. Ellie had always been the one to carry mace and keep the car doors locked when driving. Why had she left for Europe without triple checking that she'd locked up the house?

Sara put down her bags and barely stopped herself from tripping over something. She flicked on the hall light. *What's the coat rack doing on the floor?* While odd, she assumed it had toppled under the weight of the winter jackets still clinging to the hooks. She proceeded to turn on the living room lamp. Overturned couch cushions, books littering the floor—she felt panic wash over her.

"Ellie? Are you here?" She didn't expect an answer. Ellie was supposed to have left for Europe yesterday. "Ellie?" *Maybe she's upstairs.*

The stairs creaked with each step. She checked the bathroom. The contents of the medicine cabinet had spilled into the sink and onto the tile floor. The hair on the back of her neck tingled.

She saw light shining through the bottom of the master bedroom door. She gently pushed it open.

"Ellie!" she screamed. Ellie was on the floor, face down.

Sara bent down and prayed she'd hear breathing. "Ellie!" She couldn't bring herself to touch her, afraid of feeling a cold body. Nothing. No movement. No breath. "Oh my God!"

Chapter 2

Phone. Where's my phone? In my purse. Downstairs. Reluctant to leave Ellie's side, she reached for the old fashioned rotary on the nightstand. Dead. Probably hadn't been connected since Ellie's parents lived here. No choice but to run downstairs.

Sara rummaged through her bag. When she finally found what she was looking for, her heart sank. Dead. The long trip had taxed the battery to its max. Why hadn't she packed the portable charger?

She ran outside, subconsciously remembering the light in the window next door and made a beeline for the neighbor's house.

"Help! Open the door. It's an emergency!" She pounded so hard her knuckles hurt.

A cappuccino-skinned man wearing flannel pajama bottoms and a faded, holey Seattle Seahawks tee shirt flung open the door.

"What's the emergency? I just got to sleep."

"It's...it's my friend next door. Ellie. I'm supposed to be house sitting. She was supposed to be in Europe. The door. It wasn't locked. She's on the floor. She isn't breathing."

"Calm down. Did you call the police?"

"No. My phone. It's not charged."

He grabbed his phone. She looked at his face for the first time since arriving. Looked into eyes the color of chestnuts. "Not you! You're the man in the truck."

He blinked. "And you're the twit who skidded on the ice because you were swiping through Instagram."

She had no choice. She needed his help. "I..."

"I know. You're sorry. Come on. Let's help Ellie."

Infuriated over his smugness, she followed him out the back door and into Ellie's. "She's in the bedroom."

He flew up the stairs two at a time, and headed directly to the master bedroom. She later wondered how he knew the layout of the house so well.

In a flash, he was kneeling beside her, putting his ear near her face, his fingers on her wrist. "911, this is an emergency. A woman is dead. Looks like it was a break in. Yes, I'm sure. She isn't breathing and there's no pulse. No, I don't think anyone is still in the house. Okay. Hurry."

"Are they sending an ambulance?"

"Yes. And the police. Did you see or hear anyone else in the house?"

"I don't think so. I was focused on Ellie. Besides, if someone was here, they'd have taken off when I went for help."

"Did you see a vehicle in the driveway? Or pass one speeding away?"

"No. Wait."

"What?"

"Remember the car that whizzed almost killing us earlier? The Buick?"

"Shortly after you crashed into my truck."

"Yeah, after you slammed into my car. I think I heard it. The high-pitched whine...I'm almost certain it was the same car."

"This could have happened hours ago."

"Why would anyone try to hurt Ellie? She wasn't even supposed to be here. She was supposed to leave yesterday."

"If someone knew she was planning on being away, maybe this was a robbery gone bad. You didn't touch anything, did you?"

"I turned on the lights. I grabbed the bedside phone. Why?"

"Fingerprints, DNA. Leads for the police to follow."

She paced back and forth. There was a carry-on bag on the bed, and a laundry basket with folded clothes. *I'll bet she was packing for her trip. But a carry-on? For an extended trip? And she told me she was leaving yesterday.*

"He must have been waiting here for her."

"What makes you say that?"

"She hadn't turned around. She was hit from behind. Looks like she was in the process of packing. And the drapes right there by the nightstand are messed up. I'll bet he was hiding there." She pointed to the other set of drapes. "See how those others are neatly tied back?"

"Maybe she was just too preoccupied with packing to worry about the drapes."

"What's taking the police so long?"

"Neither the station nor the community hospital is around the corner, plus the roads are slick. They're careful. They wouldn't risk skidding on the ice by speeding, right?"

Jerk. With a capital J. "There's no murder weapon."

"Maybe he took it with him. Why leave evidence behind?"

"Her jewelry is lying on the dresser, and her purse is on the bed. It wasn't a robbery gone bad."

"Pure conjecture."

"When the police get here, you'll see I'm right." She wiped her eyes. "You knew Ellie?"

"Yeah. Obviously, we were neighbors. I'd see her outside shoveling the walk or getting the mail. Didn't know her well. I've only lived here less than a year."

"Where did you move from?"

He hesitated. "The Chicago area."

Fueled by adrenaline, Sara paced back and forth. Her legs felt like Jell-O. She'd never seen a dead body before. Even at the few funerals she'd attended, she could never bring herself to peer into the casket. This was Ellie, her friend. She couldn't wrap her mind around the idea that her friend was…dead.

"Where's the ambulance? What's taking so long?"

"It's only been a few minutes. They'll be here. Sit down. You're contaminating evidence walking around in those boots."

"I don't want to sit. I want the ambulance to come. I want the EMTs to say it was a mistake, that she's not dead. I want Ellie to sit up and say this is all a big misunderstanding."

"I think I hear sirens. Yes, it's them." He ran outside to meet the ambulance. When they came in, she heard him say, "She's upstairs in the master bedroom."

Sara followed them up the steps, watching as they rolled her gently onto her back and tried CPR. Ellie's eyes were open. *She looks scared. What was she thinking in those last moments? Did she know her attacker?* She felt vomit rising in her throat.

"Ma'am, there's nothing we can do. I'm sorry."

She wiped her mouth with her coat sleeve. "Then take her away. Don't leave her here like this."

"We have to wait for the medical examiner. Why don't you wait downstairs?"

Sara heard another siren. Before she could get her legs to move, the police came upstairs and started asking questions. When did Sara find her? Was she sure of the time? Did she see anyone in the house? Had she touched anything?

"Earlier tonight, a Buick whizzed past us on the road leading away from here. I thought it was strange. Where was he going in such a hurry, you know? Then I

could swear I heard it again, when I was in the bedroom with Ellie."

"You say it was a Buick?"

"A Le Sabre. Blue. I can tell you the plate number."

"Great. That's helpful. Now, why were you here tonight?"

"I was supposed to house sit and watch her cat. She was supposed to leave yesterday, for London. The house was a mess. Ellie wasn't messy."

"Ma'am, how did you get inside?"

"She'd left me a key under the mat, but the door wasn't locked. She always locked the door. Are you sure she's dead?"

"Come downstairs. Is there someone we can call for you?"

"My parents live here." She certainly didn't want to wake her parents with this news. "I have to watch the cat. Where's Panther?"

"Do you want us to call them for you?"

"No, I can't bring the cat home. My grandfather's allergic." Words seemed to float in the air, like the speech bubbles in comic strips.

The officer's voice was gentle. "Ma'am, this is now a crime scene. I'm afraid you can't stay here. There's a motel about a mile down the road."

The neighbor interjected. "I have a spare room downstairs. You can stay with me tonight.

It locks from the inside. It's practically morning anyhow."

*Locks from the inside? Stay with that arrogant piece of...*Too exhausted to protest, she followed him next door. "What's your name again?"

"Travis. Travis Jennings. And you?"

"Sara Baron."

Although the night air stung her cheeks, she felt somewhat better as soon as she walked outside. Ellie's parents! Someone had to call them. She had no idea how to reach them. Last she heard, they were doing missionary work in South America.

"Panther!" How did she forget the cat! She ran back toward the house.

"Hey, where are you going?" She heard Travis's boots crunching in the snow behind her.

"I have to get the cat."

"I'll check upstairs; you check downstairs. What's does it look like?"

"I don't know. Whiskers, four paws...It's a cat."

When they reached the house, she ran inside. She could hear the police buzzing around upstairs. "Panther. Come here, kitty."

She looked in the kitchen, in the downstairs bathroom, behind the sofa...She was beginning to feel panicky. *What if Panther ran outside in all the commotion? I have to find him.* The least she could do for Ellie was to watch over her beloved pet.

Then she opened the door leading to the garage. "Panther, are you in here?" She flicked on the light and spotted Ellie's Nissan. Sara glanced at the back seat. No cat.

She popped open the trunk. No luggage? She couldn't imagine going away for six months with only an overnight bag, having herself paid for two extra bags for her own flight from San Francisco.

She scanned the garage, spying a large suitcase perched on top of the dryer, price tag still attached to the handle. Unzipping it, she found three smaller suitcases inside, nested like Russian Marushka dolls. *I'll bet she bought this set for her trip. Why's it out here?*

A cat screeched from under the car, a black arrow flying through the open door and into the kitchen. Putting aside her superstition about black cats, she called, "Panther, come here, baby." After some gentle coaxing, Panther let her pick him up. The door squeaked open.

"Ma'am, you can't be in here. It's a crime scene, like we told you." The officer's voice was a bit less gentle than before.

"I just had to get the cat."

Travis walked up behind him. "We're going now, officer."

He led her back outside. "Let's park your car in my driveway."

She'd forgotten the case was inside. She prayed it hadn't been in the cold too long.

"What do you have there?"

"My oboe. It looks like a clarinet but…"

"But it's thinner and uses a double reed. Do I look like a Neanderthal? I love classical music."

"I'm impressed. Most people have never even heard of an oboe."

Travis drove while she cradled Panther and her oboe on her lap. They were in his driveway before the heat even kicked on. She followed him into the house.

"The bed is made up already, and there's a spare blanket in the closet."

"You have guests often?" She had no idea why that came out of her mouth.

"Not yet. I rented this place furnished. All the beds were made up when I moved in and no one's been in that room since."

"Thank you for letting me stay. I'll call in the morning, and see if the motel allows pets."

"Do you want something to drink? I've got milk and soda. Maybe even Kool-Aid."

She'd had enough of his sarcasm. "No, thanks. I just want to go to sleep."

Chapter 3

In the morning, sunlight streamed through the window. For a moment, Sara couldn't remember where she was. Panther jumped up on the bed, nudging her with his head as if to push her out of bed to get him breakfast.

"Poor baby. You must be starving!" She pulled on her flannel robe and made her way into the kitchen, following the aroma of fresh coffee.

"Travis? Are you up yet?" She saw a lonely note on the refrigerator door, held in place by a single magnet advertising a pizza delivery place. *At work. Help yourself to food.*

He'd attached the same business card he'd shoved into her palm last night—*Travis Jennings, Physical Therapist.* Panther meowed and rubbed against her legs.

"Sorry, baby." She realized she didn't have cat food and the nearest grocery store was twenty minutes away. She pulled on a pair of sweat pants and a flannel shirt. "I'll be right back."

The air was brisk, despite the sunshine. Looking across at Ellie's house in the morning light, it was hard to imagine the horror that had occurred there. She pictured Ellie lying on the floor. She shuddered. *You can do this. Breathe in and out, in and out.* She hustled across the yard to the porch and trembled, not sure she could make herself go inside. *Panther has to eat. Poor thing. I wonder if he knows Ellie isn't coming back.* She took a deep breath, and reached into her coat pocket for the key she'd retrieved from under the mat last night.

She felt like a criminal, ducking under the crime scene tape. Ellie had said on the phone she'd leave the food on the counter, but whatever had been on the counter had been swept onto the floor in the ruckus. She didn't see cat food.

The pantry. Maybe in there. Cans and paper goods rolled out in an avalanche as soon as she opened the door. On the floor, behind the boxes of cereal and pasta noodles, she spotted a nearly full bag of Purina Cat Chow. What had someone been searching for last night? Had they found it, or would they be back?

She heard a door slam. She froze, unable to breathe. She wasn't alone. Someone was in the house and like a fool, she hadn't taken her phone with her. She heard the sound of a computer booting up and saw light shining from the room. Like a bigger fool, she crept toward the den, hoping to catch a glimpse of the intruder, Ellie's killer in all probability, without getting caught.

The door den door was ajar, and peeking in, she saw a man in a hoodie sticking a jump drive into Ellie's computer. Taking a step closer, the floor boards squeaked. The man turned toward the door. Heart beating wildly, she shot herself out the front door like a bullet, never pausing to look back. When she reached Travis's house, she quickly locked the door, then ran to check the other door to be sure it too was secured. Had the intruder seen her? When she'd caught her breath, she called the police, who promised to be right over.

After she hung up, she realized she'd been hugging the bag of cat food. Poor Panther still hadn't eaten. "Here, Panther. Let's find you a bowl." In the kitchen cabinets she found a brand new Tupperware container with the lid still attached, and two shiny white mugs. She poured food for Panther, and a cup of coffee for herself. The warm cup soothed her hands. She hadn't noticed the emptiness in her stomach until she sat down at the table.

Travis said in his note to help herself to food, so she peeked in the fridge. A quart of nearly expired fat-free milk, English muffins, peanut butter, a few bottles of imported beer … *This is a bachelor pad if I've ever seen one.* She popped an English muffin into the pristine toaster. She couldn't help snooping through the remaining cabinets to occupy her time while she waited for the police.

One plain white plate, one bowl, and two medium sized glasses, lost in the ample cabinets. Travis was easily in his mid to late thirties and this was all he had on the shelves? She wished her own cabinets looked like that. Back in San Francisco, she couldn't fit all her mugs in her kitchen cabinet when they all happened to be clean at the same time—which wasn't all that often.

She heard the patrol car pull into the driveway and ran to open the door. "I'm glad you got here so quickly. Come in."

"You said someone was in the house across the way? The house that's still a crime scene?"

"Yes. I know I shouldn't have gone over, but the poor cat was starving. I just ran over to find cat food."

"And someone was there?"

"I heard a door, then heard a computer booting up. I peeked in the den and saw a man in a hoodie inserting a jump drive into the computer."

"Can you describe him?"

"Not really. The hoodie was cinched around his head. He was wearing jeans and boots with metal heels. Around my height, maybe an inch or so taller."

"Metal heels?"

"I heard him walk across the tile."

"Are you sure it was a man?"

"Well, come to think of it, I assumed so, but it could have been a woman, I guess."

"Anything else you can remember?"

She thought for a moment. "Not right now."

"We'll go over and check it out. Maybe we'll be lucky and get prints."

"I doubt it. He was wearing black, leather gloves."

"Stay inside, lock the doors. Call if you see him return to the house."

"I will. Thanks." She saw him out, locking the door as instructed.

Ellie had something someone wanted. Is that why she was killed? She couldn't stop thinking about last night. Maybe the killer was caught by surprise when he went to search for whatever it was he wanted last night. He didn't expect Ellie to be there. Or he didn't care if she was. Ellie was going to London for six months. How was she planning to do that with an overnight bag? And she was supposed to have left the day before yesterday.

Ellie's poor parents! She had to figure out how to contact them. Knowing they were 'somewhere in South America' didn't give her much to go on. She should have asked the police if they could help locate them.

She retrieved her phone from her purse. Still dead. She'd completely forgotten she needed to charge it, and didn't feel like digging through her suitcases to find it. Surely Travis had a charger lying around here somewhere.

She took a bite of her breakfast, then pulled open more kitchen drawers. Most were completely empty. She poured herself a glass of water. When she went to carry it to the table, it slipped from her hand, shattering on the stone tile. *Not now, please, I can't deal with this now.* She only had six months to get this under control. If things weren't better by then…

She swept up the mess. In her own house, she'd always left a charger by her bed. She climbed the steps to the master bedroom. The layout of this house was identical to Ellie's, undoubtedly constructed by the same builder back when housing developments took off.

Travis's room had as much character as a room at a chain hotel. No photos on the dresser, bed made up with a non-descript beige comforter…no shoes all over the floor or gym clothes in a heap, like at Brandon's place.

She saw the charger on the nightstand and bent down to unplug it. She heard footsteps behind her.

"What are you doing in my room?"

Sara shrieked. She looked up at Travis, standing at the edge of the bed, looking as imposing as a storybook giant.

"I…I thought you'd gone to work."

"I left my agenda book. I invite you to stay here and the minute I'm gone you snoop through my things?"

She stood up, charger in hand. "Absolutely not. I was looking for a charger. My phone's been dead since yesterday."

Travis's face softened. "I'm sorry I overreacted."

"You know what? I'm going to drive over to the Ramada Inn and see if they're okay with pets. I'll be out of your hair in a flash."

"No, wait. I said I was sorry. I'm a very private person and I guess my guard is always up. Stay. I want you to."

She absolutely would have gone to a hotel, in spite of his apology, if she felt she could afford it. This six-month leave didn't come with a paycheck and she'd already lost sleep wondering how to cover her bills and rent in one of the most expensive cities in the country. When Ellie said she could stay here rent free, it was a

Godsend. She'd been able to sublet her tiny San Francisco apartment to a visiting conductor.

"Yeah, okay. But only because my choices are limited. As soon as the police are done at Ellie's I'll be out of your hair."

"Grab the charger and let's get your phone juiced up."

She followed him downstairs to the kitchen and plugged in her phone. When it came alive after a few minutes, she saw she had a few voicemails. The first was from her mother. She'd called to see if Sara had gotten settled in and reminded her to come over for dinner.

The next message chilled her down to her bones. It was from Ellie, and had been left yesterday evening. *Sara.* The voice was barely a whisper. *Don't come, it's dangerous. I think someone is in the house. If anything happens to me, find the…*

"Find the what?" Sara replayed the message. "Find the what, Sara?"

"What's wrong?"

"Ellie left me a message last night. She thought someone was in the house. Listen." She put the phone on speaker. Chills ran up her back as she listened. The killer was in the house when Ellie tried to call her.

"Find the what? Do you know what she was referring to?"

"Not at all. I can't believe I didn't have my phone charged. Maybe I could have saved her."

"How? It's a good thing whoever it was had gone before you showed up."

"I could have called the police…I could have…"

"Stop. If the killer was in the house already when she left that message, the police wouldn't have made it in time."

"Speaking of the police, an officer just left. I went over to Ellie's to find cat food and there was an intruder snooping in the den, trying to get info from her computer."

"You didn't lead with that?"

"You didn't give me a chance. I need to get this phone message to them."

"Come on, I'll drive you."

"Don't you have to be at work?"

"Both of my morning patients canceled. I'm free until after lunch."

Chapter 4

Travis parallel parked in front of the old Hudsonville Police Station in the center of town. Sara had almost forgotten that her mother had recently started working there. *Mom is going to freak out over what happened last night.*

Her mother spotted her the moment she entered the station. "Sara, what are you doing here? Is everything okay?"

It felt impossible to soften the news. "Mom, it isn't. When I got to Ellie's last night, the place had been ransacked and Ellie...I found Ellie dead on her bedroom floor."

"Oh my God! That was Ellie's house? *You* found her? The officers have been buzzing around all morning talking about this case. It's the first murder most have ever seen."

"I need to talk to a detective. Who's in charge of the case?"

"There's only one detective on site. Detective Lambert. I mentioned him last night. Come on back."

Detective Lambert reminded Sara of an actor she'd seen in a traveling production of *Book of Mormon*. His neat hair and clean-shaven face made him look younger than he probably was, given he'd had time to climb the ranks to detective.

He stood up from behind his desk. "Can I help you? I'm Detective Lambert."

"Sara Baron. And this is um, Ellie's neighbor, Travis Jennings."

Travis shook his hand. "Ellie Rossi was my neighbor. The officer last night said to come by and give a statement."

Detective Lambert grabbed a legal pad off his desk. Sara had expected something more technologically up to date. An iPad, maybe?

"Tell me what you know."

"I was supposed to cat sit for Ellie. When I got to her house last night, it had been ransacked. There was stuff all over the floor. I went upstairs to her bedroom and she was lying on the floor. I saw blood. It looked like she'd been hit on the back of her head."

"Did you see a heavy, blunt object on the floor or on the bed? Something that could have been the murder weapon?"

"Come to think of it, no. Then again, I was focused on Ellie and may have overlooked it."

"What did you do after you discovered her on the floor?"

"I bent down to see if she was breathing. She wasn't, so I tried to call 911. My phone was dead, so I ran next door to Travis's house. I'd noticed a light on earlier. We called from there."

"Did you go back to the house?"

"Yes. We waited there for the police. The ambulance came and the EMT's said she was dead." Her eyes teared and the detective handed her a tissue. "My phone was dead. This morning, I charged it and there was a message from Ellie. She said someone was in the house and I shouldn't come. It was dangerous." She fished her phone out of her purse. "Here. Listen." She played it on speaker.

"Find the what? Do you know what she was referring to?"

"No, I have no idea. The way the house looked, whoever killed her was looking for something. I don't think they found it."

"What makes you say that?"

"I ran over to the house this morning to get food for Ellie's cat. Someone was in there, booting up Ellie's computer. I called an officer. He made a report."

"Were you harmed?"

"No. After I saw him, I ran back to Travis's house and called the police."

"I'll get the report later. Let's get back to the murder for the moment."

The detective scribbled notes on the yellow pad. "What time did you arrive at her house?"

"It was around 11:00. My flight got in from San Francisco last evening. I visited my parents for a bit, then went over."

"The message was left at 7:05 p.m."

"I wish I'd heard it earlier. I could have prevented this." She started to cry.

"No, there's no way of determining that. If the killer was in the house, it's better you weren't there." He looked at Travis. "You said you live next door. Did you notice anything out of the ordinary?"

"I'd been out that evening. As a matter of fact, Sara rammed into my truck last night on my way home. I checked to see that she was okay."

Sara said, "On the way to my parents, Travis crashed into my rental car with his pick-up truck. He didn't have snow tires." *I'll bet he didn't catch that I'd noticed, after he accused me of not being prepared for winter driving.* "A car flew by us in a big hurry."

"I rescued her just in time," said Travis.

"We were nearly run over, but I'd heard it approaching and was about to run to safety when Travis yanked me out of the road. My arm's still sore where he grabbed it. The car came from the direction of Ellie's house. Do you think it was the killer fleeing the scene?"

"Hard to say. Did you get a make and model? A license number, maybe?"

"It was a late model blue Buick Le Sabre. Had the redesigned back windows." She grabbed the legal pad off the detective's desk and wrote down the plate number. "And the engine made a high pitched sound which got louder as it accelerated toward us."

"You caught all that in the dark?"

"Travis had those big old truck headlights on the whole time. The glass had shattered but they still worked."

"Quite the eye for details. Have you ever done detective work?"

"No, but I'm a musician, and I grew up making handmade oboes for the family business. It's all about paying attention to details."

Travis said, "Wait. I remember something. Two days ago I knocked on Ellie's door. She'd borrowed my snow blower and I needed it back. Her window was open and I heard her arguing on the phone with someone."

"Her window was open in the middle of winter?"

Sara said, "Ellie's mom used to yell at her for sleeping with the window open in the dead of winter when I slept over there."

"Mr. Jennings, do you remember any of the conversation?"

"Something about she didn't feel safe. She said something about changing her mind. I don't know what she meant by it."

"Okay. I'll put this together with the evidence from the crime scene and I'm confident we'll find your friend's killer. Thank you for coming in. It gives us a starting point."

"You're welcome," said Sara.

"Detective, if the killer didn't find what he was looking for, do you think he'll be back yet again? What if he comes after Sara? I mean, she's staying at my house for now."

"He'd have no reason to know who Sara is and that Miss Rossi called her, right?"

"I don't think he saw me, but I can't be sure he wasn't watching when I ran away."

"He wouldn't know about the call," said Travis. "Unless he overheard it when he was in the house, before he killed her."

Sara said, "Thanks for that, Travis. Detective, what about her phone? Did you find Ellie's cellphone?"

He shuffled papers on his desk, and flipped through a report. "No phone was entered into evidence. It must not have been in the house."

"Then she is in danger," said Travis. "He'll know Ellie called Sara for help right before he killed her."

"Not necessarily. Even if he took the phone, he'd need the password to get in. My guess is if he took it, it's at the bottom of the Hudson River by now. If you think of anything else or see anything out of the ordinary…"

"You mean like someone following me?" said Sara. She felt a cocktail of fear and anger welling up behind her eyes.

"Just be vigilant," said the detective. "Maybe you should stay with your parents. Now, let me get to work on this."

On the way out, Sara's mother grilled her about what happened.

"Sara, you may be in danger. You have to stay with us for the two weeks."

"I can't. I'm cat sitting, remember? I'm going to try the Ramada Inn." *Not that I can afford it.*

"The security's terrible there. Just last month there was a robbery right in the lobby. I was here when the call came in."

Travis spoke up. "She can stay with me as long as she'd like. I have a spare room."

Sara could see her mother's wheels turning. A strong, handsome, single young man…

"I'd feel better if she was with you," said Patty Baron. It seemed to put her at ease. She segued into, "By the way, I'm making lasagna tonight for Sara. It's her favorite. You're welcome to come over for dinner."

"Mom, he's a busy man…"

"I'd like that. Haven't had a home cooked meal in…I can't even remember when." He looked at his Apple watch. "Sara, let's get your car and stop at the body shop before I go to the hospital. See you tonight Mrs. Baron."

"I can take care of myself, you know. There's a bed and breakfast past the Ramada Inn. I'll try them."

"If you want to throw away money when I've offered you a free place to stay, go right ahead. But I doubt they take pets."

She knew he was probably right. Who'd want a cat scratching the legs of an antique bed? When they got back to the house, Sara winced at the mangled bumper, then followed Travis to the body shop. They parked in the gravel lot and found the owner.

Travis took the lead. "We had a bit of an accident last night."

The owner, a middle-aged man wearing coveralls under his jacket said, "The roads were slick last night. Got to know how to handle them."

Travis smirked at Sara. She wanted to punch him. "How much will it cost to repair the bumper?"

"I've gotta take a look. I should have an estimate for you later this afternoon."

"It's a rental."

Your rental insurance should cover it. Why don't you take it back to the agency?"

"I rented it at the airport, two hours away. What am I going to drive in the meantime?"

Travis said, "You said Ellie's car was in the garage. Do you have the key? She won't be needing it."

"That's a horrible thing to say."

"I'm just being practical. The battery will die if it sits idle in the garage all winter."

The mechanic seemed to sense her unease. "There's a car rental on the outskirts of town. They even deliver. Call your insurance. They'll take care of the repairs and get you a new one."

Another rental. More money. I'd been planning to use Ellie's car while she was gone. She even left the key in the ignition. Or I can live with the bumper until I return it.

"What about my truck?" said Travis.

"The broken headlight? Come by after lunch and I'll replace it for you. That dent in the bumper doesn't look recent."

"It's not. Just fix the headlight."

So the only damage I did was shattering his headlight. Love how he made me think I'd messed up his bumper. Jerk. She made a face at him, then turned to the body shop owner.

"Can I ask you something?"

"Shoot."

"What would cause a car engine to make a high pitched whine? One that got louder as the car accelerated?"

"Could be the transmission, a loose belt, a problem in the exhaust system. Hard to say without seeing the car."

"Thanks. We'll talk to you this afternoon."

After Travis dropped her off at his house, Sara scrounged around for something to make for lunch. Doubting Uber Eats had made its debut in Hudsonville, she reluctantly slapped together a peanut butter sandwich on a raisin English muffin. She'd have to pick up some staples to fill the fridge and she needed a litter box for Panther. On the surgically clean counter, every crumb showed. She swept up the remnants of her sandwich and rinsed the plate before heading to the store.

Although she hadn't been back to Hudsonville since last Christmas, nothing much had changed. Her mother told her there was a new Starbucks in the strip mall heading out of town. She must have passed it last night, not noticing in the dark. She pulled into the ShopRite parking lot and grabbed a cart.

Canned vegetables on sale. Guess they don't have green markets in the middle of winter like they do back home in San Francisco. She threw cans of carrots, corn, and green beans into the cart. Not knowing how long she'd be at Travis's, she figured the canned goods would last.

"Sara Baron, is that you?" A sweet old lady gave her a bear hug.

Sara spun around.

"It is you. Sara Baron, one of my favorite students ever. You're still playing the oboe, right? Last I heard, you were playing in the orchestra out in San Francisco."

"Mrs. Capelli. Yes, of course I'm still playing." She'd always been a terrible liar and she felt guilty saying she had a job as if it were a sure thing. *Omitting information isn't the same as lying.* Are you still teaching?" She was sure her former music teacher was retired by now.

"Oh, I've been retired for years already. I ran into your Mom last week. She said your grandfather wasn't doing well."

"Really? He was sleeping when I stopped by last night. I'll see him tonight. Mom hasn't said much."

"Poor man. Your Mom's worried it's the start of Alzheimer's." She whispered the word *Alzheimer's* as though it was a curse word. "If the body doesn't fall apart, the mind does. When you get to be my age, you're blessed to have either."

"How's your husband doing?"

"He passed away last year after Christmas. Cancer. It's been so lonely without him. I don't like driving if the roads are slippery and you know how long the winters are here. I'm lucky if I make it out here to buy groceries when I need them."

"I'm sorry for your loss." Those words always felt hollow but she hadn't come up with anything better. She remembered how people stumbled over their words after her grandmother died and how she'd wished they hadn't bothered to say anything at all.

"Tell me about you. I suppose your mom would have mentioned if you had a husband or good Lord, if she was a grandmother."

"That's right. If and when it happens, she'll rent a billboard." *If it ever happens.*

"Do you keep in touch with any of your old friends?"

"Ellie Rossi." She looked at the floor. For a moment she'd forgotten Ellie was gone.

"Ellie. Hope she's recovered."

"What do you mean?"

"From the breakup."

"What breakup?"

"You know. From that rich boy. Everyone was shocked when she got engaged so suddenly, then even more shocked when she called off the wedding days before it was set to happen."

"What engagement?" *No way Ellie would have been engaged and not told me. From the time we were kids we'd agreed to be each other's maid of honor since neither of us had a sister. Pinky swore.*

"You didn't know? She broke it off right before the wedding."

"I should have stayed in closer touch. Are you sure? We did speak on the phone just a few days ago."

"I'd gotten an invitation, then a few days before the date, her mother called to say it was off. The whole town was gossiping about it. Her fiancé was a Montague. They practically own this town."

Why hadn't her mother filled her in? She never mentioned that Ellie had been engaged. *It doesn't matter now.* She couldn't think of a gentle way to break the news. "Ellie died last night."

Mrs. Capelli grabbed onto the cart for support. "What? Ellie died? How?"

She wished she hadn't brought it up. It was hard to get the words out. "She was killed."

"Killed? As in murdered?"

"I'm afraid so."

"I'll bet dollars to donuts her fiancé killed her. He didn't take the news well from what I hear. And she was scared of him."

"Scared? Why?"

"I ran into Ellie at church and she kept looking over her shoulder, like she was being followed. The Montagues don't go to church, but he may have snuck in the back."

"She told you she was scared?"

"Not in so many words, but she acted nervous that day. She looked stressed, lost some weight, but I figured it was from canceling the wedding."

"It's an open investigation, but I'm not sure the police know about the ex-fiancé. Maybe you should drop by the station."

"I'll do that. Poor Ellie. What's this world coming to?"

Sara said, "Hey, do you know how to get in touch with her parents?"

"No. After the botched wedding they took off to South America. I was surprised Ellie didn't go with them. Then again, she had a good job over at that company near the hospital so maybe that's why she stayed."

"Last time we talked, Ellie said they were heading there. *She said nothing about a wedding, however.* Do you know anyone who might know how to reach them?"

"You could try the church. Her parents were doing some sort of charity work. They might know."

Chapter 5

After a fruitless afternoon, first trying to locate Ellie's parents, then trying to practice, Sara put away her oboe just before Travis got back from work. Visions of Ellie lying on the floor…thinking about the Rossi's in South America, oblivious to the life changing news… she'd start playing a few measures and lose her focus. She washed her face, dabbed on a little makeup, and went into the living room.

"Sara? I'm home."

She hated to admit it, but Travis looked especially handsome in his scrubs. The blue complimented his mocha-colored skin.

"How was your day?" She didn't care, but he was letting her stay here free of charge. She'd at least try to be civil.

"Good. I love working at the hospital. Before I moved here I was in private practice and it was more isolated."

"That's ironic. You move from Chicago to small town Hudsonville and you find this less isolated."

"I went by the body shop. My headlight's fixed." He handed her an invoice. "Here's the bill."

She looked at the price and cringed. "Seriously? For a headlight? Did you have him fix the preexisting dent as well?" *Maybe they should have gone through her insurance after all. How was she going to afford this?*

"No rush if you don't have the money."

"Who said I don't have the money? I'll write you a check right now."

"Later. Don't we have to get going?"

She glanced at her watch. "Yeah. Hope you're ready for my parents. My mother will talk your ear off if you let her."

"For a home cooked meal? She can talk all night. Let me change and we can take off."

When she got into the car, she had to move a bouquet of roses from the passenger seat to the back.

"Aw…for me? I knew you felt bad about crashing into me."

Travis stammered, "I'm, I'm not admitting fault here. Besides..."

Sara said, "Gotcha. I know these are for my mother. I see the card. It's not easy to come by fresh flowers this time of year."

"I know a guy who knows a guy."

Dimples? She was a sucker for dimples. Was she trying too hard to forget Brandon and move on with her life? *Not with this tool.* "Turn right at that sign."

"Cusa farms?"

"Yeah. The land is owned by the Montague family, but when their daughter got married, they gave her and her new husband the business as a wedding gift. They own acres of apple and cherry trees. In the summer they run a farm stand right in that spot. In the winter, they sell jams and home-made pies out of the back door of their kitchen."

"Back home there were orchards like that just outside the city."

"Apple orchards outside Chicago?"

"Yeah. Hey, do I turn again or keep going straight?"

"Go straight. The road ends just about…now. Here we are—Chez Baron."

"Where's that go?" He pointed to a gravel access road. "Is that a barn?"

"A converted, repurposed barn. It goes around back to the instrument shop. *Baron Oboes* was founded by my great grandfather. We—I should say my Dad and Grandpa—craft professional quality oboes."

"And they do good business? I can't imagine how many people in this town are in the market for a professional oboe."

"Most of the business nowadays is through the internet, but you'd be surprised how many oboists have come by over the years just to see the place. Not many family run oboe-making stores around."

"I'm sure."

"In fact, we're the only one in North America last time Grandpa checked. You can park behind Dad's van."

Patty Baron must have been waiting in the foyer. She flung open the door before Sara had finished knocking. She had a habit of doing that. At least she hadn't run outside without her coat this time.

"Come in. Welcome. You must be Travis?" She wiped her hands on her apron.

"Travis Jennings. These are for you."

"Roses! They're my favorite. Thank you. Come on in."

The familiar aroma of garlic bread and homemade marinara sauce evoked warm memories of Sundays spent helping her grandmother cook. Her father threw another log onto the crackling fire.

A white-haired man wearing a Fred Rogers cardigan hobbled in from the kitchen.

"Travis, this is my grandfather, Frank Baron."

"Nice to meet you." Travis extended his hand. Frank grumbled.

"You dating a black boy, Sara?"

Sara felt her face turn ten shades of red. She watched her mother's face flush as well. "We're not dating."

What a stupid thing to say! She felt like she wanted to just melt into the floor. "I mean, we just met."

"Patty Baron said, "I'm so embarrassed. Frank has Alzheimer's and sometimes things pop out of his mouth unfiltered. He didn't mean it."

"I told you I ain't got Alzheimer's."

"Don't mind the old grump. You're most welcome here," said Sara's father. "Can I get you a glass of wine?"

"I'd like that," said Travis.

Bob Baron retrieved a bottle from the kitchen. "It's from a local winery."

Frank Baron had settled into his recliner in the corner. "What do you do for a living?"

"I'm a physical therapist. I work out of Hudsonville Regional. I hear you make oboes."

"Make oboes, like on an assembly line? I *hand craft* oboes. Emphasis on hand. Patty is that food done yet?"

"Everyone, find a seat at the table. Hope you like Italian food, Travis."

"Love it."

Frank struggled to get up from the recliner. Sara offered her arm. "Get away. I haven't forgotten how to walk." He swatted at Sara, but missed. He grumbled something about his aching hip.

Travis whispered to Sara. "He'd benefit from some physical therapy to help him with everyday functioning. That hip of his is really tight. If you can get him to come by the hospital…"

"Thanks, but Grandpa is as stubborn as a mule. No way he'd admit he needs help."

Patty Baron said, "Come on before it gets cold."

The farm style table was covered with a red and white tablecloth. Patty carried in a ceramic baking dish overflowing with melted cheese and placed it on a souvenir trivet featuring the Golden Gate Bridge. Bob Baron refilled the wine glasses, then served the lasagna.

"How was work, Mom?"

"It's been crazy at the station. Those officers never dealt with a murder before, and even Detective Lambert seems a bit uncomfortable. He's being a typical Virgo. Step by step, dotting the *i*'s and crossing the *t*'s."

"Mom, did anyone locate Sara's parents yet?"

"Not as far as I've heard. Travis, you lived next door. Did she ever say anything about where her parents are?"

"No. I didn't know her well."

"They called in that ex-fiancé of hers. The door was closed, but I could hear them and if you ask me, he didn't seem upset at all. I'd start with him." Patty always was one to take charge. Sara bet she had those police officers doing exactly what she said.

Sara remembered her chat with her former music teacher at the grocery store. "Mom, I heard Ellie was engaged and then broke it off right before the wedding. Why didn't she tell me? Why didn't *you* tell me?"

"I thought you knew. It was a whirlwind romance. One minute they were engaged, the next, the wedding was off. No one really knows why it fell apart."

"How could no one know? It had to be something pretty serious to call off a wedding."

"There were rumors he was cheating on her, but what else are people going to think?"

"Cheating. Figures." *Brandon.*

"It was his loss," said her father. "I never liked those entitled, snobby Montagues. They act like they own the town."

"They practically do," said Patty. "That family's got their hands into everything from that from apple cider to door frames."

"Sara mentioned them when we drove past Cusa Farms." Travis took a bite of meatball. "This is delicious. I'll have to get your recipe."

Patty said, "Their son-in-law runs the business now. So Travis, where's your family?"

"My parents retired a few years ago. Sold the house and moved to an over 55 community in North Carolina. Mom insisted they move somewhere that had four seasons."

"Good for them. These long winters, sometimes I wish we could do the same."

"Mom, you have too many friends here. I know you'd never leave."

Her dad said, "You know your mom. She makes friends waiting in line at the bank. Don't think that would stop her."

"Do you have any brothers or sisters?"

"Mom, this isn't an interview."

"I don't mind. Nope. An only child. Do you have other children, Mrs. Baron?"

Patty looked at the floor. Sara wished he hadn't asked. "We have a son. He's an army officer stationed in Iraq. The holidays just aren't going to be the same with him gone."

"Scott was always your favorite," said Sara. Here she was in her thirties, and it still bothered her.

"You know that isn't true," said Patty.

"Besides, you were always your father's favorite," said Grandpa. "Scott had no interest in the business or in oboe playing. You carried on the musical bloodline."

"I'd love to see your workshop after dinner." Travis reached for seconds. His plate was clean again within minutes.

Smooth. Compliment Mom's cooking and ask to see the family business. He's a player if I ever saw one.

Travis's phone rang. "Excuse me. I have to take this. I'll be outside."

"Can I get you more?"

"No thanks, Mrs. Baron. I'm stuffed. I'll be right back."

"I'll help clear the table," said Sara. She carried the baking dish into the kitchen.

Patty retrieved a Tupperware container from the kitchen cabinet and filled it with leftover lasagna before wrapping the rest in aluminum foil.

"Whatcha doing, Mom?"

"I'm going to bring dinner to Jacob next door. His wife died last spring and poor man can't boil an egg without her."

"Angie? I didn't know she'd passed." *Boy, have I been left out of the loop.*

"Yes, they were like two peas in a pod, entertaining, playing cards, hiking in the woods—you can imagine how alone he feels. I think I'm the only face he sees most days."

Sara empathized. Although throwing his butt to the curb had been the right move, she'd felt lonely at times after her breakup with Brandon.

"Travis is charming. Smart too."

"Mom, don't start. He's conceited and arrogant. Not my type at all."

"It was awfully generous of him, letting you stay at his place."

"I'll bring in the salad and plates."

Travis came in, rubbing his hands together as if trying to start a fire. "Brrr, it's cold out there."

Sara said, "Everything alright?"

"Yeah. Everthing's fine."

"How about that tour?" said Bob Baron.

Travis and Sara followed him to the shop, which wasn't much bigger than their living room. It smelled of fresh wood, and shavings littered the floor. Instrument cases and clear boxes full of keys and pads lined the shelves. On the tables, gooseneck lamps, oboe stands, knives…

"Dad, I hope you started using the computer Scott and I bought you? You're not still keeping records by hand are you?"

"Let's just say the business is in transition."

Sara spotted repair slips speared on a metal prong, just like the way they did it when Sara was in high school and helped out at the shop.

"Looks fascinating," said Travis. He pointed to one of the shelves. "Is that the wood you use?"

"We use three different types of wood. The black wood is granadilla, also known as African Blackwood. It stands up well to humidity and is easy to work with because of the fine grain. Polishes up nicely, too. This here is my personal favorite." He picked up a lighter colored wood. "This is Rosewood. It has a warm, rich sound. Of course, it's too gentle sounding for some of those orchestra players." He gave Sara a look. "Sara plays on a black one."

"I have a rosewood, too. I use it for chamber music."

"Looks like you have enough wood on those shelves to last a lifetime."

"We wind up losing about 20% when we start boring it."

"And you bend the metal into keys I presume."

"Yep. You know when my grandfather started this business, he experimented by melting down Grandma's good silverware. You can imagine what her reaction was. The story's been passed down and told so many times you have to wonder if it got embellished along the way."

"Sara, do you know how to make these?" Travis gently ran his hand along a piece of wood.

"Dad started teaching me when I was ten."

"She has a natural talent for it. Of course, when she got serious about playing the oboe, she didn't have time to hang out in the shop. I was hoping one of my kids would continue the family business but I don't think it's in the cards."

Frank Baron wandered in. "We have to get to work. Sara, grab the repair slip from the bottom of the stack. Call the customer and give him the estimate."

"Grandpa, you're confused. I'm not working here anymore."

"Why not? Shop's falling apart. We can't keep up with business."

Bob said, "Let's get back to the house."

"Dad, is he able to work at all?"

"He has good days and bad days. I'm having a hard time keeping up. Had to turn down a bunch of repair work last year and that's our bread and butter. I might have to cut my losses and sell off the business."

"You can't do that. It's our family legacy."

"I know but there's a time when you've got to be practical. Grandpa is only going to continue to decline, you're busy with your own job, and Scott, of course, is overseas. Not that he ever had interest in the shop. Come on. Mom made a cheesecake for dessert."

Chapter 6

Sara watched Travis shovel cheesecake into his mouth like he was a contestant in a competitive eating competition. *Not only is he rude, he's a pig.*

Travis stopped for a breath. "The cheesecake is delicious, Mrs. Baron."

"Call me Patty. Would you like some more?"

"I've already eaten two huge pieces, Mrs. …Patty. Don't tempt me."

"Mom, we should get going. Travis has to work in the morning."

"You'll have to come back another time then, Travis." She got up. "I'll get a container. You can take a piece to go."

"I'll take one too, Mom!"

She returned with two Tupperware containers. "It was lovely meeting you."

Mom loves him. He's quite the charmer. Then again, she loves everyone who compliments her cooking.

"Same here. Thanks for dinner, Patty. Nice meeting you, too." He shook her father's hand. He offered his hand to Grandpa, but Grandpa ignored it.

Grandpa yelled after him. "Bye, Barack. You keep your hands off my granddaughter."

Sara felt her face heating up with embarrassment. "I'm so sorry. He doesn't mean it."

Travis got behind the wheel. "He's from a different generation. I understand. Your parents are cool with me, right?"

"My Mom's in love with you. Grandpa drives them crazy when he makes outlandish comments. He's always spoken his mind, but I think his filter had eroded more since the last time I was home." She leaned her head against the window. Travis started the truck and began to back out of the driveway. "Ugh."

"What's wrong?"

"The ride doesn't feel right. I think we have a flat tire." He jumped out of the truck, Sara on his heels. *If he tries to say it's from our little fender bender and thinks I'm going to pay for a tire, he has another think coming.*

Travis checked the front tire, then circled around the truck. "They're all flat. Every one of them."

"That's impossible. The driveway is clear and you'd have noticed a flat on the way over."

Travis grabbed a flashlight. "This wasn't an accident. Look. See those holes? Follow me."

She bent down and looked at the next tire. "This has the same two holes, like it was made with a tool of some kind."

"Someone deliberately popped your tires? Why?"

"Maybe someone thinks you know more about Ellie's murder than you do."

"I'll get Dad. He's got spare tires and tools in the garage."

"He has spare tires lying around?"

"They were on sale. What can I say."

Between Sara, Travis, and her father, the tires were changed in no time. Sara kissed her Dad goodbye for the second time and crawled back in the truck.

"See, now it's smooth sailing," said Travis. What's wrong? The tires are fixed. It may have been a teenage prank. Let's not dwell on it."

"I didn't realize how bad Grandpa had gotten. I'm worried about the family business. It would be a shame to have to sell it. It's Dad's life work."

"Can't he hire help?"

"It takes years to learn the art of oboe making. The longer he falls behind, the less the business will be worth if he does decide to sell it."

She thought about the shop the whole way back to Travis's. She was exhausted, and relieved when he pulled into his driveway. *Home, sweet home.*

Courtesy of the lasagna and cheesecake, the top of her jeans dug into her waist. She couldn't wait to get inside and change into pajamas. Travis locked the car doors.

"Did you leave the guestroom light on?"

"No, I'm sure I turned it off before we left."

Sara said, "Are those boot prints? Look." She pointed at the driveway. "Big prints. They lead to the house. Should we call the police?"

"Not yet." He unlocked the door, careful not to make noise.

"Shh. Stay still. Do you hear that?"

"Hear what?"

"Someone's in the house."

"You're right. Wait on the porch." Travis tiptoed around the corner and whispered, "Better yet, go out to the car. Call 911."

The last thing she wanted to do was to be alone in the dark with an intruder lurking about. She crept behind Travis. In a flash, someone wearing black clothes and a ski mask pushed her down as he fled out the front door.

Travis bent down. "I told you to go outside."

"Yes, I'm fine, thanks for asking. Go after him."

"It's too late. I'm going to call the police."

Sara walked into the guest bedroom. Except for the lack of a dead body, praise God, the scene was eerily similar to what she'd seen at Ellie's house. Her bed was torn apart, sheets and comforter on the floor. Clothes were emptied from the dresser and her suitcases had been dumped out onto the floor.

"Looks like that's how he got in." Travis pointed to the broken window.

"Don't you have an alarm system? Close circuit camera?"

"No. Didn't think I'd need it here. Besides, I'm just renting."

"What on Earth was someone looking for? I just got into town."

"It has to be connected to Ellie's murder. They were searching for something at Ellie's the night of her murder. Whatever it was they were looking for, they must think you took it from her house."

She remembered the message. "Ellie said not to let them find...I wish she'd finished that last message. I have no idea what it is I'm supposed to have."

"Someone does and I'm guessing it wasn't on Ellie's computer."

"Or he didn't have time to download whatever he was trying to load onto the jump drive after he realized I was in the house."

"He must think you have what he's looking for. Why else would he have broken into my house and punctured my tires?"

"You think he followed us to my parent's house?"

"Possibly."

Sara heard sirens. "Thank God, the police are here." She opened the door. "Detective Lambert? I figured you'd send a patrol car."

"I wanted to be sure you're okay. I have an officer searching the grounds."

"We're both fine."

"Two attempted robberies and a murder. Has to be connected."

"He was looking for something. The guest room has been torn upside down, just like Ellie's house was. Oh, and there are men's shoeprints outside in the driveway."

An officer came inside. "Chief, we found this on the ground by the truck. Some sort of puncture tool."

Detective Lambert took the evidence bag and examined it. "Did he use it to break the window?"

"The window was broken with a rock."

Sara said, "Let me see. Our tires were punctured earlier this evening while Travis and I were having dinner at my parents' house."

"Could have been the same guy. Followed you there, punctured the tires to buy time, then broke in hoping to find whatever it is he thought Ellie Rossi had in her possession."

"Exactly my theory," said Travis. "Is Sara in danger?"

"I can help you board up the window, and I'll have a patrol car park outside in case whoever it is decides to return."

Travis turned to her. "You can sleep on the sofa. Or better yet, take my room and I'll sleep down here. You'll feel better upstairs."

She was too exhausted to protest.

Chapter 7

Exhausted as she was, Sara tossed and turned, despite Travis's downy comforter and crisp new sheets. The thought of someone deliberately puncturing Travis's tires and breaking into his place, stealing info from Ellie's computer, and, of course, the murder, made her sick to her stomach.

Then came the nightmares—Ellie begging her to find her killer. Ellie saying to keep her secret safe. She woke with a start, pulse racing, sweat soaking her nightshirt. *What's that? Voices? Is Travis talking to someone?* She listened at the door. It sounded like he was on the phone. *In the middle of the night?*

She heard parts of the short conversation. "Status quo. Under wraps. She won't be a problem."

Who won't be a problem? Ellie? Me? Her head ached. She took a Benadryl from her purse, hoping it would help her sleep. She managed to drift off and was relieved when the sun peeked through the bottom of the blinds, signifying morning.

She took a shower, then made the bed. She jumped when she heard a sudden knock on the bedroom door. *I've got to get my nerves under control.*

Travis called through the door. "Sara, you want breakfast? I've got to go soon but I made eggs."

She wondered if she should ask him about the middle of the night phone conversation. *Nothing like painting a target on your back if he was talking about you!* "Um, sure." She opened the door and followed him into the kitchen. When she grabbed a coffee mug, it slipped from her hands. "Oh no, I'm so sorry."

Travis grabbed the broom. "I've got a spare. We can share it. Are you getting help for your condition?"

"What condition?"

"Focal Dystonia, right?"

"How'd you know?"

"I'm a physical therapist, remember?"

"At first I thought it was Carpel Tunnel. It's threatening my livelihood."

"Maybe I can help. Why don't you come with me tomorrow? My office is in the hospital. I'll squeeze you in."

"You really think you can help?"

"I'll try. No promises, but there are stretches and exercises that may help."

"I was told there's no cure. I'm on a leave of absence from my job and I doubt I'll be able to return. I can't tell my parents. I can't afford the insurance premiums either, so I haven't been able to see a specialist."

"Enough with the sob story. Finish your eggs and let's go."

When they got to the hospital, a patient was already waiting for Travis. Sara sat in the waiting room, flipped through a worn *People* magazine, checked her phone, then took a walk around the hospital to burn off her nervous energy. When she passed a nurses' station, her ears perked up like a German Shepard's. Three young nurses chatted as they checked their iPads.

"I heard she refused to give him back that engagement ring. I heard it was at least eight carats."

"Bet it was worth a million dollars. That's motive all right."

"I would have kept it too. The cad goes and cheats on her the week before the wedding?"

"That's the rumor, anyway. I heard his family was going to take her to court to get the ring back."

"I've seen cases like this before. On *Judge Judy*. The ring was a gift and Preston Montague had no right to demand its return."

"So what happens now? Did they give the ring back to the family now that she's dead?"

"His mother was here yesterday for some tests. She went on and on about the ring and how she was going to sue the police if they don't find it."

"Is it their job to find it?"

"Yeah, like when a patient thinks it's our job to make the hospital food taste good."

The call button flashed.

"I've gotta go."

Sara pieced together a scenario. Ellie wouldn't return the ring. Her fiancé went to her house to ask for it back but Ellie refused to give it to him. In a rage, he hit her over the head. Ellie wanted Sara to keep him from finding the ring, but why her? She had no idea where the ring was. She hadn't even known Ellie was engaged.

She pulled out her phone and Googled local news. *Charles and Helen Winston Montague announce the engagement of their son Preston Elliot Montague to Eleanor Rossi, daughter of Mary and Anthony Rossi of Hudsonville.* The Montagues. Of course. She continued searching. Charles Montague, head of the empire, made the *Forbes* list of ten wealthiest people last year. *And they're making a big fuss over a ring?*

She headed back to the waiting room. Travis poked his head out. "I'll be another thirty minutes." He shut the door before she could respond.

She took a walk back to the nurse's station. "I heard you talking about the murder earlier. Ellie was my friend. I was supposed to house sit. I'm the one who found the body."

"Oh my God, how awful!" One of the nurses hugged her. "Are you okay?"

"I just want to know who did this to her."

"Everyone loved Ellie. I can't imagine anyone but Preston Montague being angry enough to kill her."

"You knew Ellie?"

"Sure. She was a sales rep. Medical devices—insulin pumps, artificial joints, internal defibrillators... We saw her at least once or twice a week."

"So she got along with everyone at the hospital?"

"Mostly. Except for Dr. Peters. Dr. Peters used to date Preston—before Ellie. She should be on the suspect list."

One of the nurses said, "That's a rumor. You know how stories take on a life of their own. Dr. Peters is a successful surgeon. I can't imagine her being hung up on Preston Montague."

"But we know she was. We heard her arguing with Ellie in the cafeteria that day, remember?"

"Really?" said Sara.

"I do. She said it wouldn't happen. Preston would come to his senses."

Sara's phone buzzed. "I have to get to an appointment, but I may be back. I'm on vacation visiting my parents and the gossip is a good distraction."

"I hear ya," said one of the nurses. The other nodded.

Sara ran to Travis's office.

"Where were you? I don't have a lot of time."

"You didn't tell me Ellie worked here in the hospital."

"She didn't exactly work here. She was a sales rep."

"Did you work with her?"

"She carried knee and hip joints from a local company. She showed them to me as a courtesy, but the real sell had to be to the orthopedic docs. Let me see your hand."

Travis's hand felt soft and strong as he examined her fingers, then hand, then arm. He moved her fingers with the care of an artist. "Grip my hand. Do you feel pain?"

"No pain, mostly it feels numb."

"I'm almost positive it's dystonia. It's not a common disorder, but it shows up disproportionately in musicians. Let me show you some exercises you can do at home. Then, let's set up some sessions here in the rehab room. I also want you to see an internist."

"I can't pay an internist, or you, for that matter."

"It's on the house, really. Don't worry about it."

"I can't…"

"It took me all of ten minutes. Not a problem."

"Well, thank you. By the way, do you know a Dr. Peters?"

"Jailyn Peters, sure. Why?"

"I was talking to the nurses. They said she was jealous of Ellie and told her the wedding wouldn't happen."

"I don't know anything about that. I try to stay out of gossip."

"I'm going to head to my parent's house. Dad could use some help at the shop."

"If you wait another thirty minutes I'll drop you off."

She debated over taking a taxi—one of the half dozen serving the entire town—or waiting the half hour. Again, money was an issue.

"I'll grab a cup of coffee in the cafeteria. Thanks."

She took the elevator to the cafeteria. The donuts and croissants called to her, but she mustered up her self-control and went with just coffee. A tall blonde who looked like a young Christie Brinkley was ahead of her in line, buying plain yogurt and an apple. She noticed the embroidery on the white coat she wore over dark blue scrubs. Jailyn Peters, MD. The orthopedic surgeon. Preston Montague's ex. She sat at the table behind her.

Ellie was pretty, but Dr. Peters would look at home wearing a tiara and sash. She had manicured nails, designer eyeglass frames, and an expensive haircut. Opposite of girl-next-door Ellie. Ellie came from a family of hard-working farmers who donated time and what money they could spare to the church. Growing up, Sara loved spending time at their house. Ellie's mother didn't care if they took apart the sofa cushions to build a fort, or spilled flour all over the kitchen counter when attempting to make pancakes. Somehow she got the impression that Dr. Peters had grown up quite differently—more like how she imagined the Montagues.

While she sipped her coffee, a middle-aged man in an expensive suit took a seat at the table with Dr. Peters. Despite the din in the cafeteria, she could hear bits of the conversation.

"Dr. Peters, I hope you're still on board, in spite of the unfortunate death of our junior sales rep. I've personally taken over the project. Can I count on you?"

"Of course. Having the recalled stock pulled from the shelves created a problem."

"It's under control, as you know. Looking forward to remaining business partners."

A group of nurses sat at the adjacent table. Even with her keen sense of hearing, their laughter and chatter made it impossible to continue eavesdropping. Sara looked at her watch. *Better get upstairs or I'll miss my ride.*

Chapter 8

When she got home, she went out back to the oboe shop. She straightened out the lucky horseshoe she made her father nail above the door before she left for college. While no longer a barn, the shop was notoriously drafty and several space heaters were positioned around the work area to help keep the wood from cracking.

"Dad, what can I do?" Her father was bent over a work table, holding the beginnings of an oboe. He jumped when he realized she was behind him.

"You scared me half to death. It's your vacation. Go inside and relax."

"No, I want to help. I'll start by sorting out the mess of repair tickets. Is Grandpa coming in?"

"I don't know. It's his nap time. Some days he's more in the way than he is helpful. His hip has been bothering him and he can't sit in one spot to work for very long."

She pulled out the repair tickets and lined them up on the desk. She tagged the instruments, then got to work.

"You still remember how?"

"How to unbend a key or change a pad. Child's play!" It was nostalgic working alongside her dad. Growing up, she'd always relished the time she spent in the shop with him and her grandfather.

As she was working, the phone on her desk rang. "Dad, it's for you. Frasier Woodwinds."

He grabbed the phone. "Hello. Yes, I've been looking at the contract. It's a very fair price, but I'm still thinking it over. It's been a family business for three generations and it's a lot to think about. I'll get back to you by the new year."

"Dad, who was that? You're not selling the business are you?"

"Honey, I'm not sure how much longer I can manage without your grandfather's help. The manpower has essentially been cut in half. That means I can do half as much work and I get half as much income. We're losing money."

"But you own this building."

"Our converted barn? Yes, we own it, but I'm paying for heat, electricity, and I have to lay out money for supplies before I get paid for making an instrument. It's getting to be too much."

"I can help. Look, I've already fixed this leaky pad."

"Nice, honey, but in two weeks you'll be back in San Francisco."

She didn't want her parents worrying about her and wasn't planning to tell them about her leave of absence. However, in the six months she would be here, perhaps she could make a difference and help get things back on track.

"Any idea when you'll be able to move into Ellie's?"

"The police said a couple of days."

"Any leads?"

"I was at the hospital and heard some nurses talking. Ellie broke up with Preston but didn't return the expensive engagement ring. His family is taking her to court, and the ring has gone missing. Also, there was an ex-girlfriend. A doctor at the hospital. Apparently she was overheard saying the wedding would never happen."

"Is that who he was cheating with? Your mom heard rumors."

"I don't know."

"So Preston and that doctor are the prime suspects."

"That we're aware of. Ellie had a whole part of her life she didn't share with me. Frankly, I'm miffed that she never even mentioned her engagement." She didn't mention her nagging suspicions over Travis's involvement.

Sara found herself enjoying the repair work. It was her left hand that had been acting up and she was able to work easily with her right hand. How great would it be if Travis could find a way to help her? He'd already suggested a few stretches which she'd tried out in the car. Perhaps it was the placebo effect, but they seemed to help.

Her cell rang. "Hello? Yes, Detective Lambert. No, I didn't see a phone, it wasn't in her purse? And you've searched the house? Not in her car either. I don't know. No, I didn't happen to see an engagement ring. When can I return to the house? Okay, great. Thank you."

"I assume that was the police."

"Yeah. They can't locate Ellie's phone or the ring. Dad, Ellie left me a message the night she was killed. She asked me not to let them find something."

"Find what?"

"I have no idea. I'm thinking the ring, but how am I supposed to know where it is?"

"It's not your job. The police are getting paid to do that, not you."

"Yeah, like I'm not getting paid to do this." She held up the instrument she was repairing. "Only kidding. This is a labor of love. Besides, what else am I going to do all day?"

She continued repairing instruments, finding it satisfying fixing, repairing, making something broken whole again. She watched her Dad focus on the oboe he was crafting—so careful, so absorbed. *I can't picture him doing anything else with his life. This makes him happy. Like playing the oboe does for me...*

"Hey, Dad. Do you have any more octave keys?"

"I think there are some in the filing cabinet."

She rifled through folders, rusty knives, and empty cans of key oil. Too bad her mother needed the paying job over at the police station. She'd have this mess straightened out in a heartbeat. She opened another drawer, but it seemed to be stuck. She tugged as hard as she cold, but it wouldn't budge.

"Dad, what's with this drawer?"

"It's been jammed as long as I can remember. Obviously, we've been able to manage without whatever's inside."

She grabbed tools and oil from the worktable. Then she took one of the turkey feathers they used to clean the inside of the instruments and dabbed the end with oil. Next, she slipped it into the drawer tract. It took time, but eventually it pulled free.

"Here's the problem." She pulled out a book that had been lodged in the back.

"A log book?"

"Dad, this dates back to great grandfather. Look at these records, all hand written entries."

"We used those back in the day. No worries about the computer crashing or the electric going out. Cheaper, too. There's an idea."

She flipped through the pages. The entries were careful and detailed. 1/17 *Black oboe, adjusted measurement of the bell resulting in greater resonance.*

1/20 *Started making oboe for JM. Told him it would be completed in March.* 1/30 *Date with Rosie tonight.*

"Hey, Dad. Who was Rosie?"

"Rosie? My grandmother's name was Ruth, not Rosie. Why?"

"Great Grandpa had a date scheduled."

"Let me see that. Couldn't be. He was already married by then."

"Maybe you didn't know him as well as you thought."

"Very funny. Mom should be getting back from work. Let's clean up and go inside for dinner."

When they got back inside, Sara washed the grease off her hands and pulled on sweat pants that she'd left there during her last visit home. She heard her mother's car pull up.

"Hey. I'm home!" Patty took off her coat and tossed her purse on the sofa.

"Hi, Mom."

"What a nice surprise. I'm making pork chops for dinner. Do you prefer mashed potatoes or rice?"

"Mom, you don't have to cook for me."

"It's just as easy to cook for four as it is for three. Why don't you make a salad?"

"I'd be happy to. How was work?"

"Busy. Detective Lambert has been working nonstop on Ellie's murder. We've been trying to locate Preston Montague. I'm checking credit card records for them. His family claims they haven't seen him."

"That's suspicious right there."

"It gets better. They found a fingerprint on the lamp. Guess who it belonged to?"

"Hmm. Preston Montague?"

"Bingo. They found a second print as well but couldn't identify it. Oh, and we located Ellie's parents. They're flying in tomorrow.

"Oh, no. They'll want to stay at the house, right?"

"No. They bought a condo in that new retirement subdivision last year. They gave the house to Ellie. I thought I told you."

"I suppose they'll be busy making funeral arrangements. Maybe I can help out."

"That's a nice offer. By the way, Detective Lambert was asking about you."

"What do you mean?"

"He was trying to play it cool. He asked if your husband was in town with you."

"He's a detective. He had to ask you?"

"He's a good looking fellow. Smart, too. Unless you and Travis have something going."

"Travis?" She felt her face heat up. "We're just friends. Not even friends. I don't even like him, he's rude and arrogant. Besides, I'm still recuperating from my break-up with Brandon. I'm not interested in dating anyone right now." She felt herself protesting a bit too much.

Grandpa came into the kitchen holding his right hip. "She wouldn't start up anything with someone of a different race! Their kids would be…"

"Grandpa! I can't believe you just said that."

"It was different when Pops was growing up." Bob grabbed silverware from the drawer.

"You are so racist. Times have changed, Grandpa. I don't like Travis, but it's not because he's black, it's because he's smug and full of himself." *Although he did give me a place to stay and offer to help with my dystonia free of charge.*"

Grandpa either didn't hear, or chose to ignore her. "You got any more Aleve, Patty?"

"In the cabinet over the sink. Didn't I just buy you a new bottle?"

"It's gone. Hardly helps anyway."

"Dad, you have to face up to the fact you need that hip replaced. Let's get the surgery scheduled soon." Bob Baron sprinkled salt and pepper on the pork chops.

"Nah. Don't need no surgery. Where am I going, anyhow?"

Sara spun the wet lettuce. "Travis can help. He's a physical therapist."

"Help Schmelp," mumbled Grandpa

"One of the ladies at church had her hip replaced last year and she's had nothing but trouble ever since," said Patty. "Her hair started falling out. You should see. She wears a red wig to church. Puts on a headband so it looks more real but we all know it isn't her hair."

"Grandpa, do you know anything about a woman named Rosie? I found a notation in your father's logbook about a date with Rosie."

"What are you talking about? You implying my father was a philanderer? He worshipped the ground my mother walked on. Don't you go smearing his reputation."

Bob Baron said, "Maybe he's right. No use digging up the past and blemishing our family's reputation."

"What are you talking about, Dad?"

Grandpa grumbled. "How long till dinner, Patty? I'm hungry."

"About twenty minutes. Anyone for a glass of wine?"

"Since when do you have wine in the house?" said Sara.

"It was a gift from Jacob next door."

"That was sweet of him. I'm sure he appreciates your kindness."

"I wish I had the time to keep him company. Poor man is so lonely and bored. He was a detective, you know. Now he sits and watches TV all day long."

"Too bad you can't get him and Grandpa to keep each other company."

"I don't need anyone arranging play dates for me," said Grandpa.

Sara ignored the comment. "Mom, have you heard the name Jailyn Peters?"

"Yes. She's an orthopedic doctor. That's who I took your Grandpa to see."

"I heard she was dating Preston Montague before Ellie and she was jealous."

"I may have heard that. Seems like a doctor would be more suitable as a match for a Montague than Ellie. Ellie was too good for him."

Chapter 9

When Sara got back to Travis's, she was disappointed to see the house was dark. She quickly turned off the car, ran up the porch steps, and opened the door, locking it immediately behind her. Would she always feel this shaken up? She flipped on the lights.

"Panther. Come here, Panther." He scampered across the floor and rubbed against her legs. Did he sense that Ellie wasn't coming back? She'd read a story once about a cat in a hospital that sensed when a patient was about to die. He'd curl up on the bed and keep vigil until the person passed. It became so predictable that the nurses relied on him to warn them the time was near. They called the cat a guardian angel. Sara believed in angels, and the notion that animals possess a sixth sense.

Panther meowed. She refilled his water bowl, then plopped down on the sofa to watch the news before turning in. The remote control was hiding somewhere. She checked under the cushions. She felt something sharp. A gold hoop earring. A woman's earring. *Men will be men. That's what Grandma used to say. Why does this bother me? He's handsome and successful. Of course, he goes out with women, probably lots of them. Besides, I don't even like him.*

Then she remembered how the coffee table top lifted up, revealing storage underneath. She grabbed onto the edges and lifted. *Voila, not one but three different remotes. Which shell is the pea hiding under?*

Before closing the lid, she noticed a notepad with a handful of names and phone numbers. She recognized the left-handed slant immediately. It was Ellie's handwriting. Whose numbers were these and why did Travis have them?

She closed the lid and turned on the news. Panther jumped into her lap. Poor Panther. Who was going to take him in? She wasn't allowed pets in her San Francisco loft.

The leading news story centered around the search for Preston Montague. They were calling him a person of interest in the Ellie Rossi murder case and appealing to viewers to call in with any information that could help locate him. A hotline number ran across the bottom of the screen.

The reporter said, "A white BMW was seen leaving the Rossi residence around the time of the murder." A white BMW. Not the dark sedan she had passed that night on the way to her parents' house.

She heard Travis's key in the door and felt relieved to no longer be alone. He was holding a white Styrofoam container.

"How was dinner at your parents?"

"Fine. I helped Dad in the shop this afternoon. It was fun."

"I'm sure he appreciated the help." He carried the container into the kitchen. Had he been on a date? She could smell Chinese food through the container.

She heard the fridge door close. "You doing your exercises?"

"Yep. I've got to regain control over my hand or I'm out of a job. On the news they said the police are looking for Preston Montague. Did you see a white BMW that night?"

"No. When I got home, the driveway was empty."

"The door had to have been locked, but it was open when I got there. It had to be someone she knew and let in."

"Or someone who had a key. An ex-fiancé makes sense. By the way, I had the window repaired in the guest room, but you're welcome to take my room if it makes you feel better being upstairs."

"No, I'll be okay down here. As a matter of fact, I'm going to grab my things and turn in. Goodnight."

"Goodnight. See you in the morning."

Sara scooped up Panther and brought him into the guestroom. He curled up next to her pillow and she put her ear gently against him, soothed by the purring, relaxing into sleep.

She woke up drenched in sweat, her heart racing. *Thank God, it was just a nightmare.*

She'd watched her oboe being swept down a river by a monstrous current. She jumped in and tried to reach, gasping for air as the water plunged over her. Every time she got close to grabbing it, it moved further away.

Panther was asleep next to her. She moved carefully so as not to wake him. She rummaged through her bag in the dark. *I knew it was here somewhere.* She pulled out her hand-made dream catcher, put it on the nightstand, then went into the bathroom for a glass of water.

When she came back into the bedroom, she noticed light seeping in around the blinds and peeked behind them.

Why is there a car *in Ellie's driveway? A dark sedan. A Buick. Like the one that nearly ran me over.* Her pulse raced. The car zoomed away. She heard the high pitched whine ramp up as the car accelerated. *Breathe in, breathe out. Where's my phone?* She calmed herself and called Detective Lambert.

"The patrol car is still in the area. Did you catch the license plate? Can you describe the driver?"

"It was the same car that almost ran us over the night of Ellie's murder. You have the plate number I gave you, right? Did you ever trace the number? I didn't see the driver."

"The plate was registered to an old lady the next town over. She says it was stolen, though she never bothered to report it. We'll send someone over to check it out right away. Lock the doors and sit tight."

Now she was wide awake. *I can't keep imposing on Travis, but I'm afraid of staying alone at Ellie's.* At the moment, yellow crime scene tape guarded the house and the police hadn't given her the go-ahead to move in. Maybe a cup of tea would calm her nerves. Had she even seen teabags in that pristine pantry of his? She pulled on her robe and went to the kitchen.

"Couldn't sleep either?" Travis sat at the table wrapped in a flannel robe. A bit of chest hair peeked out over his thermal t-shirt.

"I was having nightmares. Then, I saw a car pulling out of Ellie's driveway. I was going to make some tea."

"I heard a car. I think that's what woke me up. I assume you called the police?"

"Yes, it was the same car that nearly ran us over."

"Are they sending someone over to check it out?"

"Yes. I'm scared. Someone out there has a key to Ellie's. Am I supposed to feel safe staying there?"

"Tomorrow I'll call a locksmith and get the locks changed. You can stay with me as long as you like."

"Thanks. You know, Ellie called me but I never saw her phone. The police didn't find it. Do you think the killer took it?"

"Maybe so. Here, I'll put the kettle on." Then he said, "Alexa, play stress list." The kitchen echoed with Debussy.

"I've been meaning to get one of those. Can you say, *Alexa, cook me dinner?*"

"No, but you can tell her to call Dominos and have a pizza delivered."

"What made you move here from Chicago?"

"Chicago was expensive. Cost of living is cheap here, the salary is competitive. When this offer came up, I was ready for a new beginning."

"A new beginning?"

"Let's just say I wasn't expecting the curve ball I was pitched. Right out of left field."

She hated sports metaphors. "I know what you mean. Never expected my boyfriend to dump me out of the blue and start dating a co-worker. One who I considered a friend, no less. It took all my resolve not to take that violin bow of his and shove it..." *Breathe in, breathe out.* "My boyfriend—ex-boyfriend—was restless, as he put it. He told me I was too serious. Too boring."

"I can't imagine. Self-righteous and stubborn yes, but boring, no." He handed her a cup of tea, brushing his hand against hers as he did. She felt little sparks of electricity when the hair on his arms brushed against hers.

"Look who's talking. I've never met someone as arrogant as you. *Maybe that guest conductor they had last season, but no one else.* Why did you really move here?"

"It's complicated. I don't want to talk about it." He pulled his arm away. "I'm going back to bed. See you in the morning." He tugged on the kitchen door, then she heard him tug on the front door, making sure they were safely locked inside.

She stomped back to the guest room, flipping on every light switch she passed on the way.

Chapter 10

After a disturbing night, Sara downed a third cup of coffee hoping to clear her head. *Why did I open up to Travis about my job being in jeopardy? I've got to protect myself. And how am I going to hold myself together when I see Ellie's parents later?* She'd volunteered to pick up Ellie's parents at the airport this morning. What would she say to them? *I'm sorry your daughter was murdered in her own home while you were out of the country? I'm sorry the killer hasn't been caught?* She heard a knock at the door. The rental agency came to pick up the car. From now on, she'd be driving Ellie's Nissan.

The airport was more than an hour away. Once she hit the city, she crawled along the road, inches at a time. *Rush hour. I don't miss this about San Francisco.* Fortunately, with her orchestra work hours, she'd usually managed to avoid the worst of it. Even the line getting into the airport was frustratingly slow. She squinted, trying to make out the terminals and finding the entrance to the correct parking garage.

Ellie's parents have been through so much. Last thing I want to do is make them wonder if I'm going to show up. Snaking upward like a tram climbing the alps, she eventually found an empty parking spot. She rushed to the gate just as the flight from Venezuela was disembarking.

She waved. "Over here!"

Ellie's mother was about the age of her own mother, but appeared older with her gray hair, lack of makeup, and sun weathered skin. Ellie's father was tall and slender, with sandy hair and emerald green eyes like Ellie's. He spotted her first. "Sara? We're coming." He lugged an oversized carry-on bag behind him as they made their way through the crowd.

Ellie's mother hugged her. "Sara. I don't believe this. Everyone loved her. This doesn't make sense."

Her father said, "Are they positive it was her? I mean, if she was injured wasn't it hard to tell?"

"It was Ellie. I found her myself."

"*You're* the one who found her?"

"Unfortunately, yes." She wiped her eyes with her glove, hoping Ellie's parents didn't notice. She wanted to be strong for them.

"Did she…did she suffer?" Ellie's mother couldn't catch her breath, sobbing between the words as they started toward baggage claim.

"The police said it was quick and she felt no pain. She looked, well, peaceful." Wow, Sara hadn't given herself enough credit for her acting ability. She even managed to have her facial expressions match her voice. Of course, Ellie was scared. Of course, she felt pain. But her parents didn't need to know that. "Let's get your bags."

"Do they have any leads?" said Mr. Rossi.

"Preston Montague has gone AWOL."

"I never liked him. I told Ellie she could do better. He was angry that she didn't return the ring. I was with Ellie when he confronted her about it. Ellie swears she gave it back." Ellie's mother wiped her tears with her coat sleeve.

They grabbed the luggage and made their way to the car.

Mrs. Rossi said, "Ellie wasn't herself the last time I talked to her."

"My wife kept saying, 'Ellie sounds like she's hiding something.' I should have listened."

"There's nothing you could have done, I'm sure," said Sara. "Come, the car's over here."

"While we were in town, I heard Ellie talking on the phone. Whispering, really. It sounded like some sort of drug deal, except I know my daughter and would bet my life it wasn't that."

"What do you mean?"

"I heard her say 'I've got more but need more time.' When she saw me, she hung up and looked like she'd been caught stealing from the cookie jar."

"Tell her about the closet." Mr. Rossi nudged his wife.

"Ellie had a lock installed on the closet door in the guest room."

"So she had something of value she was guarding."

"No, she had the lock installed on the *inside* of the closet."

"On the inside of the closet? She must have felt someone meant to harm her."

"I think she created one of those safe rooms. I saw that in a movie," said Mrs. Rossi.

"Whoever killed her was looking for something. I think it was the ring. Do you have another idea?"

"It could have been that, but who was she talking to on the phone? She also said she was thinking of buying a gun. She always hated guns."

"Was she afraid of Preston?"

Mr. Rossi said, "That little wimp. Ellie wasn't afraid of him. She had the upper hand in that relationship. I can't see Preston having the guts to confront Ellie, let alone kill her."

"Honey, his family is very powerful. The ring is an heirloom and their children...no one was going to mess with a Montague heir." Mrs. Rossi blew her nose. "I tried to convince her to come to Venezuela with us. I almost had her convinced but at the last minute she said they needed her here."

"Who's *they*? Her job?"

"I assume that's what she meant."

"So you're saying a member of the Montague family may have gone after Ellie either for revenge or to get back the ring." *I know she's understandably upset, but I have to be clear on this so I can help.*

"Calling off the engagement was a huge embarrassment to the Montague family. Let alone all the money they lost canceling at the last minute," said Mr. Rossi.

"Money isn't an issue for that family. Social standing and embarrassment are," said Mrs. Rossi.

"Why did Ellie call it off? Was he cheating on her?" *Why was that my first guess? Maybe she found him boring and called it off. Good for her.*

"There was an ex-girlfriend in the picture. A doctor at the hospital. She never said directly that was why."

"Jailyn Peters."

"That's right. Ellie was tight lipped about a lot of things, but she did let that name slip out more than once." Mr. Rossi directed her to turn.

Sara pulled into a recently constructed retirement community. "Which unit is it?"

"The first on the left," said Mrs. Rossi. "I'm thankful we got out of that house. I couldn't bear living there knowing what happened."

"Come on. I'll help you with your bags."

"I've got them, said Mr. Rossi. "You've been kind enough to pick us up. You must have things to do."

Yeah, she'd be practicing her oboe or making reeds if her life was back to normal. Truth was, her hand ached and she was having trouble unclenching her fingers even with the stretches Travis recommended.

"Here's my number. I'm staying next door to your house—your old house—until the police say it's okay to go back. Do you want me to bring Panther over?"

Mrs. Rossi started crying again. "We can't have pets here. Condo rules. I forgot about Panther. What's going to happen to him?"

"I've got him for now," said Sara. "If you need help with the arrangements, please call me. My parents offered to help as well. Mom says she and the ladies at church already have the food covered for after the service and the church says the basement is available whenever you need it for after the service."

"Thank you. This town is a security blanket for all of us. If this had happened in the middle of a city somewhere no one would blink an eye."

She's right about that. At least in my limited experience living in one. "We're all family here. No one goes it alone. Remember, call if you need me."

Sara wondered if Ellie's parents would ever be able to move on after losing their only child in such a violent way. At the least, her killer had to be caught. As if her thoughts had transmitted themselves, her phone vibrated.

"Sara, it's Detective Lambert. I wanted to let you know the crime scene has been cleared. You are free to go back there if you wish."

"Is it…is there blood…?"

"We can send a crime scene cleaning service over if you'd like. I'd recommend that."

"Okay."

"I have a few more questions for you. My morning is booked, but how about lunch at the diner? By then I'll let you know when the cleaning service has arranged to come to the house."

"Um, okay. I'll meet you at the diner."

"12:30 then."

Was her mother right? Did the detective have an interest in her, or was this strictly business?

Sara stopped at home and walked around back to the shop. She was thrilled to see Grandfather sitting at a worktable making an oboe.

"Hi, Dad. Grandpa, look at you working like a pro."

"Don't placate me, Sara. I've been making oboes my whole life. Why shouldn't I be doing so now? I'm old but I'm not dead."

Her father, working at the table behind Grandpa, simply shook his head.

"Can I help? I have a few hours to spare."

"We can use all the help we can get. Can you work on repairs?"

"Sure." She grabbed an oboe case and started working. The screwdriver slipped out of her hand onto the floor.

"And I'm the one who can't do this anymore?" said Grandpa.

"It just slipped out of my hand. No big deal."

"Leave her alone, Pops. This is like old times, the three of us together in the shop."

She had a flashback to a snowy Saturday afternoon back when she was in middle school. "Dad, do you remember the time the electric went out and you had to finish those two oboes for the principal of the New York Philharmonic?"

"Sure do. He was coming to pick them up the next morning. If he wasn't satisfied with the oboes he could have ruined my business."

"Mom brought a thermos full of hot chocolate from the house so you could keep working. She sat down and began sorting the invoices. Scott was scared being in the dark, so he came over, too. Grandpa showed him how to polish the keys; remember, Pops?"

"The boy has two left thumbs. But he managed better than I'd expected."

"It was nice working together as a family," said Sara. "And those oboes got glowing reviews."

Her father laughed. "I could barely keep up with the new orders long afterwards."

"I picked up Ellie's parents."

"How are they holding up?" Her father kept working while he talked.

"They're barely holding it together."

Grandpa announced, "I saw young Barack over at the hospital this morning when I had my hip appointment."

"Who?"

"That boy that came around for dinner the other night. I had an appointment with Dr. Peters. I was in the waiting room and I could hear them arguing through the door, even with my bad hearing and all."

"You mean Travis. His name is Travis, not Barack."

"Whatever. You know who I mean."

"What were they arguing about?"

"He was saying stuff like *if you had anything to do with this...*"

"Are you sure that's what you heard?"

"Yeah, he said he knew she was happy to be rid of Ellie. Ellie was a threat."

"A threat to what?"

"How do I know? Just sayin' what I heard. Anyhow, Barack blew right past me, didn't even notice I was sitting there." He continued to work.

Bob Baron shrugged his shoulders. Without missing a beat, he said, "Pops hears lots of things these days."

Sara continued working on the repairs, leaving herself enough time to run by Travis's to pack her things before meeting Detective Lambert for lunch. She fed Panther, then went upstairs and got to work.

The coffee had worn off and her head throbbed. She searched her purse. *All out of Excedrin. Now what?* She tossed the empty bottle in the trash. Panther followed her into the master bathroom on a hunt for aspirin.

The medicine cabinet was as pristine as the kitchen cabinets. Shaving cream, Tums, Excedrin Migraine, and a small prescription bottle. "Look, Panther. *Migraine medicine. Take as needed. Cameron Stokes.* "These expired two years ago. Who is Cameron Stokes?" She noted the doctor's name and instinct told her to snap a photo of the bottle. She shook two caplets out of the Excedrin Migraine and headed downstairs.

"Panther, I've got to get out of here and meet the detective. I'll come by and pick you up after lunch." She was probably being overly optimistic, thinking the crime scene clean-up would be done by then.

She changed into a new pair of jeans and a red pullover, then dabbed on a touch of eye shadow and face powder. Checking herself in the mirror, she turned to the side, then loosened the pullover so it didn't cling to her stomach.

Chapter 11

The noisy diner was beginning to fill with the lunch crowd. Sara pushed past the glass case with cream pies and Greek pastries. She spotted Detective Lambert in a booth drinking a cup of coffee. He stood up when he saw her.

"Hello, thanks for meeting here rather than at the station. My schedule's packed but I managed to carve out a lunch hour."

"Well, my schedule's rather sparse at the moment. In fact, there's no schedule. I'm on vacation."

"The snow's plentiful this year. The nearby resorts are packed with skiers."

"I'm not much of a skier. I'm in town to help my family make arrangements for my grandfather's surprise 80th birthday party."

"Your mother says you play in an orchestra. I play a little electric guitar myself. What instrument do you play?"

"Oboe."

"Is that the giant brown instrument with the mouthpiece that looks like a plumbing pipe?"

"No, that's a bassoon. It's the instrument that looks like a clarinet and plays the duck in *Peter and the Wolf.*"

"Peter and the what?"

"Never mind. Did you order yet?"

"No, but I always go with the lamb gyro."

She stared at the menu, searching for a healthy choice. The aroma of fried falafel tempted her as the waitress approached the table. *Stick to the plan or these new jeans won't fit for long.*

"I'm going to have the grilled chicken on pita. Go light on the mayo. And can I get a side salad in place of the fries? Dressing on the side."

"Yes, ma'am, but our fries are really good."

"She's not kidding," said Detective Lambert. He had a million-dollar smile.

"I'll just steal some of his." She handed her the menu. "So what did you want to ask me?"

"The night of the murder, you said you passed Travis Jennings on your way into town. Correct?"

"That's right. I'd skidded on the ice after a deer darted across the road and he pulled over to make sure I was okay."

"Was he going toward or away from the Rossi place?"

"He was behind me, so he was going toward it."

"And when you got to the Rossi's, what time was it?"

"Around 11 p.m."

"And Travis Jennings was at his house at the time? Was his truck in his driveway?"

"Yes. His light was on and I'm pretty sure his truck was in the driveway. Wait, maybe it wasn't. He has a garage. I can't remember. Why do you ask?"

"There were fresh tire tracks in the murder victim's driveway."

"I told you a Buick Le Sabre nearly killed us. The same one that pulled away from Ellie's house last night. I'll bet it was those tire tracks you saw."

"I had forensics check. They came from a truck."

"You think Travis was parked in Ellie's driveway sometime the evening Ellie was killed? Did you check what you found against his tires?"

"He refuses to let us take a mold without a warrant. It was sleeting earlier in the evening. Tracks made earlier in the evening would have been washed away with the freezing rain."

"Did you talk to Travis about it? There must be an explanation."

"He denies being there. Says he was home all evening after 8:30. He's not being very forthcoming."

"Travis was home when I discovered Ellie's body. I ran to him for help."

"So he says. Never mind."

"Do you doubt him?"

"Certain things don't add up, that's all. He said he hadn't ever been in her house, yet we found his fingerprints all over the living room and kitchen."

She wondered if his prints were in the bedroom as well. Of course, they were. He followed her upstairs to where Ellie was. Wait, or did she follow him? No. He led her directly into the master bedroom. If he'd never been there, how did he know the way to Ellie's room?

"And we found a man's sweatshirt in her closet. Seattle Seahawks. The neighbor was from Seattle."

"The neighbor? By *the neighbor* you mean Travis Jennings?" *Of course, he does. I should have known Travis was a player right from the start.*

"That's the assumption, though we can't be sure."

The waitress brought the food to the table.

"That was quick," said Sara.

"We try to get the lunch crowd in and out since most work downtown and have limited time."

"Did you ask him where he was earlier in the evening?"

"He said he was out of bread and ran to the store."

It was true that he'd run out of bread She'd made a sandwich on a stale English muffin for lunch. *I'll bet the store closed early due to the weather.* She took a bite of her sandwich.

"How is it?"

"Delicious. Haven't had Greek food for a while."

He made a symmetrical circle of ketchup and arranged the fries around it with his fork.

"Here. Try this." He stabbed a fry and offered it to her.

"You're right. These are good." She alternated a bite of salad with a fry from the detective's plate.

"If you notice anything that could possibly link Travis Jennings to the murder, would you give me a call?"

"Of course, Detective Lambert."

"Phil. Call me Phil—unless we're down at the station."

"Okay, Phil. Let me treat you to some Baklava since I ate half your fries."

"I'm pretty full. Let's share one instead. Enough shoptalk. Tell me about you. What do you like to do when you aren't working?"

"I'm fortunate that playing the oboe isn't something I consider work. I like to read."

She couldn't remember the last book she'd read.

"Do you like snowboarding?"

"Haven't tried it. I did a little skiing growing up, but like I said earlier, I'm not very good at it."

"We'll have to give it a try sometime. It isn't hard. Easier than skiing."

She'd made a habit of avoiding any activities where she could possibly injure her hands. Should she even worry about that anymore?"

"By the way, the crime cleanup service finished. You can go back to the Rossi house now."

"Finished already?"

"It's not like they had a lot of work ahead of them, and there wasn't much blood. They almost sounded excited when I called to arrange it. I'd better head back." He grabbed the check and left a generous tip. "Thanks for meeting me. We'll have to do it again."

She wouldn't mind seeing him again. It was nice to talk to someone her own age. Someone pleasant and with manners. Should she trust Travis or not? She'd trusted Brandon and see where that left her. Her gut wanted to believe Travis was on the up and up, but there were some discrepancies in what he'd told her, not to mention the earring she'd found. And why wouldn't he allow the police to take a mold of his tires unless…she didn't want to go there. *Just because he's private doesn't mean he's guilty.*

She stopped at Travis's house to pick up her things and to get Panther. The more she thought about it, the happier she was to get out of that house. For all she knew, she'd been staying with a killer.

"Panther, you'll be happy to be back in familiar territory, won't you?" She grabbed her things, then noticed a text from Travis. *Locksmith came. New key is on kitchen table.* She'd almost forgotten. "Well, Panther, should we do a little investigating before we leave?"

She listened to be sure they were alone, then went to Travis's closet in his bedroom. Half a dozen shirts and pants, a three-piece suit, and a bath robe hung from the bar. No woman's clothing. Then she opened the drawers, one by one.

The boxers were neatly rolled and sorted by color. Going through the t-shirts, she found the holey one he'd been wearing the night of the murder. She unfolded it. There was a dark stain at chest level. Could it be a blood stain? She trembled.

"Let's check the bathroom, Panther." She opened the drawers under the sink. Amongst the neatly arranged shaving cream, razors, and deodorant, she found a curling iron. Surely that didn't belong to him. *Ellie used to love to curl her hair when we were in high school...*

She looked at her watch. Travis might pop in at any moment. She scooped up Panther and scurried downstairs.

It took longer to load her things into the car than it took to drive next door. She stood on the porch, trembling. "We can do this, Panther."

She walked into a ransacked mess, exactly like the last time she'd been there. She picked up the couch cushions and tossed them on the sofa, clearing the path to the stairs. She trembled going up the steps, picturing Ellie on the floor.

She pushed open the bedroom door, expecting the worst, but the bedroom was devoid of any traces of the murder. The carpet looked brand new. Not a trace of blood anywhere. She could detect the faint odor of bleach, but other than that, you'd never know a crime had taken place here.

She went to the dresser. Ellie's brush...a cosmetics bag...deodorant. All traces that Ellie had indeed been here. Her eyes teared.

Ellie's watch and gold necklace are sitting right here on top of the jewelry box. If this was a robbery, it wasn't valuables they were after. What did they want?

She'd have to have Ellie's parents come get her things when they felt up to it. On top of the jewelry box, she spotted a gold hoop earring. The match to the one she'd found at Travis's house.

Caught off guard, she felt heat on the back of her neck a second before feeling a hand clamp over her mouth. Strong arms pinned her own arms against her body. *Travis! He caught me snooping. He followed me and he's a murderer!* She struggled like a bear in a hunting trap. Her heart punched and tried to rip its way out of her chest. *How could I be so stupid as to trust him?*

"Stay still. I'm not going to harm you. I have to talk to you."

She continued to struggle. Now his gloved hand partially covered her nose. She couldn't breathe. With all her energy she flung forward, but might as well have stayed still. The vise around her torso tightened.

"I didn't kill Ellie. I loved her. You have to convince the police to look in another direction. Shake your head if you're willing to listen to me."

He loosened his grip. *What other options do I have? It's agree or suffocate.*

He peeled his hand off of her mouth. She turned and faced him, arms like Jell-O, legs numb.

"You're not Travis."

"No, I'm not."

She caught her breath. "You're Preston Montague, right? How did you get in here? The locks were just changed."

"The back door was unlocked. So much for security. If you know who I am, then you've done your homework. You should have concluded I'm not a murderer."

"If you're innocent, why have you gone into hiding?"

"Because no one will believe me. I'm not getting locked up for something I didn't do."

"Are you going to kill me too?"

"Of course not. How many times do I have to tell you I'm not a killer? I just want to see justice done; I want to find whoever did this to the love of my life. I owe it to Ellie."

"Let me go. I'm friends with the lead detective investigating this case. I'll talk to him."

"Don't run right to the police. Dig further. Ellie and that neighbor were involved. I saw them together. I think he killed her. Just look into it, that's all I'm asking."

She found herself being swayed by his sincerity. "Okay. I'll keep searching on my own. Will you leave now?"

"Give me your phone."

"What?"

"I'll leave it on the front stoop. Stay here until I'm gone. Promise, or you'll be coming with me."

"Okay. I promise."

Chapter 12

She flopped on the bed and heard heavy boots clomp down the steps. She waited to hear the front door close. She didn't hear a car, but hadn't seen one parked anywhere near by when she first entered the house.

He must be on foot. If he killed Ellie, certainly he had the resources to hoof it out of town. He couldn't be stupid enough to have stayed in town and taken a chance by coming to her house, which he knew the police were all over. Unless...he was still searching for the ring. Maybe he thinks I found it? No, he didn't even mention the ring. What if he's right and Travis killed her? I've been staying with a murderer. No. In her heart, she didn't believe Travis could have done that.

When she was convinced of her safety, she locked the back door, then went out front to retrieve her phone. She started to call Detective Lambert, then reconsidered. Maybe she should do a little digging first. *If Preston realizes I called, I could be putting myself in danger. Besides, he'll flee the country if he gets a whiff of the fact that the police know he's still in town.*

She summoned her courage, and took her bags from her car.

She lugged her things in from the car. *Can I handle staying in this house*? The expense of staying in a pet friendly hotel for six months was out of her budget, leaving her without an option. Besides, if Preston wanted to kill her she'd already be dead. Same with Travis. They both had the opportunity.

She unfolded the black dress she'd packed in case they went out somewhere fancy. Now she'd be wearing it to Ellie's funeral. Ellie loved dresses. It would have been a lot of fun going wedding dress shopping with her. Too bad she hadn't gotten the chance.

Senior prom. She and Ellie took the train to the city and shopped for the perfect dresses. Frustrated at the prices, Ellie had dragged her into a second-hand shop and for the price of Chinese takeout, Ellie had walked away with a blue satin gown and a cameo brooch. She herself found an ivory, off the shoulder, tea-length which she imagined was once someone's wedding dress. All the girls at the prom wanted to know where they'd found those vintage gowns. She hung the black dress in the closet and unpacked her shoes.

When the doorbell rang, Sara felt the hairs on her arms stand up. *Calm down, the bad guys don't announce themselves by ringing the doorbell in broad daylight.* She grabbed Panther and went down the stairs.

"Who is it?" She tried to line her eye up with the peephole but couldn't make out the distorted image.

"Home Security Systems. We have a work order." She undid the chain and talked through the small opening. The man in the gray uniform showed his ID badge and presented her with paperwork. "Are you Ellie Rossi?"

"Just a minute." She unlocked the door. Reluctant to explain that Ellie was dead, she said, "I'll sign for it. How much is this going to cost?"

"It's already been paid for. No worries. We'll start with the motion sensors." A second man grabbed equipment from the van. A new security system, new locks. She'd be safe here, wouldn't she? *Ellie had bought an expensive home security system after turning her closet into a safe room? She had to have been terrified.*

Her phone vibrated. "Mom, everything okay? You're swamped at the station? Sure, I can pick up Grandpa and bring him to his appointment. Lunch was nice. Yeah, he's nice. Yes, he is a gentleman. Yes, he could be in a toothpaste commercial with those pearly whites. I'll swing by and get Grandpa."

The security workers assured her they didn't need access to the inside of the house. Sara drove to her parents' house and picked up her grandfather. It took so long for him to answer the door, she was beginning to panic that he'd fallen, or worse. The door creaked open.

"Sara? What are you doing here?"

"Mom said she told you. I'm here to bring you to your appointment."

"I could've skipped it."

She ignored the comment. "Here, I'll help you. The walk is slippery."

Pulling away, he said, "Don't you think I know? I've walked this path nearly every day for the past eighty years." He tossed his cane into the back of her car. "When are you going home?"

Sara's stomach turned every time she lied to her family, but with party planning, Scott away in Iraq, and now the situation with the family business, she couldn't pile more problems on her parents. "When my vacation is over." Technically that was true.

"You can take off whenever you feel like it? You're lucky to have that job you know."

"They're on a month long tour. I'm not the only oboist. I had vacation time coming."

"I never take a vacation from work."

"You own your own business. You can take time off whenever you want." She watched him limp toward the door. "What's going on with your hip? I don't remember you limping last time I was here." She handed him his cane.

"Nothing I can't handle." He threw the cane on the floor. "Your father wants me to have a hip replacement, but I don't want no operation."

"Travis might be able to help. He's a physical therapist. Want me to talk to him?"

"Barack? Like I said, I don't want surgery."

"Then after your appointment with Dr. Peters, I'll bring you by to talk to Travis."

He mumbled. "Yeah, yeah."

"We'd better get going." She grabbed the cane and tossed it in the back seat of her rental. When she neared the entrance, she followed signs to the parking area, surprised they managed without a separate medical tower for offices like the hospital back in San Francisco. After she parked, she grabbed the cane from the back seat and opened the passenger side door.

"Here. Take this."

He knocked the cane out of her hand. "I don't need that. I can walk. I'm not ready to be thrown out to pasture."

She tossed it back in the car. "Come on, then. You'd better prove it and keep up with me."

She walked more slowly than usual as she took her grandfather to the orthopedic floor.

"I can go in with you," said Sara.

"What, like I'm going to see the pediatrician and need my mommy to hold my hand? Come back in an hour."

"You got it." *How do my parents have patience with him?* Although she loved him dearly, she couldn't imagine living with him 24/7. She walked out into the corridor, where she saw someone come out of the back door of a neighboring office. *Wait. That's the back door to Dr. Peter's office, I'm almost sure.*

The man looked both ways, pulled up the collar of his jacket like a turtle retreating into his shell, and started toward the elevator. *That's Preston Montague!* She didn't want to lose sight of him, especially given the police hadn't been able to locate him. *How did he get by security? Surely the turtle act wouldn't have cut it.*

Keeping her distance, she watched him veer toward the stairs, not the elevator. She slipped through the door and followed him. Her heart raced. She summoned up every ounce of bravery she could, and kept on his tail. He was about to go through the emergency exit. If she left, she knew she couldn't get back into the building. If she stayed, he'd be off in the wind. *I have to do this for Ellie. Here goes.*

She followed Preston up and down the rows of cars. *He's heading toward the stairs. He's going to another garage level.* While cars went in and out of this level, she knew the stairwell was likely to be deserted. Anyone parking for the hospital would take the elevator to the correct floor, not park a level or two away. It wasn't San Francisco. It was possible to find a parking space close to your destination. *Breathe in, breathe out.* She followed him, careful not to clang her boot heels on the metal steps

Where's he going? She followed him down two flights to the ground floor. She caught herself from tripping, but her heel clanked against the stoop. Preston stopped. He turned as if he'd heard a sound, and she immediately ducked behind an Audi, afraid to breathe. *This is a possible murderer I'm following. Is he going to take off on foot?*

In a flash, she heard chirping and saw headlights. Preston sped away. No way could she keep up, and her phone wasn't getting a signal. The police were looking for his white BMW. Preston drove off in a black Tesla. The electric car barely made a noise. *Maybe that's why*

I didn't hear Preston drive away from Ellie's after he cornered me.

She was out of the garage before she got a signal. Preston was still in town and he had an accomplice. Whoever owned the Tesla was working with him, and it had been parked in the spaces reserved for doctors! *So much for the noisy Buick registered to an old lady in the next town.*

"Detective Lambert please." *Please let him be there.* Maybe they could be on the lookout for the car if they went for it right away. "Yes, Detective, Phil, I just spotted Preston Montague at Hudsonville Community Hospital, He left in the Tesla. Five or ten minutes ago. I'm at the hospital now with my Grandfather who's at a doctor's appointment. It was parked in the reserved doctor spaces in the parking garage and I saw him leaving out the back door of an orthopedic office." She stopped to breathe. "I got some of the plate numbers. What? I will."

She was about to hang up when he asked her one more question. "Dinner? Tomorrow night?" She was caught off guard by the abrupt change of topic, but the words slipped out of her mouth without effort. "I'd like that." *I'm sure Mom had something to do with that.*

She took a deep breath to calm herself before fetching her grandfather. *In and out, in and out. Maybe Preston Montague and Dr. Peters got back together now that Ellie is out of the picture. They had broken up before his engagement to Ellie, but exes get back together all the time. Well, maybe not all the time. It'll be a cold day in you know where before I'd ever take Brandon back. I would make a bet that the Buick belongs to the doctor.*

Montague knows the police are on the lookout for his BMW so he's using her car. Does she normally drive a Tesla? Is he staying at her place? *I forgot to say it was Jailyn Peter's office Preston came from.* Should she call Phil back and suggest checking it out, or would it seem like she was trying to tell him how to do his job? She'd casually mention it at dinner tomorrow night.

She glanced at her watch. *Grandpa!* Surely he was done by now and wondering where she was. She slipped into the elevator just as it was closing. A neatly dressed gentleman was talking to one of the doctors. *He's the man from the cafeteria. The one who was sitting with Jailyn Peters.*

"These hold up longer and are less expensive than the previous models."

"What about the clinical trials? Did the data support these?"

"Absolutely. Patented and FDA approved." He pulled a pamphlet from his briefcase.

"Great. I'll look into it."

"Here's my card if you have any questions."

When the elevator stopped at the orthopedic floor, the gentleman followed her into Dr. Peter's waiting room. The receptionist didn't even ask his name.

"Dr. Peters will be with you shortly. She's expecting you." She buzzed him in. *He must be a frequent visitor. She didn't even ask for ID.* Grandpa struggled to get up from the plastic chair. Sara handed him his cane.

"Where've you been, Sara? I've been waiting here twenty minutes."

"Sorry, Grandpa."

"Come on, Sara. I've got things to do."

Things to do? Like take a nap? "Let's go. Oh, do you want to talk to Travis about the physical therapy?"

He grumbled. "Let's make it quick."

She led Grandpa to the other end of the floor where the physical therapy facilities were located. The receptionist was on the phone. Grandpa drummed his fingers on the counter, louder and more quickly as time progressed. Then he said quite loudly, "I guess she doesn't see us waiting."

"Shh, Grandpa. Making appointments and answering the phone is part of her job. She knows we're here. Stop being so rude." She looked through the window to the other side of the counter and saw a business card. Craig Danalchek, Medivision Medical Devices.

With a deliberate motion and a look that could kill in spite of an appropriate customer service tone, the receptionist hung up the phone and said, "Can I help you?"

"I was wondering if we could talk to Mr. Jennings for a moment. I'm a friend."

The receptionist looked her up and down. "He's busy with patients."

A nurse was filing papers behind the reception desk and spoke up. "His patient just left. He's available."

The receptionist made a disapproving sound and called Travis. She glared at Grandpa. "Go on back."

Grandpa mumbled, "It's about time" as he followed Sara back.

Travis was jotting notes in his iPad. "Is everything okay?"

"Yes. Grandpa wants to talk to you about physical therapy for his hip. He'd like to avoid surgery if it's possible."

"Sure. I can't operate on a damaged hip, but I may be able to ease the pain. At least you may be able to delay the surgery."

"How much does this cost? Do you take Medicare? I got Medicare."

"Yes, no problem. The receptionist can help you with that. Make an appointment with her on your way out."

Oh, I'm sure she can't wait to help Grandpa now that he made such a great first impression. "Thanks, Travis."

"Did you settle in at Ellie's? You got the new key, right?"

"Yes, and some security company showed up. They're installing motion sensors and monitors. Ellie must have felt threatened, what with making her closet into a safe room and purchasing an expensive security system."

"As it turns out, her instincts were spot on."

"Travis, I saw Preston Montague right here in the hospital. He was leaving the back way out of Jailyn Peter's office. I followed him into the parking garage."

"You did what?"

"He didn't see me. I watched him get into a black Tesla that was parked in the doctor's area. I'll bet it belonged to Jailyn Peters. Then I called the police but I'm fairly sure it's too late to catch him."

"That was pretty brazen. Don't try to be the hero here."

"I'm not. I just happened upon him. He and Dr. Peters must still be seeing each other. I think she lent him her car."

Grandpa said, "If you two lovebirds are done, I've got things to do. Get me home, Sara."

Travis's phone buzzed. "Okay. Send him in." He rose from his desk. "I have a meeting with the CEO of Medivision. Come by the house later."

"Okay. Thank you." She mouthed, 'I'm sorry' on the way out.

Grandpa waited until they were outside the office to say, "We could have been home already if you didn't keep flirting with Barack."

She felt her cheeks heat up. "I wasn't flirting, He's a jerk. And don't call him Barack; it sounds racist." *And it's an insult to Obama.*

"Twirling your hair like a teenager? I wasn't born yesterday. And he ate it up. He was looking at your chest, you know."

"Let's get you back home." *The sooner, the better.*

Chapter 13

The next day, Sara pulled her black dress over her head and brushed her hair into a low ponytail. Ellie's parents had gotten the funeral arrangements together in record time. Travis offered to give her a ride, and she dabbed on some face powder and pale pink lipstick.

When they got to the church, the parking lot was nearly full. She recognized her parents' car and wondered if they'd brought Grandpa along. Small candles in colored glass jars were lined up along the sides of the church, filling the air with the aroma of incense. Sunlight streamed through the stained glass windows.

"Where do you want to sit?" asked Travis.

"Wherever there's a spot. Who are all these people?"

"Looks like she had a lot of friends. I see Detective Lambert over there. Sometimes the police check out a murder victim's funeral for possible suspects."

"Or maybe he's just paying his respects to her family?"

"Don't think so. I watch a lot of detective shows. That guy over there owns the company Ellie worked for. The Montagues are heavily invested in it."

She recognized him from the hospital. "He was at your office and I saw him talking to Dr. Peters at the hospital. Craig Danalchek, CEO of Medivision. Isn't that Dr. Peters he's talking to now?"

"Yeah. She uses their products in her surgeries."

"Why was the busy CEO of Medivision on the orthopedic floor yesterday?"

"He's CEO but he hustles, just like Sara did. It's one of those companies where they motivate employees with shares of stock. Seems to work. The company is thriving."

"Are they local?"

"Yeah, Montague owns the office building next to the hospital and warehouse at the edge of town. Looks like they're starting the service."

If the words at a funeral didn't make her cry, the music always managed to. When a soprano who'd gone to school with Sara and Ellie sang *Be Not Afraid* from the choir loft, Sara couldn't hold back the tears. To her surprise, Travis took her hand in his, then just as abruptly pulled it away.

Sara's parents sat a few rows ahead of them. She knew her mother was empathizing—she'd picture herself in Mrs. Rossi's shoes. Her mother wiped away tears. Ellie was an extension of her own family, with all the time she spent at their house growing up. Grandpa had stayed home. Thank God. He'd have told Mom to stop bawling or something similarly inappropriate. Sara looked to the front row. From behind, she saw Mr. Rossi hugging his wife as she fell apart.

Having grown up Catholic, Sara found the funeral services comforting, though less personal than others she'd been to. Rituals, order, the promise of an afterlife—reassuring when your world has been turned upside down. She recited the prayers from rote which she'd learned as child, sang the hymns she knew by heart, and followed the progression of stand, kneel, sit, make the sign of the cross.

After the service, the congregation followed the casket to the cemetery behind the church. Sara took a turn saying goodbye and tossed a rose on the casket. *Her poor parents. How are they going to bounce back from this?*

Afterwards, they headed downstairs to the church basement. Sara's mother and members of the church had set up a buffet. Finger sandwiches, potato salad…brownies, cakes, cookies…a huge urn of coffee with a tempting aroma…

She hugged Ellie's parents. "I'm so sorry for your loss. You know she was the sister I always wanted."

Mrs. Rossi said, "She thought of you that way, too. She loved you, you know."

"I loved her. I wish we'd stayed in closer contact recently. I didn't even know she was engaged or anything."

"Well, it happened so quickly—the relationship, the engagement, the breakup…all in the blink of an eye."

Travis said, "I was Ellie's neighbor. Didn't know her well, but she always had a smile on her face whenever I saw her outside."

The man Travis had identified as Ellie's boss, the one from the cafeteria, came up to them. "Craig Danalchek. I'm so sorry for your loss. Ellie will be sorely missed. Such a hard worker, and great with the customers. Walked the fine line between persistent and pushy. She has some things at the office. No rush, whenever you're ready to pick them up."

Two co-workers came over, also offering condolences.

"I'm Camaya Campbell. Our cubicles were side by side. She used to bring banana bread to share with us. In the fall it was pumpkin bread." Tears dripped from Camaya's eyes. She pulled out a tissue. "I can't do this. I need some air."

"I'm going to see if she's okay," said Sara. She climbed up the stairs and into the church garden where Camaya was huddled on a metal bench.

"Are you going to be okay?"

"I miss her so much. I should have been there for her."

"What do you mean? You were her friend. I'm sure she knew that."

"I knew something was wrong. She said nothing was wrong but I should have pried. I saw her slip out to take phone calls. She'd always taken calls right at her desk before. Instead of going to happy hour at Ralph's she was always in a rush to get home. It wasn't like her."

"She must have been upset when the engagement broke off."

"She was acting strange before that happened. I wish I'd done something."

"I grew up with Ellie. She was one of the most stubborn people I'd ever met. If she didn't want to talk, no amount of coaxing would change her mind."

Sara heard a rustling coming from behind the shrubs. "Did you hear that?"

"Yes. It's probably a stray cat. I'm going to head home now."

After Camaya left, Sara heard the sound again. She got up and searched the garden. There. Preston Montague! He was wearing a hat and doing the turtle number but she recognized him. He ran toward the parking lot.

You're not getting away this time. Travis came outside just in time.

"Quick, let's get your car and follow that man."

"What man?"

"Preston Montague. He just ran toward the parking lot."

Travis wasted no time. They ran for his car.

"I can see him. Let's go."

Travis followed the Tesla. The paved road leading to the church turned into a gravel path.

"Where's he going? There's nothing but farmland down that road."

"Stay on him." Sara hung onto her seat as the road became bumpier and bumpier.

"I'm going to ruin my tires." The gravel turned into a one-lane dirt path. "What are we going to do when we catch up to him? He may have a weapon."

"If we see where he's hiding, we can go back and tell the police. Phil thinks he's left the country already."

"Phil?"

"Detective Lambert. They've seen no sign of him. Of course, they were looking for a white BMW. I think he's driving Dr. Peters' car. A black Tesla."

"Really? Look, he's turning." The dirt road became a grassy path. "He's sure to see us if we go down there."

"Park."

"What?"

"Park behind that tree and we'll go on foot."

"Are you nuts? It's freezing out and look at those shoes you're wearing."

"I can walk in these." She looked down at the pumps that had been hurting her feet since she put them on. "I'll be fine."

Travis pulled the car behind the tree. "Come on."

Sara slid before she got clear of the car. "I didn't see that patch of ice. I'm fine." She'd felt more secure balancing on her figure skates than she did in these heels.

Travis held her hand. "Look, There's a hunting cabin. He's going inside. We can turn around now."

"Let's see if we can peek in the window. See if he's with anyone."

"I don't think it's a good idea."

"Then go back to the car and I'll meet you back there when I'm done." If it wasn't so darn cold, she'd lose the shoes and go barefooted. Travis followed her.

When they got to the cabin, they ducked below one of the windows. Sara could hear Preston talking to someone. Was it in person, or on the phone? She peeked above the ledge.

Travis pulled her down and whispered, "What are you doing?"

"He's talking to someone."

"I don't hear anything."

"Trust me, he's talking to someone."

"Let's not tip our hand. If he knows we found the cabin he'll just hide somewhere else. Come on. Let's go back. You can call Phil and tell him what we found."

The touch of sarcasm made her warm inside. *He's jealous.*

"You're right." She felt like her feet had sprouted a dozen blisters. Maybe going barefoot would be better after all. She took off her shoe.

"Are you crazy? You'll get frostbite. Come on." He picked her up and slung her over his shoulder like a sack of potatoes.

"Put me down. I'm too heavy. You'll rupture a disc or something." His hair smelled like fresh linens. His shoulders were sturdy.

"It's faster this way. The car isn't far."

His hands, which were wrapped around her thighs, moved to her derriere as he shifted her weight. *His hands are so strong. Stop. You're trying to escape a psycho killer and you're thinking about how Travis's hands feel?*

When they got to the car, he put her right in the passenger seat and took her shoes out of his pocket. "You should burn these."

"Done."

On the way back, she called the police. Detective Lambert wasn't in. The receptionist said he'd gone to a funeral. Duh. She'd forgotten she'd seen him in the back of the church.

"Tell her you want to speak to an officer if he's not there."

How would she explain why she and Travis followed Preston to a hunting cabin? "I'll try his cell."

"Why do you have his cell number?"

She turned away from him. "Phil, I tried the station but you weren't there. Look, we stumbled on something really important. Preston Montague is hiding out in a hunting cabin on the outskirts of town. I'll text you the directions."

Chapter 14

When she got home, she went to her room, changed into comfy sweats, and pulled out her oboe. *I'm almost afraid to try.*

She soaked a reed and dug music out of her suitcase. *If I recover, this will be the first piece I play with the Philharmonic. Brahms 4th Symphony.* One of her all-time favorites, with beautiful but exposed oboe solos. *Here goes.*

She crowed on the reed, causing Panther to dart from the room, then warmed up on the opening bars of the Mozart Concerto. *The reed's not great, but my hands are working just fine. I miss playing so much. If I can't return to my job, I'm not sure what I'll do with my life.*

She played a while, scraped the reed, then played some more. Just when she was beginning to feel optimistic, the fingers on her left hand froze in an unnatural position. Tears fell down her cheeks. She pulled apart the oboe, threw the reed against the wall, and buried her head in her pillow. When her pity session had run its course, she thought about the events earlier in the day.

Did Phil catch up to Preston Montague? Maybe by now he'd confessed and the case is closed. And he sounded so sincere the day he snuck into the house and pinned me. It won't bring Ellie back, but at least Ellie's parents will learn why he killed their daughter. She'd see Phil in a few hours. Should she call, or wait? She dug in her purse for her lucky penny. *Heads I call, tails*

I wait. Tails. She got in the shower, leaving her phone on the bed.

Between the shower and when Phil picked her up promptly at 6:00, she fussed with her hair and tried on three different outfits. *I almost forgot.* She swabbed out her oboe and tucked the pieces back in their case just before the doorbell rang.

Phil wore a tan crewneck sweater and dark jeans. His hair was neatly combed to the side, held in place with a touch of gel. She got a whiff of citrus cologne when he helped her into her coat. *He's neat, clean, smart, well-dressed...why don't I feel butterflies around him?*

"You look nice," said Phil. "Red's a good color on you." He handed her the tattered scarf.

"Thanks. You too. I'm dying to know. Did you catch Preston Montague?"

"No. We found the cabin but there was no sign of him."

"He had to have left some clue behind. That proves he hasn't left town."

"Or hadn't yet. I wish you hadn't followed him. It tipped him off and gave him a chance to escape."

"Seriously? We were doing you a favor. Besides, he didn't see us. Maybe he'll come back later. You should post an undercover patrol car out there."

"Thanks for the advice. Want me to tell you how to play that instrument of yours?"

She rolled her eyes like a passive aggressive teen.

Phil pulled into the parking lot of La Pergola. It had a reputation supported by restaurant reviews for being the best Italian food in the county. Sara salivated like one of Pavlov's dogs when she smelled the garlic bread the moment she stepped inside the restaurant.

The dining area was nearly at capacity. Sara and Phil followed the hostess to a linen-covered table with a robust, glowing candle in the center. She was glad she'd packed a second dress at the last second and didn't have to wear the black one she'd worn to the funeral. She'd accessorized with a colorful statement necklace and diamond earrings that hung like filigree ropes and she could see them sparkle out of the corner of her eye as they caught the candlelight.

Phil ordered a bottle of wine. "What are you in the mood for?"

Sara read through the menu. It'd been a while since she'd eaten here. "I think I'll try the gnocchi." *No-key, or no-chee?* She could never remember which was correct so she mumbled over it. *I've never eaten Italian food that could hold a candle to Mom's.*

"That sounds good."

"Did you check for prints? What about tire marks?"

Phil closed his menu. "Like I said, the cabin was abandoned. Looked like no one had been there in quite some time."

"Are you sure you got the right place? And did you check out Dr. Jailyn Peters? I hear she was the jealous type."

"I'm sure. And Dr. Peters has an alibi for the night of the murder. She was volunteering at the clinic across town. Now, can we find something more pleasant than murder suspects to talk about? How's your grandfather's party coming along?"

She'd almost forgotten about it. "I'm ordering the cake tomorrow and I have to check on the hall. Mom and I are going decoration shopping." She wished Scott could be there instead of in the middle of a desert on the other side of the globe.

"Sounds like fun."

"You should come. The more the merrier."

"I'll probably be working, but if not, I'll stop by."

"Mom makes way too much food and she loves to show off her cooking. That gene must skip generations."

"I'll check my schedule. Thanks. How's the family business going?"

"It's getting hard for my dad to keep up. Grandpa isn't able to help much anymore. He's talking about selling the business, which I know would destroy him."

"Can't he hire help?"

"It's not so easy. If you know a skilled oboe maker who will work for peanuts, send him on over."

"Maybe he'll enjoy being retired. My father and his new wife spend their days in Utah on the ski slopes or riding horses."

"We don't have that kind of money. If he retires, they'll barely make ends meet."

The waiter set the food on the table. "More wine?"

Phil lifted his glass. "Yes, thanks." He reached across the table and gently took Sara's hands. "I hope I'm not being too forward, but I'm really attracted to you. I'm hoping we can get to know each other better."

Sara gently pulled her hands away. "I just got out of a bad relationship, and I have a job waiting back in San Francisco. Let's take it a step at a time and see where things go." She hoped she'd have her job waiting. So far, the exercises Travis had recommended seemed to help, but nowhere near enough to eradicate the problem. She remembered her frustrating practice session earlier today.

"Here's to seeing how things go." He raised his glass. "I got out of a bad relationship not too long ago also. I've dated a little, but nothing serious. You get to that age where you want to put down roots, have a family. You know what I mean?"

"I do. I feel that way myself at times. With my symphony schedule and having to keep up my playing,

I didn't think about it so much. Now that I have time on my hands, I can picture myself as a mother."

"I'm at the point where I'd like nothing more than to come home at the end of the day and eat dinner with a wife and a couple of kids. And a dog or two. Do you like dogs?"

"I'm more of a cat person. I can't have pets in my place."

"Do you like living in San Francisco?"

"Yeah. There's always something going on, and the weather is pleasant, other than some rain."

"So you don't miss the snowy, gray winters?"

"A little snow now and then would be nice—as long as I didn't have to drive to work in it. What I do miss is the sense of familiarity here—having people around that you've known your whole life. I don't even know my neighbors back home. Then again, with my schedule, I have to spend a lot of time alone practicing and making reeds. I don't have time to get to meet people outside of my orchestra colleagues." *And that turned out well. It was awful being in the same room as Brandon and the violinist he was still dating.*

"Have you ever considered moving back and helping with the family business?"

Unfortunately, she *had* been considering it. It might not be a choice. "I'd miss playing in the symphony. It's who I am. Do you think you'd be happy doing something other than law enforcement?"

"No. Well, maybe." He took a bite of food. "When I retire, I'm going to breed standard Poodles."

"Those cute little puff balls? My aunt had one."

He took out his phone. "Not the little toy poodles, the big ones. See?"

"They're—cute." What else could she say? Raising dogs wasn't on her bucket list and the oversized poodles just looked wrong. Then again, it must be nice to have a passion outside of work, like he did. She watched the hostess seat a couple next to the window.

"Are you ready for dessert?"

She was about to utter a rude *excuse me,* then realized he meant it literally.

"They have Italian cheesecake. And cappuccino."

"Sure." She looked toward the kitchen. "Isn't that Jailyn Peters? And the head of Medivision, Ellie's boss."

Phil turned to look. "Yeah, that's her. And the man she's with is Craig Danalchek. We interviewed both of them."

This was the second time she'd seen them talking together. He looked different, dressed in corduroys rather than a suit and tie. "And they're dating?"

He turned around again. "It doesn't look romantic to me. They're probably talking business. He runs the medical device company; she uses artificial joints and such."

They ordered a cheesecake to share. Sara watched Jailyn Peters head towards the ladies' room. "I'll be right back."

When she neared the rest room, she heard Jailyn whispering on her phone. *"I'll come by tonight. Stay put and stop panicking. Nothing's changed."*

She ducked past her into a stall. *I'll bet she's talking to Preston Montague. Stay put? He must have gone back to the cabin.*

When she got back to the table, Phil had divided the slice of cake into two identical halves. "I waited but it wasn't easy."

"Looks delicious." She took a bite.

Phil leaned over. "You have a little bit of..." He pointed to his outer lip.

She patted with her napkin. "Better?"

"No, let me." He dabbed gently at the corner of her mouth. "There."

She watched Jailyn Peters and Ellie's boss, Craig Danalchek, leave the restaurant. *If that was a date, it mustn't have gone well. They were in and out in record time and looks like she didn't even finish her dinner.*

Phil pushed back from the table. "I'm stuffed. Maybe a little walk in the night air? Or we can go back to my place for a drink."

"I had a lovely time but I'm beat. Maybe next time."

"Let's get you home."

The whole ride back, Sara was nervous Phil would try to kiss her goodnight, but he simply walked her to her door and told her he'd had a great time. She locked the door and set the alarm. As soon as she heard his car pull away, she went to work.

If Jailyn is heading to the cabin, this may be the only chance of nailing her. She called Travis. No answer. *Where is he? Surely he hasn't gone to bed yet, and he doesn't work nights.* She put her coat back on and walked across to his place. The porch light was on, but the rest of the house was dark. She knocked. *Maybe he's gone to bed.* When she didn't get a response, she retreated back to Ellie's.

Should I go it alone? This can't wait. She called Travis one more time and left a message. She took out the penny in her pocket and gave it a flip. *Heads. I'm going. I hope I can find this place in the dark.* She threw on sweats and stuck her lucky penny in the pocket of her jacket. Shaking but determined, she headed to the cabin. What choice did she have?

Snow flurries melted as they hit the windshield. The roads were dark and she didn't pass a single car. Not one. She did, however, keep on the lookout for deer crossing the road, and fallen rocks. If she got stuck out here, she'd be stranded. *I think I have to turn up there.*

Her hands were shaking as they gripped the steering with a death hold. *Breathe in and out, in and out.*

Found it. She got out of the car. *It's not too late to go back.* The driveway was empty, but she noticed tire tracks in the dirty snow. *I have to do this for Ellie.*

Pulling her scarf tighter, she worked her way closer, stepping on dried branches that had fallen off the bare trees. *One step at a time. You can do this.* She crept to the window, ducked underneath, and carefully peered inside. Too dark. As much as she strained, she couldn't see inside. Creeping around to the back, the wind blew snow flurries onto her face. Wiping them away, she saw something on the ground. A hospital ID badge. Jailyn Peter's badge. *This is proof she was here!*

She couldn't wait to call Phil and tell him to get a squad car out to search. She grasped the badge in her cold hand and was ready to head back to the car. Then everything went black.

Chapter 15

She woke up shivering, her hands numb, her face burning. The back of her head throbbed.

"Wake up! Come on, Sara. We have to get you out of here before you get frostbite. Wake up." Travis shook her gently, then more aggressively.

"I'm...I'm okay." She tried to sit up, felt nauseous, then lay back down.

"We have to get you home." Travis helped her up. "What happened? What are you doing here?"

"I tried to call you. You weren't home." She rubbed her head.

"I got your message." He put his arm around her and started walking her toward the car. "I thought you had more sense than this."

"I had to. I overheard Jailyn. I know Preston is staying here. Had to find proof before they fled."

"According to the detective, if he was ever here, he's long gone. They searched here, remember?"

"Look, I found this. Jailyn's ID badge." She opened her fist. "It's gone!"

"Are you sure? Look around."

"No, I had it right in my hand. She must have taken it."

"Or Preston did."

"Where were you, anyway? I called, I knocked at your door."

"I was out." He hesitated. "Playing Poker with the guys."

She hadn't heard him mention a single friend since she'd gotten into town, let alone a Poker game. He was on a date. I know it. *Stop; it's not your business.* "How did you know where to find me? Or that I was in trouble?"

"I told you. I got your message and knew if you headed to the cabin it might be trouble. Come on, let's get you to the hospital."

"Hospital? No, I'm okay, really. I just want to get home."

"You might have a concussion."

"And if I do? There's not much they can do at the hospital. If I start seeing double or throwing up, I'll call you ASAP. You will be home, right?"

"I'll be home. Come on, let's get out of here."

Sara fell asleep the moment she hit the bed. She hadn't had the strength to brush her teeth or change out of her clothes. When she woke, head pounding like she'd been out on a drinking binge, Panther was purring, asleep on her pillow.

"You stood guard all night, didn't you, kitty?"

Panther opened his eyes and nuzzled against her, butting her with his head.

"I know, you're hungry." She looked at the alarm clock. An hour later than her usual wakeup time. After gulping down a few Excedrin, she formulated a plan. Shower, breakfast, head to the police station. Oh, and fill up Panther's bowl with a can of Fancy Feast. He deserved a treat for keeping watch over her last night.

By the time she got in the car, her tsunami of a headache had ebbed into a strong rip current. She thought about her 'date' with Phil and hoped he'd be busy when she arrived. Not that he wasn't a *good catch*, as her mother would say. She'd had a perfectly pleasant time, but the chemistry wasn't there and Phil as much as told her he was hungry for a serious relationship.

Besides, at this moment two important issues were foremost on her mind. Would she be able to continue her career as an orchestral musician, and who murdered her childhood friend?

When she walked into the station, she went directly to her mother's desk. Phil's office door was closed.

"Sara, what are you doing here? Did someone try to break into Ellie's again?" Her mother's face wrinkled with concern.

"No, Mom. I just need your help."

"Detective Lambert said he took you to dinner last night. I think he likes you."

"It was a first date, if you'd call it that. Look, I don't want him to know I'm looking into this, but can you run a check on Dr. Jailyn Peters?"

"Grandpa's doctor? Why? Did Detective Lambert date her? She went out with Preston Montague and well…you don't need to be involved with anyone who has a psycho ex-girlfriend in the closet."

"Oh, no. Nothing like that. I think she may have a connection to Ellie's murder, but Phil swears she has an alibi. If I probe him further, he'll think I don't trust his competence."

"What do you want to know?"

"Can you start by seeing if she has a police record? Maybe do a background check?"

"I can see if she's in the system. Jailyn. Pretty name. How does she spell it again?"

Sara spelled it out and waited while her mom searched. *Mom looks like she's worked here forever rather than a few months. Maybe she'd have been happier having a career in addition to raising me and Scott. Can you be fulfilled being only a wife and mother in this day and age? Montagues and company aside, can anyone afford to raise a family on one income?*

Patty slapped the desk. "Sara, your hunch may be right. According to this report, Jailyn Peters was brought in on battery charges a while back. She attacked a man and was ordered into anger management classes. I should've checked her out myself before taking Grandpa to her."

"I knew there was more to her. Does it say his name?"

"Will I get arrested for telling you? I'm sure this is confidential information."

"Mom, it's me. I'm not going to tell anyone. It's for Ellie. If Jailyn Peters had anything to do with Ellie's murder, I have an obligation to get the info to the police, but right now, I have no evidence."

"Okay. His name is David Coleman. You can't let on where you got this or I'll be fired or worse. Here's the address I have. Can't promise he hasn't moved since then."

"Thanks, Mom." She kissed her on the cheek.

Phil Lambert's door flew open. A woman dressed in a fur coat shouted, "If you don't find that ring soon, I'm going after your badge. We have connections in this town. Important connections." She slammed the door and strutted past Sara and her mother, leaving the heavy scent of Opium perfume behind her.

Sara let out a sneeze, reviving the pain in the back of her head. "What was that all about?"

"That's Mama Montague. She's been in here practically every day since the engagement was called off. The ring was an irreplaceable family heirloom and she wants it back."

"They didn't find it when they searched Ellie's house?"

"Apparently not. It takes all kinds. You wouldn't believe some of the folks who walk through those doors. It could be a reality TV show. *The Real Wackos of Hudsonville.*"

"Think they'd keep you on as the office manager turned narrator?"

"I'd insist. Can you stop by for dinner? You can bring Detective Lambert."

"I'll have to play it by ear. No Detective Lambert, though. I just saw him last night and don't want to seem over anxious." Truth is, she didn't want to let it slip she was investigating the good doctor.

Sara looked him up and verified the address. David Coleman was a real estate agent whose office was downtown near the Greek diner. She headed straight there. She immediately recognized him from the picture on his website.

"Can I help you?"

"Hello, my name is Sara Baron. I'm hoping you can."

"Have a seat. Want some coffee? It's vanilla peppermint." He poured her a cup before she had a chance to decline. "How many bedrooms and baths are we looking at?"

"Oh, no. I'm not here to find a house." *Although if my leave of absence from the symphony becomes permanent, I'll likely be back. No, I take that back. I'll more likely be broke and living in my parents' basement.*

"Then what can I do for you?"

"I'll get right to the point. My childhood friend has been murdered. I was supposed to house-sit for her, but when I got there, I discovered her body."

"Ellie Rossi. You're the one who found her? I'm so sorry."

"Thanks. I have some questions regarding Dr. Jailyn Peters."

"Are you with the police?"

"Do I look like a detective?"

"A reporter?"

"No, I promise"

He was easily convinced and eagerly started to talk. "That witch. Excuse my French. What do you want to know?"

"I know she dated Ellie's fiancé at one time and I was wondering if it was possible she became jealous and retaliated."

"Killed your friend? She popped my tires, all four of them, when she saw me out on a date after we broke up."

"Go on."

"Then a week or so later, she followed me home from a date. Pulled in behind me in my own driveway and started beating me with a tire iron. Caught me by surprise so she did some damage."

"That's awful. Did you report her?" She knew he did, but wanted to hear it from his own lips.

"I called the police immediately. She was charged with battery and the court ordered her to attend anger management classes. Got a hefty fine as well. Just to be safe, I filed for a restraining order."

"And she's stayed away?"

"Shortly after that, she took up with the Montague kid. Then I saw the engagement between Montague and your friend in the paper so I figured things didn't work out with him either."

"Thank you for the information."

"Hope it helps. Sorry for your loss. Oh, there's one more thing."

"What's that?"

"The judge mentioned something about this not being her first offense. Something about how she got off easy last time because she was a med student and if he ever saw her in his court again she'd be facing felony charges." He looked at the clock over his desk. "I have to meet a client at a property. Hope I've been helpful."

"Very much so."

Sara sat in her car and contemplated her next step. *Med school. I wonder if she went to med school locally?* She googled Jailyn Peters and read through her credentials. *Jailyn Peters graduated from Irving Medical College, less than an hour away.*

Chapter 16

She wasn't sure what she'd gain from visiting, but here she sat at the entrance of Irving Medical College. While sitting in front of the real estate office, she'd turned on the car radio, trying to decide whether or not to make the trip. A well-timed commercial convinced her. The announcer said, "Begin a fulfilling medical career at Irving Medical College." A clear sign she should pursue this lead.

Evergreen trees lined the entrance to the college, which consisted of several stone buildings, covered in ivy. It had been years since Jailyn Peters was a student here. Sara pulled open the heavy, oak door to the admissions office.

"Excuse me. I was wondering if I can get a catalog? I'm considering a career change." *Ha. Maybe not so far off the mark.*

The receptionist said, "So all the programs are listed in here along with the courses needed to complete the program."

"I have to apply, then pick classes?"

"Yes. If you're accepted into a program, you can access the course offerings, meeting times, and professors online."

"I had an old friend who did her medical degree here. Has the program changed much in the past 15 years or so?"

"We have new offerings such as radiology tech, and we began a physical therapy assistant program back a few years ago, but the standard medical school program hasn't changed. You can find the outline beginning on page 20."

"I'm sure there's turnover, but are some of the same professors here from when my friend attended?"

"Our professors tend to stay until they retire, so yes. There are some."

"And do your students ever return to teach here?"

"It's happened, but only after they're in practice for a while."

"Thank you."

"Best of luck. Get your application in early!"

Sara wandered into the coffee shop and browsed through the catalog. She had no idea where to start. She was hoping to find more evidence that Jailyn had a history of violent behavior fueled by jealousy, and all she had to go on was a vague comment about an incident she had in med school. She flipped through the section on faculty bios.

Here's a woman who's been here for the past twenty years. She teaches anatomy. And here are two more that would have been here when Jailyn was a student. What next? Go up to them and ask if they remember a student who beat up her ex-boyfriend or his new girlfriend in a jealous rage?

She wandered through to the faculty offices and read the names. The first one she'd marked, Dr. Shaw, had hours posted, but none today. She checked her list. Dr. Floyd, anatomy. Now what?

As she was deciding her next step, the door opened.

"Can I help you?" The professor was middle aged and wore tortoise shell glasses.

"I'm Sara Baron. I know this sounds weird, but my friend has been murdered and I'm doing all I can to help the police look in the right direction. My friend had ties to a Dr. Jailyn Peters, a past student here. It's a long shot, but I was wondering if you remember her."

"Blonde, looked like a model? I do."

Sara's adrenaline kicked in. "That's great. Did you ever hear of an incident where she threatened another student? Or that student's significant other?"

"I'm sorry, but it would be unethical to give out that sort of information, even if I knew something."

"She was in your anatomy class, right?"

"Yes, and she took anatomy lab as well. I can't help you, I'm sorry."

As she turned to walk away, Sara said, "Did she have lab partners, or a TA that knew her?"

The doctor hesitated. "The secretary in charge of the lab has been here a long time and fancies herself the med school historian." She added in a whisper, "She's a bit of a gossip." She nodded at a map hanging in the corridor. "Good luck. I have to get to my class."

Excited at the obscure clue, Sara looked at the wall map and found where the lab was located. She walked across the courtyard, into an older brick building, and down a flight of stairs where she ran right smack into the receptionist's desk. It had to be a sign.

"Excuse me, I was told you are the go-to person in regards to the history of this place."

A plump blond wearing a Jets football sweatshirt looked up from the romance paperback she was reading. "What can I do you for?"

"My name is Sara. Sara Baron. I grew up near here and am back for the holidays. I'll cut right to the chase. My childhood friend was murdered."

"Oh my God. Are you talking about that poor girl in Hudsonville?"

"Yes. Ellie Rossi. I think she may have been murdered by a jealous ex, or more likely, the girlfriend of a jealous ex."

"How can I help?"

"The woman's name is Jailyn Peters. She was a student here quite a few years ago."

"Blond? Looks like a Barbie doll?"

"That's her. What do you remember about her?"

"She and her lab partner were an item that whole first year...well, up until I'd say April or May. He broke up with her and started dating another first year student. That student nearly died. A hit and run. Everyone suspected it was Jailyn."

"Why did they suspect her?"

"Cause she ranted about how she was going to get even. They had a big shouting match right here in front of my desk. Then she went into the lab, grabbed a gurney and rammed it right into the poor girl. That was the day before the accident."

"Did they arrest her?"

"Nope. No proof. What does that have to do with your friend's murder?"

"Jailyn Peters dated Ellie's fiancé. I'm trying to make a connection. There's little to go on since everyone liked my friend."

"A leopard doesn't change its spots. And they're hard to catch. I added that part myself."

"Clever. Leopards run fast, hard to catch...I appreciate your help."

"Anytime. Hope you find whoever killed your friend."

Sara got back into the car. Now what? She'd found more evidence pointing at Jailyn as the killer, but it was all hearsay. If only she'd have been able to hold onto that ID badge...

Not having much of a schedule, she thought about going home and practicing, but she didn't have the energy to cope if her hand acted up again. *Dad said the business is running behind. Maybe I can make myself useful.* She headed toward her parents' house. No one was home, as she'd suspected. She walked around back to the shop.

"Hey, Dad. Need some help?"

"I won't turn down help. Especially if it means working alongside my daughter. I miss having you around."

"Where's Grandpa?"

"Probably went for a walk. He does that sometimes, tries to keep his hip from freezing up. Can you polish the new oboe I just finished? It's on the stand."

"Sure. Looks beautiful. Who's it for?"

"The young guy who just got the principal position in Atlanta."

"I saw an entry about Atlanta in Great Grandfather's logbook. I'll bet he made the instrument for the former principal, too." She grabbed the logbook and flipped through. "Here it is. Sent to Atlanta. I recognize the name of the oboist."

"It'll make for continuity for sure."

She continued reading the logbook. "Dad, what's this?" Two of the pages were filled with numbers left to right. She handed it to her father.

"I don't know. Too many numbers to be a combination or phone numbers."

"They aren't perfectly straight, either. It's kind of a pattern, yet it isn't."

"I don't know, honey. My grandfather loved spy books and puzzles. He was probably doodling."

The door creaked open. "Ya'll workin' or chit chatting? There's a pile of repairs over there. I gotta finish the new rosewood for the guy at the Met. Promised he'd have it after the holidays."

"Where were you, Grandpa? I checked the house and you were gone."

"Needed some fresh air, that's all." He hung his wool coat on a hook by the door. He walked past Sara to his worktable.

"You smell like garlic. You worried about vampires or something? I know you weren't in the house making sauce."

"Mind your own bee's wax. If you want to help, be quiet and start varnishing."

Sara dropped the brush, this time out of her good hand. *What am I going to do? Now I'm having trouble with my right hand, too? No, just butterfingers. From worry. The dystonia is supposed to stay isolated, not affect both hands.*

Her father came over with a rag. "You okay?"

"Tired, that's all. I'm sorry, let me clean it up."

His phone rang. "Patty? Yeah, I'll make a ShopRite run. A roast, carrots, and some sort of dessert. I'll try to remember."

"Mom wants you to go shopping?"

"She says you and that Travis fellow are having dinner with us tonight."

She'd completely forgotten to invite Travis. "I'll run to the store while you and Grandpa get some work done. I heard roast, carrots, and dessert. How's she going to make a roast that quickly?"

"I bought her a pressure cooker for her birthday. Surprised the heck out of her that I came up with such a thoughtful present. She'll get it done."

A pressure cooker? If my husband bought me a pressure cooker as a gift, I'd have a fit. Sara grabbed her jacket and got into her car. She pulled her phone out of her purse. *Do I want him to come? He's hiding something. The only way I'll find out if he had something to do with Ellie's murder is to spend time with him. Surely, something will slip out.*

"Travis, it's me. Mom invited you over for dinner tonight. I forgot to mention it. 7:00. Text me or call me back when you get this message."

She got to ShopRite before the 'pre-dinner rush', as her Mom always called it. The rush meant waiting behind one or two others to checkout instead of walking right up to the register. Back in San Francisco, you couldn't find a parking space from 4 p.m. until well after 8:00. She knew she had to stop comparing everything to her old life—the life she didn't know if she'd ever recoup.

She felt like a lost child, standing over the meat case. It'd been a while since she bought a roast. What size was she supposed to get? A rump roast? A pork roast? It was all very confusing.

"Hi, Sara. You spend as much time at the grocery store as I do, I see." It was her old music teacher.

"I'm on a mission to buy dinner ingredients and have no idea what to get."

"How many people?"

"Four or five. And she wants carrots."

"Well, if she's cooking carrots, she probably means a pot roast. Here's one that should fit the bill. I always buy more than I need so I can have leftovers the next day."

"Thanks! Hey, what are you doing for dinner tonight? Why don't you come over?"

"I don't want to intrude."

"Are you kidding? You know Mom. The more the merrier."

"Well, I'd like that. As long as the roads stay clear. I'll bring dessert."

"Great. One less choice I have to make."

"I was heading to that aisle anyway. My friend, Lillian, just got out of the hospital."

"Is she okay now?"

"Yeah. Very strange. She had her hip replaced last year. For a while she felt great—no pain when she walked. She even started doing Zumba with the exercise channel. Then she got this strange rash, and she was tired all the time. Then her hair started falling out. Not all of it, but enough where you could see her scalp through it."

"What caused it?"

"Her daughter made her see a specialist in the city. It was metal poisoning."

"Really?"

"Yeah. She underwent treatment and she's much better now, although the hair doesn't seem to be growing back."

"Glad to hear they figured it out in time." She pushed down her glove and looked at her watch. "I'd better get moving. See you tonight."

Chapter 17

Sara put on her skinny jeans and a bright red sweater. Skinny was a misnomer. In fact, she had a bit of trouble zipping them up, though they'd fit just fine before this trip. She took time straightening her naturally unruly hair, and put on a bit of mascara. *I look way too pale.* Her California tan had faded and she remedied it with a little blush and bright lipstick. Travis honked. She took a last look in the mirror, grabbed her coat and went outside.

Travis unlocked the car door. "Glad I checked my phone messages."

"Where were you? It took you long enough to return my call."

"So all day long you've been longing to talk to me?"

"Shut up. That's not what I meant. It's just…Mom had to know how many she was cooking for."

"What happened when you went to Jailyn's medical school? Did anyone remember her?"

"Yes, they did. Jailyn had been a suspect in a hit and run. Girlfriend of her former lover/lab partner. Of course, they couldn't prove anything, but everyone at the school thought she was guilty. Jailyn has a temper and is vindictive. It establishes a pattern."

"It's hard to imagine a successful doctor with this serious of a fatal flaw. If you hadn't found the ID badge at the cabin, I'd be skeptical."

At least he believes me about the badge and doesn't think I'm crazy. She took off her glove and rubbed her hand.

"It's bothering you. Are the stretches helping?"

"They were, but I've been slacking. I tried practicing. I was fine for a while, then my fingers clenched. I can't imagine not playing in the symphony. It's my whole life."

"Sometimes we're given a detour, or wind up choosing a better route."

"Did you read that in a fortune cookie? You sound like you're talking from experience. Is that what happened to you?"

"I don't want to talk about it. Hey, I forgot the bottle of wine I was going to bring."

"Don't worry. My parents seldom drink wine, they're quite the teetotalers. You can bring it next time if you want." *Am I counting on a next time*? "We're here."

Her mother flung open the door and ran outside. "Sara, honey, come in. It's freezing out. Travis, let me take your coat."

"And where's your coat, Mom? I told you not to go running outside in the middle of winter in shirt sleeves. You're going to get sick."

"Smells wonderful in here. Pot roast?" Travis took off his coat and gloves.

"One of my specialties. I made it in the pressure cooker. Can I get you a glass of wine?"

"Sure." Travis followed Sara into the living room while Patty carried the jackets into the kitchen.

Sara said, "Travis, this is my former music teacher, Mrs. Capelli. One of my greatest fans."

"Gail, please. Sara, you can call me that too you know."

"She encouraged me to go into music." Her father cleared his throat. "Of course, Dad fed me a musical diet from the time I was born. He taught me most everything I know. Mrs. Capelli was like extra vitamins."

Grandpa came in from the kitchen. Was she imagining it, or did his eyes sparkle when he saw Mrs. Capelli sitting on the sofa?

"You bought the wrong kind of carrots, Sara. Your mom doesn't buy them pre-sliced you know."

Patty Baron interjected. "It's fine, Sara. Saved me a step or two, and cooked with the roast who would know the difference?"

"How you doing there, Barack?"

Travis didn't bat an eye, just answered. "Hungry. Nice eating something other than fried chicken and collard greens."

Sara felt mortified. Her grandfather hadn't even caught Travis's sarcasm. *He can't be that rude, can he? He's deliberately pushing my buttons, like he used to do to Grandma. Grandma didn't let him get away with it.* "Grandpa, do you remember my old music teacher, Gail Capelli?"

"Yeah. We know each other."

Sara felt surprised. "You do?"

Gail said, "Your Grandpa and I run into each other on our lunch time walks. Sometimes we hit the diner for coffee afterwards."

"Grandpa, you walk? With your bad hip? I thought you were kidding when you told me that earlier. I thought you took your nap after lunch."

"Am I supposed to report when I leave the house now? Is there a sign out sheet?"

"Your grandpa and I have a lot in common," said Gail. She rested her hand on his shoulder and he seemed to relax immediately.

A lot in common? Funny, I don't recall my beloved music teacher being a racist old coot. She jumped when the doorbell rang,

"Who else are you expecting, Mom?"

Sara's mother went to the door. "I invited Detective Lambert."

" I asked you not to."

"I know, but he was talking about going home and opening a can of Spaghetti-O's for dinner. He wasn't even going to bother heating them up. Cold Spaghetti-O's straight from the can? You'd have done what I did if you were in my shoes." She opened the door.

"You look lovely, Patty. These are for you." Phil Lambert handed her a bouquet of carnations and a bottle of wine."

"Beautiful flowers, thanks. And wine. We love wine."

Phil took off his coat and gave Sara a kiss on the cheek. "Nice to see you again so soon."

Travis shook his hand. "Glad you could make it."

"Phil, this is my former music teacher, Gail Capelli."

He kissed her hand. "Former? You don't look old enough to have been teaching when Sara was in school."

Gail blushed. Grandpa grumbled. Sara could read his thoughts. *Don't go flirting with my lady.* She had to chuckle. *Grandpa and Mrs. Capelli?*

Phil sat on the sofa, planting himself between Travis and Sara.

Sara felt uncomfortable with the silence. "So, Phil, where was Jailyn Peters the night of Ellie's murder? Unofficially, of course."

"She has a solid alibi. She was volunteering in a clinic across town."

"I don't buy it. I think she and Preston Montague worked together to get rid of Ellie."

"Why? Preston Montague broke up with Jailyn Peters well before he started seeing Ellie. Then, Ellie broke up with Preston. That's not a love triangle. I don't see motive."

"Preston was angry Ellie called off the engagement. His family was pressuring him to get the ring back, but Ellie refused. There's motive."

"A weak motive at best," said Phil.

Travis said, "He ran away after the murder. You were barely able to question him. If he's innocent, why hide out in the cabin?"

"I've seen it before. A suspect is innocent but knows it looks bad for him so he avoids the police. I've got to admit he was the first person we considered."

Sara didn't buy it. She hadn't completely made up her mind over whether Preston was sincere when he asked for her help. *Preston may be getting close to Jailyn because he suspects her of killing Ellie.* "Then what about Jailyn Peters? She lent Preston her Tesla and she's helping him hide out at the cabin."

"We found no evidence of that," said Phil.

"I told you she dropped her ID badge at the cabin."

"We didn't find…"

"She has a history of reacting poorly to being jilted."

"And she saw a way of getting back together with Preston," said Travis. "I mean, without Ellie in the picture…"

"Who said she wanted Preston back? You don't even know who initiated the breakup. It's all conjecture. We have nothing linking Jailyn Peters to the crime scene, or Preston Montague for that matter. The only prints we found in the house were yours, Travis."

"We were neighbors. Of course, I'd been over there."

He said he barely knew Ellie. Just said hello to her when he saw her outside. And what about the earring I found in his sofa? The one that matches Ellie's? And the curling iron?

Phil said, "And there were tire tracks in her driveway. They match your truck."

"I didn't give you permission to test my tires. Did you have a warrant?"

"Didn't need one. Tires on that truck of yours are fairly standard."

"In other words, you have tire tracks matching the tires of the model of truck I drive. Not my specific truck. Besides, I drove over when Sara found the body."

No, he ran over and drove my car back to his place. "We were nearly killed by a speeding Buick on my way here from the airport."

"And Sara, you're sure it's the same Tesla you saw Preston drive away in at the parking garage? One hundred percent sure?"

"Yes. Top of the line. I'm sure."

"Even if it was the same car, it could have been speeding for a million reasons other than that the driver had just killed your friend. Maybe he was late getting home to his wife, or late to start the night shift where he worked, or he had too much to drink."

Patty Baron stood in the doorway wearing the 'Kiss the Cook' apron she'd bought at the craft fair years ago. "Dinner's on the table."

Phil sat next to Sara. Grandpa was about to sit on her other side when Travis said, "Why don't you switch with me so you can talk to Gail more easily?"

Grandpa grumbled, nodded, and hobbled over to where Gail sat.

Bob Baron, head of the household, was perched at the head of the table like a king on a throne. "Patty, come on in before it gets cold."

She poked her head out of the kitchen. "I'm just packing a care package for Jacob next door. I'll take it over after dinner."

Bob said, "Our neighbor is a recent widower. Poor guy doesn't know which end is up. If Patty didn't bring him food, he'd likely starve himself to death."

Gail said, "How considerate. I know how he feels. It's so lonely in the house with my Charlie gone. It was some time before I could get out of bed to make myself meals."

"Patty and Bob took care of me after Mary died. They still do, though they don't need to treat me like a baby."

That's about the mildest I've ever heard Grandpa complain about being babied. Usually it involves yelling and stomping—more like a temper tantrum.

"Well," said Gail. "Getting to know your grandfather has really brightened things up. Maybe your neighbor would like to join us on our walks sometime."

Patty said, "That's a great idea. I've invited him over but he always refuses. Maybe if you and Grandpa went and knocked on his door it'd be different."

"More wine?" said Bob.

"Not for me. I'm technically off duty but you never know when I'll be called in," said Phil. Sara could have sworn he puffed out his chest in an inflated sense of importance as he spoke.

"Pass the salt," said Grandpa. Sara reached for it, but couldn't grasp it. It spilled on the placemat.

Sara instinctively threw a pinch over her left shoulder. *I can pick up a pinch of salt but miss the shaker. My hand has a mind of its own now.* "I'm so sorry." She picked up the placemat and went into the kitchen.

Her mother called after her. "Honey, there's another placemat in the drawer next to the stove."

She was about to go back inside, when she heard a phone vibrate. It was coming from Travis's jacket pocket. She slid it out. *Unknown caller. Probably a telemarketer.* She went back to the table.

Phil said, "Your father was telling me about the family business. How interesting. Do you know how to make those things too?"

"You mean oboes? Yes. It's been a while but Dad taught me back when I was little. I'm a little out of practice."

Bob said, "Nah. It's like riding a bike. Look how you stepped right in doing repair work. We're already making a dent in the backlog since you've been home."

Travis pulled his phone out of his pocket. The ring tone was the opening of Beethoven's *Fifth Symphony*. "Excuse me, I've got to take this." He went out the back door, allowing the frigid air to sweep in.

His phone just rang. In the kitchen. In his jacket pocket. I saw it with my own eyes. He has two cell phones! Her creative mind raced through the list—*wife, secret girlfriend, a child. Or optimistically, a slew of patients he stayed connected to in case they required emergency physical therapy.*

"Right, Sara?" said Patty.

"Huh?"

"I was telling Phil how you used to play in the marching band. You looked like a toy soldier in that tall hat and the pants with the gold stripe running down the sides."

"Those uniforms were the worst! Especially when it got warmer and we had to march in the Memorial Day parades. I have Mrs. Capelli to thank for those memories!"

Gail laughed. "I didn't like it any more than you did. You think I liked giving up my Saturdays to be at football games all fall. I don't even like football."

Patty said, "Remember that time it was so hot and you threw up right during the ceremony at the cemetery?"

"Mom, please. Let's change the subject." She was glad Travis was out of earshot, not wanting him to picture her dressed like a toy soldier with vomit in her hair. He definitely wouldn't have let that go by without a sarcastic barb. She shuddered.

Travis came back inside. "I have to go."

Patty said, "We haven't had dessert yet."

"I have to go out of town tomorrow, early. I'll need to pack. Ready, Sara?"

"I'll take her home," said Phil. "Go on and get ready for your trip."

Sara felt torn. She didn't want to eat and run, yet she wasn't keen on Phil driving her home. And why had Travis's demeanor changed so drastically after the phone call? He'd been relaxed and happy, now he was all business. She saw worry lines deepen across his forehead and his jaw was clenched.

"Maybe I can swing back later."

"Really, Travis. No problem at all." Phil put his arm around Sara's shoulder. She pulled away.

"Wait a minute." Patty went into the kitchen and returned with a plate of brownies. "Take these, for the road."

"Thanks, Mrs. Baron. Dinner was delicious."

"I told you, call me Patty. And you're welcome to come over any time."

"Sara, you going to be all right?"

"Of course. I'll see you when you get back. When do you get back? And where are you going?"

He didn't answer, just slid out the door.

Bob Baron threw a new log onto the fireplace while Patty carried a tray of brownies and cookies into the living room.

Gail passed around plates. "So, Sara, what's on the next symphony program?"

"*Marriage of Figaro Overture, Brahms Second Symphony,* and *Rachmaninoff Piano Concerto.*"

"Nice. Wish I could hear it."

Bob said, "You can stream it live. I'll show you how."

I hope my father doesn't do that. He'll know it isn't me playing oboe, even if they don't zoom in on the oboe section. Then again, she couldn't keep her secret much longer. *I'll have to tell them sooner rather than later that I'll be here for at least six months.* The thought of disappointing him squeezed her heart like a garlic press.

Sara yawned. She hated that Travis was leaving town, only because she felt safer having someone right next door. One minute she needed him, the next she suspected him of murder. *What's wrong with me, anyway? How long does he plan to be gone? What sort of emergency? He didn't say his parents were sick or that there'd been an accident. Two phones? Haven't you learned your lesson? That right there is a deal breaker.*

When Gail got up to leave, Sara suggested they head home as well. Phil grabbed their coats and graciously accepted the care package of cookies and brownies from her mother. He held open the car door while she scooted in.

"Let me know if you need the heat turned up," said Phil. He backed out of the driveway.

"Do you think Preston would kill over not getting the ring back?"

"Where'd that come from?"

"Sorry. I can't stop thinking about it."

"His mother is the one really pushing the whole missing ring drama. It was passed down from her family, yada, yada, yada. Preston never came in and reported it missing after the engagement was called off. She's the one who filed the police report."

When they pulled into the driveway, Sara saw light in Travis's bedroom window. With so few belongings, she didn't imagine it would take him long to pack. What emergency? The migraine medicine! Cameron Stokes was the name on the prescription. *I'll bet she's a secret girlfriend and he's going to see her tomorrow. Maybe she has a husband. Maybe Travis has a wife. Or two wives!*

"Here we are. I had a really nice time tonight." Phil inched closer to her.

"Me too. I'm pretty beat." She opened the car door and hopped out.

"Wait. I'll walk you to the door."

She wasn't thrilled about it, but then again, staying alone, even with the super security system still gave her the jitters. "Okay." She waited for him to turn off the engine.

When they got to the front door, she was thankful for the detective escort.

"Oh, my God! What's that?"

The menacing message was clear. *Stay out of it or you'll be next.* Spray painted in red across the entire front of the house.

Phil immediately grabbed his phone. "This is Detective Lambert. We need a team at the Rossi house ASAP."

Chapter 18

Travis appeared as soon as the police cruiser flashed its lights in the driveway. *He's always just around the corner when these threats happen.*

"Sara, what happened?"

"Look at the door. Someone thinks I'm getting close to finding something."

"Who could have done this? Jailyn Peters? I'll bet someone at the med school tipped her off that you'd been asking questions."

"Maybe she followed me out there." The cold night air made her shiver; the thought of Jailyn following her and spray painting the message chilled her bones. She was struck by the incongruity. *A Barbie doll, country club surgeon wielding a can of spray paint? Then again, she slashed someone's tires and came after him with a tire iron...*

"Why don't you stay at your parents, at least while I'm gone."

"I'll be okay. I must have forgotten to set the alarm system. The motion sensors should have been activated." She had to admit she was glad he cared.

"No one broke in, did they?"

"Phil's checking." Something shiny caught her eye. She bent down and picked up an oblong gold pin. "Travis, look at this."

Phil ran over. "Door was still locked from inside. No broken windows. We found an empty can of spray paint under the porch. You should stay with your parents tonight."

"I can't leave the cat. Besides, it will be no better tomorrow night or the night after. Whoever did this was just trying to scare me."

"Then heed the warning. Stay out of this. We've got it covered," said Phil. "He's right," said Travis. "You can't put yourself in danger."

"I'd recommend sleeping elsewhere."

"No, I'll have to get used to it sooner or later."

"I can have a patrol car keep an eye on the place."

"You can stay with me tonight," said Travis. "I had the window in the guestroom repaired."

"You have to leave early. I'll be okay."

Phil said, "I'm going to have my men check the closets and under the beds. Wait here."

Travis whispered in her ear. "I wish I didn't have to leave." His warm breath on her neck made her tingle.

"Can't you postpone your trip?"

"It's non-negotiable. I'm sorry."

The officers drove off. Phil returned. "Coast is clear. Set the alarm system, and make sure your phone is charged. Call if you think anything seems amiss or if you just feel scared. I can be here in a flash."

She hustled inside, immediately turned on every light in the house that Phil hadn't, hugged Panther, and carried him upstairs. *Phil's crew checked under the beds. No monsters in the closet. Alarm is set.* She plugged her phone into the charger and turned on the bedroom TV. She closed her eyes, but opened them every few minutes just to be sure.

The bed felt too warm, then too cold when she turned down the comforter. She considered adjusting the thermostat, but felt paralyzed. She listened to *The Late Show*, hoping for a laugh or two to lighten the mood. She stayed awake through *The Late, Late Show*, *Murder She Wrote* reruns, and finally, *The Early News at 4:30*.

When sunlight streamed through the bottom of the blinds casting shadows on the floor, she was relieved it was morning. She peeked out the window hoping to see Travis's car in the driveway, but he was already gone. Why did she feel so empty knowing he wasn't there? She pulled her phone off the charger and noticed a voicemail from Ellie's mother.

Ellie's boss called and asked if I'd go by and pick up her things. I can't do it. I was wondering...you said if there was anything you could do to help and this would be a tremendous help.

She immediately punched in the number. "Mrs. Rossi, I got your message. Of course, I'll pick up Ellie's things. She worked in the building next to the hospital, right? Got it. I'll head over there after breakfast."

She was thankful to have something to focus on this morning. After downing an entire pot of coffee, she headed over to Medivision and found Ellie's desk.

"Can I help you with something?"

She recognized Ellie's friend from the funeral. "Camaya, right?"

"Yes. We talked at the funeral. Are you here to get her things?"

"Her mother called and asked me to come by."

"Looks like someone rifled through her desk. The contents are right there in that box. I don't know who would have taken the initiative, but it wasn't me."

She rummaged through the box. A framed photo of Ellie's parents, a globe shaped paperweight, a black sweater..."Do you want to keep this?" She held up a picture of Ellie and Camaya on a boat. "When was this taken?"

"That was last year's company picnic. Our boss rented out the yacht club. He's a boating aficionado. I'll keep it if you think Ellie's parents wouldn't mind. We had so much fun that day."

"I'm sure her parents would want you to have it. You said Ellie had been acting strangely before she died."

"Yeah. One day I saw her stuff a file into her bag on her way out."

"Maybe she was taking it home to line up clients or something."

"She had her regular clients. And any new prospects would have been discussed with all of us at our morning briefing."

"Did her ex-fiancé ever drop by?"

"Preston Montague? His family owns a large share of this company. Both he and his father came in regularly for board meetings. Preston took Ellie out to lunch afterwards a few times, when they were still together. And he picked her up after work to go to the gym together once or twice."

"Is that how they met? At work?"

"Yes. He was here for a meeting one day and they got to talking. Things moved fast after that. Next thing you know they were engaged."

"After they broke up, did he still come by?"

"For meetings, but not right here. The board room is clear on the other side of the floor."

"What about Preston's old girlfriend, Jailyn Peters? Do you know who I'm talking about?"

"The Barbie doll doctor? Yeah. She came around a few times. I saw her in Craig's office on occasion. Gossip was they were secretly seeing each other."

"Jailyn Peters and Craig Danalchek?"

"What about Craig Danalchek?" Ellie's boss appeared out of nowhere.

Camaya stuttered, "We're just…"

Sara said, "I came by to pick up Ellie's things for her family. This box, right?"

"Yes, that should do it."

"It's very light. That's all the personal stuff she had?"

"I have a feeling she had one foot out the door," said Craig. "I think she was looking for another job on the sly, though I don't know why she'd have wanted to leave. She was one of our top representatives and she'd just gotten a substantial raise in salary. Anyway, give my regards to her parents."

He shook her hand and disappeared down the corridor.

Camaya said, "That was embarrassing. I hope he didn't hear the part about him and Jailyn."

"Was Sara was looking for another job? I thought the company was sending her to London to pitch the new product or something."

"London? That's the first I've heard about it. I don't think the company even has an overseas office."

"You sure she wasn't going away on business?"

"I don't know."

"Was she job hunting?"

"She was being secretive, like I said, but she'd always been happy here. I don't know what changed."

"What about the engagement ring? Do you have any idea where Ellie would have kept it?"

"Personally, I don't think she had it. She would have returned it if she did. She didn't even like the ring. She called it gaudy."

"Well, I'd better get this box over to Ellie's parents. If you think of anything that may be helpful in finding Ellie's killer, please get in touch. Here's my card."

Sara placed the box in the back seat and drove to the Rossi's condo. The sky had turned darker and the weather forecast predicted snow later that afternoon.

Jailyn Peters and Preston Montague both made appearances in the Medivision office. Preston was invested in the business, and Jailyn may have been seeing Craig Danalchek. She was also linked to the business in her role as an orthopedic surgeon. Travis mentioned that she used their products. Why wouldn't Camaya and her boss know that she was going to London on business?

She parked in front of the condo and carried the box up the stoop. Ellie's mother, wearing faded sweats and no makeup, opened the door.

"Sara, thanks for doing this for us. I just couldn't face it."

"No problem. Looks like there wasn't much there. Did Ellie say anything about looking for another job?"

"No. As far as I know, she liked her job. She'd even gotten a raise recently."

"Did she tell you she was going away on business?"

"She mentioned she'd be out of town for a while. She wasn't clear on the details."

"Another thing. If Ellie still had that engagement ring, where would she have kept it? Did she have a safety deposit box?"

"A safety deposit box? I doubt it. Ellie wasn't the spiteful type. She would have returned the ring. If she had it, and I doubt she did, it'd likely be right in her jewelry box. Did you look there?"

"No. I...I haven't opened the door to her room since that night."

"I understand."

"I'm going to go back and check the jewelry box. If you need anything, call me."

"Thanks, Sara."

Sara drove back to Ellie's, then cautiously checked the ground for footprints as she walked to the door. The graffiti was still there. She didn't know whom to call to remove it. If Travis was home, he'd know. She listened at the door before opening it, then jiggled the handle. Locked, like she left it. She turned off the alarm and went in.

You can do this. The body is gone. It's just a room. She climbed the stairs, jumping with each creak. When she got to the top, Panther darted out of the bathroom with a loud meow, scaring her half to death.

It's just a room. And it's daylight. And the alarm was set. She opened the door to the master bedroom. She stood there for a moment, imagining the scene the night she'd first been in here.

Breathe in, breathe out. Do it for Ellie. She shook off her fear and made her way to Ellie's dresser. The jewelry box was open, necklaces half in and half out. The police were finished in here so she supposed she didn't need to worry about leaving fingerprints. After untangling the necklaces, she lifted a velvet-covered section containing rings. *Ellie's high school ring. After all these years. I should bring this to her mom.* She slipped it into her pocket.

Sifting through it, she came across several rings—a turquoise and silver one, a band shaped into the infinity sign—but no engagement ring. *Maybe she hid it in the drawer.*

Sara searched the drawers, finding a checkbook, an American Express credit card, and a passport. *Where was she going without a passport? Certainly not London.*

She checked under the mattress, crawled down to peek under the bed, then foraged through the closet hoping to find some sort of hiding place. She pulled down a decorated box from the closet shelf. Rummaging through, she found scarves, belts, and under all that, a folder full of papers. It looked like some kind of inventory list. KJ, HJ, HV, IP...all with dates and numbers next to them. *What kind of list is this and why did she hide it?*

Interesting, but no ring. She spotted running shoes on the closet floor and remembered seeing running tights in the drawer. *Think. Ellie was a workout freak. Maybe she stashed the ring inside a pair of running shoes? The ones on her top shelf look brand new.* She pulled down the shoes and reached into the toes. No ring.

One last thing. She checked the freezer. She'd heard of people hiding valuables in the freezer. No luck. She looked at the sink where she'd placed her coffee mug, a plate, and a butter knife, meaning to wash them later. *Butter knife, the kitchen drawer…wait! There was a key in that drawer!* She opened the junk drawer. *Come on, I know you're in here.* If this was Travis's place, she'd have found it right away. On second thought, Travis didn't have a junk drawer. *Got it.*

The tiny silver key looked as if it could open a safety deposit box, or maybe a locker. *Where would I even start? It'll be like searching for an earring post on a football field.* Her hand froze and the key fell to the floor. Her stomach knotted in anger. *This is getting worse, not better. This condition is supposed to be specific to my oboe playing. So much for MedUcate. Should've known better than to trust an internet medical blog.* Vowing to step up her sessions with Travis and spend more time on the stretches, she picked up the key from the floor.

Determined to make progress, but clueless as to what direction to take, she got in her car and drove. Following her intuition, she found herself parked in front of her parents' bank.

"Can I help you?" The teller was cheerful, smiling. *She must have aced the customer service training.*

"Yes, I found this key, and I wondered if it might be the type that opens a safety deposit box." She slid it under the glass.

"No, this is definitely not a safety deposit box key. It's too big."

"Even for a big box?"

"Yes, the keys are all the same size."

"How about a safe?"

"Any commercial safes I've seen have combination locks, but I suppose you could find a home safe that uses a padlock."

"You think this key goes to a padlock?"

"A small padlock. You know, it looks like the key I have for my gym locker."

"Gym locker?" She felt the adrenaline ramping up. "How many gyms are there in town?"

"Just one commercial gym. *The Forward Fitness* near the hospital. I'm surprised they stay in business. The YMCA is much cheaper, but it doesn't have a pool or locker rooms."

"And *Forward Fitness* has lockers?"

"Yeah. You pay extra to rent one, but it's worth the convenience if you're exercising on the way to or from work."

Sara did that herself back home. She'd use the gym before rehearsals. *Make that used the gym. It's been over a year.* "Thanks. You've been very helpful."

She raced over to the gym and pulled in next to a Jaguar. Given it was the middle of the afternoon, she had her pick of places, but since the Jaguar driver had parked diagonally, hogging two spots, she felt compelled to park within inches of it. She had a six-year-old Nissan Sentra sitting in her own driveway back in San Francisco. She admitted to a slight pang of envy looking at the slick, sexy car.

The modern gym was entirely metal with big glass panes. Through the glass she saw members lined up like mice on a row of treadmills. As soon as she opened the sleek, chrome door she was bombarded with pounding techno music. She instinctively covered her ears to shield herself from hearing loss. The reception desk was unmanned. *This is my lucky day.* She followed the arrow on the wall and the scent of chlorine, then slipped right into the small locker room.

That was incredibly easy. Now what? Try every key? The rows are three deep in lockers. Thankfully, the majority have combination locks. She listened. No chattering. No water running in the showers. *Here goes.*

She worked fast, silently, and methodically, with her ears on high alert in case someone entered. After she'd gone through half a dozen locks, most of which didn't even come close to fitting with the key, she made her way to the bottom row. Voices. Coming from the pool entrance. Flip flops slapping against the tile floor. Her pulse quickened.

"So, how many laps did you do today?"

"Enough. I'm still sore from yesterday. Wish I could go home instead of back to work."

Sara ducked into the changing stall, holding her breath. She could have pretended she was simply a member opening her locker, but this was a small gym and she was afraid they'd notice hers wasn't a familiar face. *It can't take long for them to change if they have to be back at work.* When she heard water running in the showers, she came out of hiding and finished her mission. Nothing.

What if this isn't her locker key, but Preston's? I should check the men's locker room! Wait, am I crazy? But this is probably my only chance. Maybe there's a hint to where he's hiding out after fleeing the cabin. Her heart thumped like a bass drum. She followed the wet footprints to the pool entrance. If she went in through the pool area, she'd eliminate the risk of being seen if the front desk person had returned.

She poked her head through the metal door and seeing the coast was clear, stepped inside. The sticky chlorine-infused air stuck to her skin and irritated her nose. She eyed the men's locker room across the pool, and quickly scooted over. *Not a soul taking advantage of the heated pool in the middle of winter? Insane.* She opened the door, listened, and convinced herself it was safe to enter.

More combination locks, fewer padlocks than in the other. Finding a rhythm, she quickly weaved her way through the aisles. *Nope. Not this one. Definitely not.* About to give up, she surprised herself when one of the lockers clicked open. Her heart pounded faster as she opened the door. A black gym bag was squished inside.

Do I take this out, or just grab a look inside? From the crime shows she'd watched, she knew she could blow the case if there was anything of value and it wasn't obtained following the letter of the law. She pulled her gloves back on, and unzipped the bag, still listening for signs she wasn't alone. She stuck her hand inside and felt around. Gym shorts, a tee shirt, and yuck, a pair of white boxers. *Please God, let these be clean boxers.*

Then, she felt something in the bottom of the bag and pulled it out. Bingo. It was a ring. A big, gaudy diamond ring!

Chapter 19

She shoved everything back into the bag and slipped out of the gym. *How do I get Phil to put this together and search the locker?* She drove across town to the police station.

"Can I see Detective Lambert?" She'd barely finished asking when Phil came out of his office.

"Sara, what a nice surprise."

"Phil, can I talk to you?"

"Sure. Come in."

She'd never been a good liar in the past but she'd been honing her skills daily since arriving in town. "I found a key in Ellie's kitchen drawer. I knew it looked like a key to a gym locker—*yeah, right. I just knew it.* It occurred to me that Ellie loved the gym, and her co-worker mentioned that they worked out together, so I think you should go over there and investigate."

"Over where?"

"*Forward Fitness.* It's by the hospital."

"I know the place. You have the key?"

"Yes, here it is." She placed it in his palm. "Maybe there's a clue as to where Preston went."

Her mother knocked and came in. "Sara, what are you doing here? I was in the bathroom and guess I missed you coming in."

"Just visiting." She saw her Mom's eyes twinkle.

"Detective, I have paperwork for you to sign. Mrs. Montague is insistent about getting a police report detailing the stolen engagement ring so she can submit it to her insurance company."

Sara's heart paused. "Maybe you shouldn't sign that just yet."

"Why not?" Both Phil and her mother looked confused.

"I don't know. Maybe something will turn up. You were on the way to search his locker, right?"

"Yes. Put the paperwork on my desk for now, Patty."

"Will do. Talk to you later, Sara."

"Phil, how sure are you about Jailyn Peter's alibi?"

"I told you she was working at a clinic across town. Her colleagues verified it. Are you still on that?"

"I just have a gut feeling she's not being truthful. She had motive to kill Ellie."

"What motive? We've already been through this. Jealousy over her ex-boyfriend's ex-fiancé? Ellie had already dumped Preston. She didn't have a reason to kill her."

"I guess you're right. It's just, I don't know. She seems to have a mean jealous streak. Maybe she was getting back at Ellie for hurting Preston?" *And the ring motive is off the table.*

"Sounds like grasping at straws. Besides, I told you multiple times she has an alibi."

"Yeah. You're right."

"Can I pick you up for dinner?"

She weighed the options. Restaurant dinner with intelligent conversation or eating with Panther in front of the TV. "Sure. I'd love to."

"I'll pick you up at 7."

Maybe by then he'll have found the ring. She headed back to Ellie's. *What am I missing? There has to be a clue somewhere in this house.*

She had just kicked off her shoes and grabbed the Mint Milanos she'd impulse bought at ShopRite when her phone rang.

"Sara? This is Camaya, Ellie's coworker from Medivision."

"Hi, this is Sara."

"Look, after you left, I remembered something. I was outside on lunch break after a board meeting. I heard Preston talking to Ellie. I guess I was hidden by the trees because they didn't notice me. Ellie was saying he should do the right thing and how she would 'blow the whole thing apart' if he didn't."

"Really? I wonder what she meant."

"I don't know, but then Preston's voice got really serious. He told her if she even tried, she'd be sorry. It's the way he said it, like he was threatening her."

"When was this?"

"Right before she called off the wedding. I'd forgotten all about it until you asked about Preston earlier. It may be nothing, but I figured I'd let you know."

"Thanks, Camaya. It could prove to be important. Call me if you think of anything else. Anything at all."

She finished her cookies, plotting her next move. Ellie's phone was never found. Was there a chance it was still in the house? She'd turned much of the house upside down looking for the ring already. *If it's not in the house, maybe it's in the garage.* Ellie's car! That's one place she hadn't thoroughly checked.

She put on her shoes and opened the garage door. The car was unlocked, as it was left. Sara checked the trunk, rummaged through the overnight bag, and felt along the back seat. Nothing.

She checked the glove compartment and under the passenger seat. When she reached under the driver's seat she found it. Ellie's phone.

Sara grabbed her charger and plugged it in. *What do I do about a password?* She tried the most common ones. 1234; 0000. Nope. Her birthday. After all these years she hadn't forgotten Ellie's birthday. Month and day? Nope. Day then year? Nope. What about the year she was born? She was the same age as Sara. *Wait. I saw a pocket calendar in the junk drawer. That's where I write my passwords.*

She found the shiny day runner and flipped to the back. Birthdays, phone numbers, passwords! She ran back to the garage and tried the one next to 'phone.'

Bingo. The phone came to life. Texts galore. Ellie begging Preston to make things right. Preston telling her to keep her mouth shut.

Ellie: *If you don't come forward, the engagement is off.*

Preston: *Over my dead body.*

Ellie: *Lives are at stake.*

Preston: *Open your trap and you're dead.*

Then, the messages stopped. Until the day Ellie died.

Preston: *It's over. Watch your back. I'm coming for it.*

His voice was different. Not threatening this time, more like…nervous. *Didn't he mean coming for you? It? What's it? The ring? It had to be more than that.* Was Preston Montague still in town?

She looked at the time. Before she knew it it'd be time for her…date. She listened to the phone messages one more time. Wait. A sound in the background. It sounded like church bells on Preston's end. Was he hiding in a church? She'd have to turn the phone over to Phil. Maybe he'd have an idea.

A quick shower, make-up, and her comfy jeans. She'd told Phil she'd prefer a casual dinner, and, in fact, was craving pizza. He rang the doorbell at exactly 7 p.m.

"You look pretty. I like your hair pulled up like that."

"Thanks."

"By the way, we found the ring! Right where you thought it would be, in Preston's gym locker. We picked up his mother and it didn't take much to get her to confess that Preston had it all along. She was turning it into an insurance scam, claiming it was stolen."

"I knew it. Ellie wouldn't have kept that ring. Even her coworker said Ellie called the ring gaudy. Hey, before we go, I have to show you something." She grabbed Ellie's phone from the coffee table. "Listen to the messages."

"Ellie's phone? Where'd you find it?"

"It was in her car. Here." She played the messages.

"He's clearly threatening her."

"Listen again. To the background noise when Preston is speaking."

"It sounds like chimes."

"Exactly. Do you think he's hiding out in a church?"

"There's only one church with those elaborate chimes. It's on the way out of town."

"Is it anywhere near the restaurant?"

"No, but we can swing by and then head to Antonio's. Get your coat."

The road to the church was the same one she'd taken into town from the airport. In fact, she pointed out the spot where her car had skidded. They passed Cusa farms, a Christmas tree farm, and an abandoned fruit and vegetable stand. Few houses appeared along the route—even less when they turned onto a gravel road. She could see the steeple well before they parked in the church lot.

"Here we are. Come on." He took a flashlight out of the glove compartment.

She followed Phil into the deserted, dark church. They marched through the pews and up into the musty choir loft. Nothing.

"What about the rectory?"

"Two elderly priests live there. I don't want to disturb them at this hour. I can guarantee you they'd have nothing to do with harboring a fugitive."

"What about the area behind the altar. You know, where the priests get dressed?"

Phil led the way. Sara moved aside a pile of robes. She found a black, leather glove. "Phil, look. It has his initials embossed. PM. Has to be…"

"Preston Montague." He wrapped it in a paper towel he'd pulled from a roll on the table housing the robes.

Sara continued searching the room. "Look! A phone charger. It's still plugged into the wall. I'll bet Preston Montague was hiding in here but why? He must have made that last phone call from here while the chimes were ringing."

"I'll take that, too. Good eye! And kudos for recognizing the chimes on the message. Otherwise, we'd never have come here."

"Has he left town? You've got people covering the airport, right?"

"Been covering the shuttle and limo services to the airport, the train station, even the bus terminal since shortly after the murder. No sign of him. No purchases on his credit cards either."

I should have told him about my encounter with Preston. "You checked his parents' place?"

"Of course, we did. And we have a patrol car keeping an eye on it. You have to stay out of this, Sara. We're getting closer and it's getting more dangerous now that the stakes are higher. Trust me to do my job. Promise."

"Okay, okay. I'll back off."

"Good. Come on, let's eat."

Chapter 20

The next morning, Sara woke drenched in sweat, heart pounding. She'd been jogging through Cusa farms and came upon an abandoned barn. She knocked on the warped, wooden door. Animal cracker animals poured out of the barn and ran into the wilderness. Behind them, Preston Montague, laughing and saying, 'you can't catch me; I'm the gingerbread man.'

Either I'm losing my mind, or that dream is a message. Wait! Travis said the Montague family owned the business, and gave it to their new son-in-law. It was a farm business, but in the winter it appeared abandoned. I'll bet no one has thought to search there for Preston.

Maybe I should call Phil. Just last night he discouraged her against pursuing the case. Even made her promise to stay out of it. *Better to have evidence before alerting him so I won't have to eat crow if I'm wrong.*

Plan B. She looked out the window, hoping to see Travis's car in his driveway. She wished he'd told her when he'd be back. *It's broad daylight. I can drive to Cusa farms and just nose around—see if there's any sign of Preston there. Maybe it wasn't a dream, but a premonition that woke me up.*

Sara took a quick shower, fed Panther, and jumped in the car. Cusa farms was on the way to her parents' house. Travis pointed it out the night they went over for dinner.

She easily found the entrance to the desolate farm. A chain blocked the dirty, snow-covered road through the orchards. Glad she'd worn boots, Sara parked the car and proceeded on foot.

The sun reflected off the snow and was at work melting the path through the orchards. The sky was a bright, robin's egg color blue, so rare during these winter months. *It's a sign. I'm on the right track.*

Her legs ached. She'd trekked quite a while before spotting the warehouse. Along the way, she searched for a sign that Preston was on the premises. The snow squished under her feet as she approached the warehouse.

It certainly looks like it's boarded up for the winter. She fingered the rusty padlock chaining the door shut.

She walked around the outside of the building, trying to peek into the few barred windows, but even stretching on her tip toes they were too high to reach. No trucks, no cars...no sign of Preston Montague or anyone else. *I was so sure. All this effort has to pay off in the end. Or does it?* She turned back feeling defeated but aware of a schedule-less day stretching in front of her. *Dad's killing himself trying to catch up on work. Might as well do something useful. The morning was a waste of time.*

She got back in her car and drove to her parents' house. She checked inside first. Empty. Then she went around back to the shop where she found her father at work. She was proud of his skill, his work ethic, and his creativity. Proud that she'd inherited those traits.

"Dad?"

"Sara? I didn't realize you were coming in today." Her father was hunched over his desk, measuring and drilling the beginnings of an oboe. The smell of fresh wood shavings brought back memories.

"I thought you could use a hand."

"Yeah. Your grandfather went out to lunch with your Mrs. Capelli. He reeked of cologne and had even combed back his hair. You may have a step-grandmother one of these days."

Sara laughed. She was pleased as punch that those two were spending time together. Any signs of early dementia seemed to disappear when he was with or talked about Mrs. Capelli.

"I'll continue the repairs if you want."

"Yeah, and afterwards, I'll give you a refresher course in drilling tone holes. I have to get moving on this backlist before I lose customers. These oboes are great, but who can afford to wait a decade to get one?"

She felt a bit excited about helping. Although there was a process and it involved accurate measuring, definitely in her skill set, instrument making was creative in its own right. Taking your stored experiences, connecting the dots, making something from nothing…the process was familiar even when transposed to a different activity.

The repair she was working on required a seldom-used tool. She opened the drawer where she thought she'd seen an assortment earlier. *It must not have been this drawer.* This drawer was where her great grandfather had stashed the logbook.

She opened to the page of numbers and examined them again. *Some are darker than the others. Does that mean something?*

"Dad, can you toss me a pen?"

"Catch."

She traced the outline made by the darker numbers and a shape emerged. If she flipped it sideways, it looked like a narrow cone. She leafed through the logbook looking for a reference or any clue as to what this could be.

"Listen to this, Dad. 'Rosie is mine and I'll keep her hidden as long as I have to.' What does that mean? I thought we'd established he wouldn't cheat on your grandmother."

"Is it before they were married? Check the date."

"Nope. After the wedding date. If Rosie wasn't a mistress, maybe he was hiding a fugitive or an illegal alien."

"I'd swear on a bible my grandmother wouldn't have cheated. Man, I'd forgotten just how creative you are. It could mean anything, or nothing at all."

"Aren't you curious? And what about those cryptic numbers? Look at this. If you trace the darker numbers and turn the page sideways, it makes a shape."

"Let me see." She brought it closer to her father. "You, know, it almost looks like an oboe."

Patty pushed the door open. "Sara, what a nice surprise."

"Mom? I thought you were at work."

"Lunch hour. I forgot my lunchbox so I thought I'd come and eat with your father. Now that you're here, even better. Come in the house."

She and her father neatened up their areas and followed Patty inside.

"How about grilled cheese and tomato soup. Comfort food for a chilly day."

"I haven't had grilled cheese in ages. Have you got pickles?"

"Of course. There's an open jar in the fridge."

"So what happened with Mrs. Montague? Was she arrested?"

"No, but I'll bet her insurance company drops her like a hot potato. Imagine, blaming Ellie for keeping the ring when all along she knew exactly where it was. And shame on Preston, too."

"I don't suppose they found him between last night and now?"

"Last night?"

"I had dinner with Phil and he said they'd been watching for signs of Preston's whereabouts but were drawing a blank."

"You and Phil had another date?" Patty smiled with her eyes.

"Leave her alone, Patty. It's her business; she's a grown woman."

She loved how her father always had her back. "I wouldn't call it a date, just two friends sharing a pizza."

Patty said, "You know, I like Travis a lot, but things would be simpler, you know, if you got together with Phil."

"Mom, seriously? I have no interest in dating Travis. We're like oil and water."

"I'm just saying you and Travis come from different backgrounds. You'd have to be sensitive to that. And I wonder if his parents would accept him dating out of his race?"

"Mom, you're crazy. I told you we're not dating. Please change the subject."

"I was wondering how long you can stay? I assume you're leaving right after Grandpa's party."

"Actually, I'm not. There's something I have to tell you."

"You're worrying me."

"There's nothing you can't tell us." Bob scooped out a bowl of soup for each of them.

"I'm on medical leave. I'm having a problem with my hand—focal dystonia."

"Like that oboe player in the Chicago Symphony had?" said her father.

"Yeah. I took six months off to see if it improves. So far, it's not looking promising, even with Travis's help."

"I forgot he's a physical therapist. Poor baby. Come here." Patty hugged her. Sara could feel the love all around her. Thank God she had the greatest parents in the world.

Sara's eyes teared. "You know how much I love my job. And how fortunate I was to win the audition. What if I never play again?"

"Don't go thinking like that. You have six months. See what happens. Dad and I are here for you. Grandpa, too. He acts like an old fool for attention but he loves you and Scott dearly."

"I know."

"And the guy in Chicago was able to work his way back into the orchestra. I made a new oboe for him."

"I know. We'll see what happens."

Patty cut the grilled cheese sandwiches and set them on the table. "By the way, Phil thinks they found the murder weapon."

"Really? Why didn't you lead with that?"

"Frankly, I was more interested in your love life than some nasty weapon."

"Well, what did they find?"

"A tire iron. The blood matched Ellie's and guess what else?"

"Don't keep me in suspense."

"They got a fingerprint off it. Preston Montague's fingerprint. If they were searching for him before, you can bet they're sending out the posse now."

Sara couldn't believe she hadn't heard this from Phil. Then again, why would he tell her? First of all, he's been busy with this new clue all morning. Secondly, he didn't want her in danger and had clearly told her to stay out of it.

"Will you let me know if they find anything more?"

"Okay."

"Where did they find the weapon, by the way? I thought they'd done a thorough search of the area already."

"Apparently they missed it. They received a phone call saying it was in the woods behind the house."

"A phone call from whom?"

"The person didn't want to leave a name. Phil thinks they may have been worried for their safety."

"I hate to eat and run, but I'm going to head home now. I didn't sleep well and I'm going to try to take a nap. Dad, I'll be back tomorrow to help. Mom, I'll order the cake on my way home."

"Okay, honey. See you then."

Sara stopped at the bakery and leafed through the book of birthday cake designs. *Too many choices.* She decided on the design with musical notes and balloons. *I'll have them add a great big number 80.* Buttercream, of course. Yellow cake with chocolate pudding between the layers. Grandpa's favorite.

When Sara got home, she found a note stuck in the front door. *It's not how it looks. I know who killed Ellie. Call me. Preston M.* She read the number. Her pulse raced. *He's still professing his innocence? I'm supposed to call the prime suspect in my friend's murder and chat? Is he crazy? Especially now that they found the tire iron with his fingerprint on it?*

She unlocked the door and tossed her purse on the sofa. *On the other hand, it's not like he can strangle me through the phone or anything.* Hands shaking—from nerves, not the dystonia—she punched in the numbers.

"Hello. Is this Preston Montague? It's Sara. Um, you said to call you."

"You called. Thank God. Look, I know you're Ellie's friend and I know I'm the prime suspect in her murder, but you have to believe me. Like I told you before, I didn't kill her. I loved her."

"Preston, your prints were on her back door. And on the murder weapon."

"What murder weapon?"

"The tire iron. With your fingerprint on it."

"I'm being framed. They searched that yard before and now they come up with a weapon? With my prints? I was coming to rescue Ellie the night she was murdered. You have to believe me."

"Rescue her from what?"

"I can't tell you over the phone."

She had wondered herself how they'd missed the murder weapon. "How did they get your tire iron with your prints then?"

"It was stolen out of my car. I'd fixed a flat tire a week ago."

"You went into hiding instead of telling the police. And you had her ring in your locker."

"That was my mother's idea. I told her I didn't want to do it, but arguing with her is like climbing Mt. Everest in flip flops. Look, I have some important information to give you. Information you can turn over to the police. Ellie begged me to do the right thing and I didn't listen to her. Now she's dead and I think I'm next. I know who killed Ellie. Can you meet me at Cusa Farms?"

She hesitated. *Seriously? I was just there a few hours ago.* Then again, there was something sincere about him. Why leave a note when he could have ambushed her at the door had he wanted to kill her?

"Please. For Ellie. No police—they won't give me a chance to explain. Meet me at the warehouse at Cusa farms. 4:00. I know you know where it is. I have something to give you."

She couldn't believe it. *Preston, a murderer on the lam, wants to meet me at an abandoned warehouse.* Was she seriously considering this?

"I don't know that I can do that." *Then again, it's not like I have any solid evidence against him. I'm not a threat. Cusa farms is a perfect place to hide. Why risk reaching out to her if he wasn't being sincere?*

"You're my only chance. I'll give you everything you need to show the police who really killed Ellie. And please don't go to the cops. They'll arrest me before I can explain."

Should she call Phil? He'd have the place crawling with cops and Preston would go back into hiding. It was still daylight. "I'll be there."

Chapter 21

She was trembling, not sure if it was the cold, fear, or pure adrenaline in anticipation of learning who killed Ellie. *Preston Montague is innocent. I feel it in my gut. I believe him when he said he was framed. With the careful searching the police did, how come they didn't find a tire iron? If Preston used it to change a tire last week, of course, his prints would be on it.*

Travis still wasn't home. She knew it was a Hail Mary, but she hoped that when she went into the driveway to get into the car and go meet Preston, Travis would see her, run over, and offer to come with her. *Am I crazy? For all I know he's the killer.* Offer? Travis would insist she not go alone. He's the one who rescued her when Jailyn conked her over the head at the cabin. Or was it Jailyn after all? Travis just happened to be on her tail?

Between this morning and now, the sky had gone from blue to gray. Freezing rain pelted her windshield. A sudden turn of events, like the sudden change of weather. It had to be an omen. *Should I turn back? Breathe in, breathe out.*

When she reached Cusa Farms, the rusty chain barrier lay on the ground and she drove through the same road she had been forced to hike this morning. She turned around a bend and spotted the warehouse. A white BMW was parked next to it.

Here goes. She pulled up alongside the BMW and slammed her car door shut in a false gesture of bravery. *I can do this. I'm finally going to learn the truth.* She shivered as she walked toward the door. Then, she looked down at the snow. Pink snow. She froze. *Oh, my God. This can't be happening.* For the second time in her life she was staring at a lifeless body. A gun was lying on the ground a few feet away.

Her instinct was to scream, though she realized rather quickly no one was going to hear her. She bent down to feel for a pulse, something she hadn't been able to bring herself to do when she discovered Ellie. Dead. No question about it. Preston Montague stared up at her with blank, lifeless eyes. He had something in his hand. He was clutching a gold, oblong pin.

My phone! She ran back to the car and called 911.

It seemed like forever. She waited in the car, doors locked just in case. Preston was about to tell her who killed Ellie. Now he was dead too. *If he was guilty, he wouldn't be dead. Someone wanted to insure he didn't spill the beans. Sirens. It's about time.*

Phil ran out of the car and knocked on the window. "Sara, open up. We're here now."

She got out of the car, falling into Phil's arms. "He's...he's been shot. He's dead. Preston is dead."

Arms squarely planted on her shoulders, he said, "Stay here with the officer." It was more of a command than a request. Phil ran over to the body. Within minutes, the ambulance was on the scene and in a blur, she was taken to the police station to give a statement. The first person she ran into at the station was her mother.

"Sara! What happened? You said you were going home to catch a nap and next thing I know you find another dead body? Are you okay? Come here, honey." Her mother's arms wrapped around her, making her feel less alone.

"When I got home, there was...there was a note. On my door." Her mother handed her a tissue from her desk. Sara blew her nose and caught her breath. "Preston wanted me to call him. He wanted to meet with me. He said it wasn't what we thought. He was going to tell me who killed Ellie."

"Why didn't you call the police? Going out to an abandoned farm to meet a killer? You're smarter than that."

"I called him. He was scared the police would arrest him before he had a chance to tell his side. He was going to tell me who killed Ellie."

"Since they found the murder weapon this morning with his print on it, I'd say it was pretty clear who murdered her."

"No. It doesn't make sense. He explained it. They'd already done a thorough search right after Ellie was murdered. They would've found it back then. He was being set up."

Phil Lambert came into the office. "We've got the crime scene unit out there. Come in and let's get a statement." He held the door open, motioning for Sara to enter. She remembered the note and took it out of her jacket pocket. "This was on my front door."

Phil took the note. "Why didn't you call me right away?" The veins in his forehead popped out.

"You told me to stay out of it. I wanted to hear what Preston wanted to say and he was adamant. No police."

"Still, Sara. Technically you interfered with police business."

"Can you trace the gun?"

"What gun?"

"The one that was lying a few feet from the body. And he had said he'd have evidence with him. Did you find a box or something—maybe in his car? Did you check the trunk?"

"There was no gun. Preston Montague clearly was shot, but we didn't find a murder weapon. And no magic box full of evidence either."

"That's impossible. I saw the gun with my own eyes. *First I say I found Jailyn's badge, then the gun. Both times the items disappeared before the police saw them.* Unless…"

"Unless?"

"Unless the killer was still on the scene and grabbed it after I went to the car. Oh my God. I could have been next."

"You did the right thing locking yourself in the car, but clearly, you never should have gone there alone. What were you thinking?"

"I didn't want him to get scared off and run again."

"I hope you learned your lesson. I told you to leave the police work to the professionals. I don't try and play clarinet in that symphony of yours. I know I don't have the necessary skills."

"Oboe. Not a clarinet. Let's get this over with. All I want to do is take a hot shower and get into my pajamas."

"I'll have someone escort you."

"No. I'll be fine." She didn't want to sit around waiting for an officer to become available.

When she finally left the station, it was dark. She stumbled to her door in a fog, fumbled with the key, and then felt arms grabbing her from behind. She couldn't breathe, couldn't get the air needed to scream.

"Sara, it's okay. It's just me. Travis."

"Travis? Where have you been? When did you get home?" She felt angry that he hadn't been there for her.

"A few hours ago. I heard the story on the news and immediately called your mother. Your phone went to voicemail. I figured you forgot to charge it. She told me what happened and said you were on the way home. I wanted to be sure you're okay."

"You scared me half to death." She opened the door and flicked on the lights.

"Reset the alarm. Tell me what I missed."

"I got a note from Preston. It was stuck in the front door. He had something to tell me and wanted me to meet him at the warehouse, but when I got there, he'd been shot. It's safe to say he's off the suspect list. I saw the gun. It was right next to the body."

"Then they'll be able to trace it and find the owner."

"Not exactly. I saw a gun by the body. I'm positive. But the police didn't find a gun. The killer had to have still been on the grounds while I waited."

"You shouldn't have gone alone. You know that."

"Well, I went looking for you, but you never told me where you were going or when you'd be back. I had no choice. If I waited, Preston might have changed his mind."

"Thank goodness you're safe now."

She didn't want to talk about it anymore. "So, where did you go in such a hurry?"

"I'd rather not say. I was taking care of business."

"Secret physical therapist business?"

"No need for sarcasm. Are you hungry? I'm sure you haven't eaten dinner yet."

Her stomach growled. "The last thing I want to do is cook."

"I'll order us a pizza."

Sara changed into comfy sweats and when she came downstairs, Travis had started a fire. She grabbed Panther and sat down in front of the fireplace. "If Preston didn't kill Ellie, who did? The ring motive is out the window, as is Preston seeking revenge. That leaves Jailyn Peters."

"And the motive is jealousy?"

"She has a history. Maybe it's more than jealousy. Maybe she's hiding something and Ellie was about to expose her. Ellie told Preston to come clean and he threatened her not to say anything. Perhaps Preston and Jailyn shared a secret not related to romance. Maybe whatever Preston was going to hand over to me exposed that secret. Jailyn found out he was contacting me and got to him first. How can we find out if Jailyn Peters owns a gun?"

"There's the pizza." Travis answered the door and came back in with a piping hot box of pizza.

"How solid is her alibi?"

"Phil says she was volunteering at a clinic across town."

"And he's absolutely sure?"

"He seemed sure."

"I think our next move is to take a ride to the clinic."

"Our next move? We're in this together?"

"Well, I see what happened when you tried doing it alone. By the way, I hope your detective finds out if Jailyn Peters has a gun permit."

Her phone rang. "Hi, Mom. I'm fine. Travis is here and we're sharing a pizza. Tomorrow? Okay. Can I invite Travis? Okay. See you then."

"Your mom?"

"My parents want to take a trip to the winter craft fair. I think she's trying to lighten the mood. Want to come?"

"Tomorrow's Saturday. Sure. Why not?"

Chapter 22

Another nightmare. Sara kicked and pawed at the icy water, grabbing for her oboe. Every time she clasped her hand around it, it slipped away like a serpent taunting her. She felt the dark water pulling her under. As she struggled, she watched a box of papers sink to the bottom of the freezing lake. A gun toppled out of the box and floated to the top. She sat straight up, gasping for air.

Breath in, breathe out. Panther, sharing her pillow, rubbed against her face. She nuzzled her face in his black fur. *Don't need Freud to interpret that dream.*

Looking at the alarm clock on the nightstand, she realized she'd slept a good hour past her normal wakeup time. Even when the symphony was in season and she was playing concerts late into the night, her internal clock seldom allowed her to sleep much past sunrise. It didn't matter much when or if she got up now that she was on leave. *Stop it. Don't succumb to depression on top of fighting the dystonia.*

"Come on, Panther. Let's get us some breakfast." She went downstairs, started the coffee, and popped a few frozen waffles in the toaster. "I didn't forget about you, Panther." While she waited for the waffles, she poured food into the cat's bowl. "We're getting low. I'll have to pick up another bag next time I'm at the store." Panther meowed, then dug into the food, barely coming up for air. She wondered if he realized Ellie wasn't coming back.

Travis picked her up an hour later. In spite of the recent nightmare and Travis's shady secrets, she'd slept better knowing he was right next door. The air of mystery almost made him more attractive. Almost.

"Did you sleep okay? You were really zonked out last night. Who could blame you? Two dead bodies inside of a month?"

"I know. And they say small towns are boring."

"So, are we looking for something particular at this place?"

"They sell unpainted furniture. My parents are looking for a new dresser for the guest room. Maybe you'll see something for your place."

"I'm good. I've got everything I need."

"Turn left at the light. It's right down the road."

"Close to Cusa Farms?"

"Yeah. I guess it is." They pulled into the crowded lot. "Looks like my parents are here already. That's their car."

They spotted Sara's parents as soon as they entered the gate. "Mom, Dad, ready to hunt for a dresser?"

"Yep. Just like old times. Remember when we bought that second dresser for your bedroom?" She followed her father down the path.

"Travis, are you buying furniture, too?" said Patty.

"I was telling Sara I don't need anything in particular. But we'll see."

Patty said, "It was awful, Sara finding Preston yesterday like she did."

Yesterday a dead body, today, shopping for arts and crafts. Just going with the flow.

"You've got one tough daughter there Mrs. Baron."

"I sure do." She turned to Sara. "I'm so glad you're all right. I hope you'll refrain from snooping now that you see how dangerous it is. I hear stories from the officers at work. There's nothing glamorous about investigating crimes."

"I know, Mom. It's not like I'm trying to play Nancy Drew or anything. Preston reached out to me and I owed it to Ellie to see what he had to offer." She only wished she'd been able to hear him out.

Bob Baron found fault with every dresser. One was too skinny, another too fat...Sara's nose was so cold she worried she had frostbite. *Let's wrap this up already*.

"Mom and Dad, how about Travis and I investigate the other side of the fair? Let us know if you find a good one and we'll do the same."

"Divide and conquer," said Bob. "I like that idea."

Sara and Travis broke away from her parents, immediately approving almost every dresser they saw along the new path. Sara inhaled the aroma of fresh wood. "This one's so pretty as is. Dad shouldn't ruin it by painting it."

"He could stain it and it'd retain the beauty while being protected from damage," said Travis. "This one fits the bill, right? Not too big, not too small, and the wood is so smooth he'd hardly have to sand it."

Sara opened and closed the drawers. "The price is within their budget. Let's see if they approve."

Sara recognized voices she knew coming from behind. She turned around to see Jailyn Peters and Craig Danalchek, Ellie's boss.

Jailyn said, "Travis? I didn't know you liked arts and crafts."

"Kind of. You and Craig shopping?"

Craig said, "Yes, and no. I mean, we're looking for an umbrella stand for the office. My wife and I were here yesterday and bought one for our house. I came by to pick up another and ran into Dr. Peters."

Wife? I missed something. She was convinced he and Jailyn were together. *Camaya said Jailyn came around and went to lunch with Craig after the board meetings at Medivision. I guess it was just business after all.*

Jailyn said, "I heard you were the one who found Preston Montague yesterday. Poor Preston. Must have been awful finding him in front of the warehouse like that. What were you doing at Cusa Farms in the dead of winter?"

Sara felt her face turn red, this time from heat, not the cold wind. "I, um…"

Travis interjected, "I'm sorry for your loss. You and Preston were once close according to the hospital grapevine."

"Yes, well. It was quite a shock hearing he was dead."

Sara spotted her parents. "We'd better get moving. My parents are on a mission and we promised to help."

Travis brought the Barons over to the dresser they'd found. "What do you think?"

"It's perfect," said Patty. "How about we get this one, Bob?"

"It's as good as any I suppose."

"Come over tonight for dinner and you can see how it looks in Scott's old room."

When Travis nodded, she said, "Okay, Mom. We'll be there."

Back in the car, Sara replayed the interaction with Jailyn and Craig. She was still shocked to find out Craig was married. He and Jailyn seemed to share a bond. 'Awful finding the body in front of the warehouse…' *Those were the words Jailyn used.*

"Travis, the news didn't release the exact location of the body."

"And?"

"Jailyn said it must have been awful finding Preston in front of the warehouse. How did she know that's where I found him?"

"You're right. I'm telling you, with Preston out of the picture, I'm convinced Jailyn Peters warrants further investigation. Alibi or not."

"Do you know the clinic Phil was talking about? The one where Jailyn was the night Ellie died?"

"I do. Feel like taking a ride?"

"As long as we're back in time for dinner at my parents' tonight. I'll go tell them."

While Travis drove, Sara checked the hours. Given it was Saturday, she was afraid they'd close early. "Open till 5:00. We have plenty of time."

The outside of the clinic looked like it had survived both world wars. Sara couldn't in any way picture Barbie doll Jailyn Peters working here. The paint, probably containing lead, peeled from the walls, and the carpet in the waiting room was so stained that it was impossible to discern the original color. A baby screamed in his mother's arms. An elderly man coughed so hard he could barely catch a breath. Travis took the lead and stepped up to the counter where a nurse was juggling several tasks at once.

"You must be in charge, here. I'm Travis Jennings, a physical therapist at Hudsonville Community."

"If you're not here to volunteer, move on. We're very busy as you can see."

"I won't take up much of your time. I want to ask you about a colleague. Jailyn Peters. I understand she volunteers here."

"She does."

"You must have some sort of sign in sheet. I have to check her hours, verify that she was here."

"I'm not turning over that information to a stranger. You should know better than to ask."

"She's up for an award based on community service. It's a secret. If she doesn't meet the requirements, I won't bother nominating her."

That lie came out of his mouth seamlessly.

The nurse hesitated.

Travis leaned in, flashing his warm smile, dimples showing. "We'd appreciate it so much. You know how hard it is to get recognition in this world. We do our jobs day in and day out like we're invisible. Isn't it great when someone takes the time to notice?"

She said, "Give me a minute."

Sara whispered, "If you get tired of physical therapy, Broadway's an hour and a half away." *Those dimples are irresistible.*

An old man who reminded her of Grandpa sat sandwiched between a young mother and the wall. He clutched his head, leaning back against the wall. *Poor man is by himself. Looks like he's in a lot of pain.* Since she'd come home, she'd seen too many examples of lonely, elderly folks. It had to be the same back in San Francisco, but she hadn't ever thought much about it.

The nurse came back to the counter. "Okay, now. Here are the logs from the night you questioned."

Travis and Sara leaned in for a closer look.

"She signed in at 6 pm, and out at midnight."

"Are you sure?"

"She means, did Dr. Jennings go out for a dinner break, or leave to run an errand maybe?" The nurse glared at her. She should have kept quiet and let Travis do the challenging.

"If she did, she didn't sign out. I gotta get back to work."

Sara bathed her hands in hand sanitizer the moment they left the germ infested waiting room.

"So, there was a window of opportunity. That place was wall to wall patients and it's a Saturday afternoon.

Imagine it at night when doctors' offices are typically closed."

"I'd guess these patients come here because they have no insurance and can't afford a doctor. I'll bet it's packed all the time. Jailyn could have slipped out unnoticed. I doubt that detective of yours simply verified by looking at the sign in sheet. He must have had witnesses, or close circuit TV to back up her alibi, don't you think?"

"I suppose so." She hated to admit defeat. "Hey, we'd better get going. My mom will be waiting at the door for us you know."

Chapter 23

"Sara, Travis, come in before you catch the death of you." At the door, as predicted. Without a coat.

Sara almost tripped over the unpainted dresser. "Do you need help getting this upstairs?"

"We tried but it's too heavy. After dinner you and Sara's dad can move it," said Patty. "It's exquisite. Don't you think so, Travis?"

"Absolutely. And hearing the crackling log in the fireplace, feeling how it warms up the room makes me feel safe."

Safe? What a strange choice of words. She hugged her Dad.

"I've got cookies, but save room for dinner." Baroque music played softly in the background.

Travis said, "Bach Concerto for Oboe d'Amore, right?"

"You know your Bach," said Bob. "Impressive."

"Sara, can you play one of those?"

"If I made a reed for it I could. I don't happen to own one."

Travis's phone vibrated. Not the one with the Beethoven ring tone that he carried in his pocket, but the second one he had stashed in his jacket the other night. "I've got to take this outside."

"I hope it isn't an emergency," said Patty.

"He's a physical therapist, not a trauma surgeon. I can't imagine what sort of emergency we'd be talking about."

"I was thinking a family emergency," said Patty.

Grandpa came down the step. "Maybe it's his wife. I heard about this before. Betcha Barack's got a family in the city and a little hideaway in a small town where he meets up with his mistress. Or his second wife."

She knew Grandpa loved to bait her, but she bit every time. "Grandpa, that's awful. Travis isn't like that." *Though I did find the earring in the sofa. And who's Cameron? Why was she jumping to his defense?*

As if just now noticing, though he'd already nearly tripped over it, Grandpa said, "When did a dresser grow in the middle of our living room?"

"Amazing," said Bob. "Yesterday it was but a tiny acorn sitting on the carpet." Patty gave him a light swat.

"It's temporary. We'll get Travis to help us move it later."

Travis came back in, rubbing his hands together like a boy scout trying to start a fire.

"Everything okay?" asked Patty.

Travis's tone turned cool and distant. "Yeah. Everything's fine." He picked up a cookie and gave it a chomp.

The doorbell rang. "That must be Gail. Frank, why don't you get that? My hands are full." Patty carried a pitcher of cider into the room.

Frank grumbled all the way to the door. As soon as he opened it, his sour face turned sweet and his voice lost the gruffness. "Come on in."

Gail wore a green sweatshirt that said *Meowy-Christmas* under her ski jacket. The coarse white strands around her temples were newly a soft brown, and Sara caught a whiff of floral perfume. Gail handed Patty a Tupperware container. "I baked sugar cookies. Slice and bake, I'll admit. It's been a while since I used the oven."

Frank hung her jacket on the coat rack, bumping into the dresser on the way. "Did you go see your friend at the hospital?"

"I did. She's feeling better. They're getting the excess metal out of her body with a drug they're putting in her IV. Chelation therapy, she called it. I hope she winds up with a healthy bit of compensation from the company that made the hip joint."

Sara said, "Why?"

"The manufacturer is being sued left and right. The parts they manufactured weren't safe."

"Was the manufacturer Medivison by any chance?" *Medivision, Jailyn Peters—orthopedic surgeon...*

"I don't have any idea. Whoever was making them isn't doing it anymore. There was a massive recall, I remember seeing it on the news."

Grandpa grumbled. "See. Told you I didn't want my hip replaced. You all want me to die so I'll be out of your hair. Knew it all along."

"This isn't a pity party, Grandpa." *Out of our hair, maybe. Dead, definitely not.*

"We want you mobile, Pops. I'm not pushing a wheelchair down the church aisle if you ever get married again." He winked at Gail.

Gail's cheeks turned red. "The fire is lovely."

Travis answered, "Yes, it is." Sara thought he looked a bit uncomfortable. He continued, changing the subject. "We went to the craft fair this morning. Have you been?"

"Not this year. Last year I bought a set of handmade placemats. Four of them. Not that I need more than one, but they do look pretty sitting on my table. Did the weather hold up?"

"Yeah, we had a welcome sunbreak. Sara and I helped pick out the perfect dresser."

"Yes, I couldn't help but notice when I walked in. By the way, did you watch the news? Preston Montague was murdered," said Gail.

"And guess who found the body?" Patty nodded toward Sara.

"Sara?" Her hands flew over her mouth. "Another dead body? Are you serious?"

"I'm feeling a little cursed."

Patty said, "They say death comes in threes. You better be careful, honey."

"Thanks for the warning, Mom. I'll be on the lookout." Her mother went into the kitchen and Sara doubted she'd caught the sarcasm.

Patty came back with a bowl of popcorn. "There's more hot apple cider inside so drink up."

With the care of a jeweler cutting a diamond, Sara rearranged the pictures of her brother on the mantle. Scott in his baseball uniform, Scott graduating West Point... *Do they have baseball in Iraq?*

Grandpa said, "Making room for more pictures, Sara?"

"No, nothing to add. Just missing my brother."

"There's plenty of space for pictures of my future grandkids," said Patty. She smiled at Sara, who turned her head, feeling embarrassed in front of Travis. It's not like she didn't want kids, and, yes, she was aware of the whole biological clock issue. One more year and she'd be considered a high-risk pregnancy. She'd briefly considered freezing her eggs. That was when she was sure she'd have a salary coming in.

Gail said, "Travis, how are you liking it here? It's been what, a year or so since you started working at the hospital?"

"I like it. Easy commute, friendly people."

"I'll bet you miss having professional sports at your doorstep, though. I mean, you have to travel to the city to take in a game here," said Bob. "Are you a Bears fan?"

"Um, yeah. It was an easy commute to the stadium. I'm more of a baseball fan. Last summer a group of us from the hospital took in a couple of Mets games."

"Not a die-hard Cubs fan? Or are you team White Sox? Most Chicagoans I've met are loyal to the core, no matter where they move."

Sara reached for her glass of cider. "Oh, no. I'm so sorry." She had spilled her drink all over the rug. "I'll clean it up."

"What's with the butter fingers?" said Grandpa. "You've got the steadiest hands I know. I remember how easily you scraped reeds. Hands of a surgeon. Remember I used to say that?"

"Leave her alone, Frank. I'll bet she didn't sleep well last night after discovering Preston Montague."

"Are we eating dinner anytime soon?" said Grandpa.

"It's ready. I made chili in the crock pot."

Gail said, "The glow from the fireplace—slice and bake cookies—life is good."

"Enough with the sappiness. Can we eat already?" Grandpa hobbled toward the kitchen.

The pot of chili was demolished in no time. Patty had bought paper plates and utensils. Sara was glad to see she'd become more practical since becoming a working woman. When she was home last Christmas she had to help her mother hand wash the china her grandmother had passed down to them.

Travis whispered, "Sara, do you mind if we get going? I'm beat." He looked at the dresser. After we move the dresser, of course."

Feeling worn out herself, she was eager to comply. "I'll help." Together they put the dresser in its new home, Scott's old bedroom turned guest room.

"Mom and Dad, we're going to head home."

"Okay. This was fun. You'll have to be back soon."

"Of course." She kissed her parents and grandfather goodnight.

"Thanks for including me," said Travis. "Goodnight."

Travis didn't say a word the whole way home. He looked more serious than she'd ever seen him, or perhaps that's how he looked when he was worried. Not his usual self. Snow fell on the windshield.

"Home, sweet home," said Travis. "I'll walk you in."

Travis turned on the lights and walked through the rooms. "I don't see any boogey men in the closets." He made sure the interior door to the garage was locked. "Turn on the alarm behind me. Goodnight."

As she was closing the door, he turned around and said, "I had a really nice time tonight." Then continued walking to his car.

Although it felt a bit lonely after being with her family, Sara was glad to be home.

Her hand had been stiff and bothering her all night. She scooped up Panther. "I might have to stay after all. I don't know how I'll cope, giving up the orchestra, but I'm getting worse, not better. Come on. Let's go to bed." She put Panther near her ear. His purring always soothed her.

Just before she turned out the bedroom lamp, she looked out the window at the snow floating through the night sky like wisps of cotton. She had an excellent view of Travis's driveway. *What's that black car doing parked in his driveway?*

The front door opened and a man in a trench coat stood in the doorway talking to, more like arguing with, Travis. She couldn't hear from across the yard, even when she cracked open the window. Travis slammed the door shut, then she heard the engine rev. The stranger sped away. *Who was that? Am I being completely stupid by trusting Travis.*

Chapter 24

Sara woke up with two goals for the day. She planned on going by the shop to help her father, and she wanted to touch base with Travis over pursuing Jailyn's alibi. Could anyone who was at the clinic that night vouch for her being there all evening? She couldn't directly ask Phil or he'd accuse her of telling him how to do his job. She'd already made that mistake.

Peeking out the blinds, she was surprised Travis's car was already gone. *It's early for him to go into work. Does his early departure have anything to do with the private phone call he took outside in the freezing air last night? Or the argument he had with the stranger wearing the trench coat? I know he's hiding something, and he's an amateur at it.*

She knew how it felt to harbor a secret. *My parents showed no signs of suspecting I have a health issue or that I may be leaving behind the career I've worked so hard to attain. Not until I told them. It felt good to have it out in the open.*

After breakfast, she scraped the snow off her windshield and drove over to Baron Oboes. Both her grandfather and father were huddled over worktables, tools in hand. She paused at the door, catching part of their conversation, feeling her heart sink.

"I don't think we have a choice. We can cover our bills for only a few more months."

"If we work quickly enough, we can deliver the oboes on our backlist and that'll cover the bills," said Grandpa.

"But we haven't been keeping up. Look how far behind we are. We're losing business because no one can wait that long for an instrument. Frasier Woodwinds made us a generous offer."

Sara walked in. "You can't throw in the towel, Dad. I'll help. Once I get a bit of practice, I can work fast."

"We're swimming against the tide, Sara."

"Let me see the list."

"You're better off helping with repairs. The learning curve on instrument making is steep."

"But it's not like I don't know how to do it. I worked alongside you my whole life before I left for college."

Her father hesitated for a moment. "Okay. Come on. Let's start with measuring the wood. The bore has to be exact. Not that I have to tell you. Attention to detail has always been your strong point." His tone suggested he would take all the help he could get to have the family business survive.

He handed her a list of coordinates on a graph. She hoped she could keep her hand in check, now that she convinced her father she was capable. She took a piece of wood and started the process. *It's like riding a bike. I've got this.*

While she worked, she thought about the case. Jailyn Peters had a convincing enough alibi to keep her off the police suspect list. If she and Travis could poke holes in her alibi, Jailyn would be right back on that list. She hoped to ride over to the clinic later with Travis and find witnesses who worked alongside Jailyn Peters the night of the murder. In spite of the alibi providing sign-in sheet, could witnesses verify Jailyn Peters was at the clinic every minute of that shift? Or was it possible she slipped out unnoticed, killed Ellie, and returned to work?

She felt Grandpa breathing on her shoulder. "That's good. Turn the lathe just a bit."

"Like this?"

"Yeah. Now check the measurements for the next section."

She looked at the graph. "Wait a minute!" She opened the drawer with the logbook and flipped to the page of numbers. Connecting the darker numbers created an oboe shape. She'd been interrupted last time she realized it.

"Grandpa, do these numbers make sense as measurements?"

"Not really. The proportions are similar, but the numbers don't work."

Her father said, "How's the practice oboe coming along?"

"Dad, I'm wondering if the dark numbers in the log book are measurements. Grandpa thinks the numbers wouldn't work. What do you think?"

Her father held the book under his lamp. "The ratios aren't what we use. Grandpa's right about the numbers."

She was sure there was a connection. "Great Grandpa liked puzzles you said. Maybe it's some kind of a code."

"You can play around with it when you have time, but if you truly want to help…"

"Sorry, Dad. I'll get back to work."

Once she got her skills up to par, she knew they could conquer the backlist. Especially if Grandpa was able to work too. He may have off days, but she was impressed with the speed and accuracy he exhibited this morning. In fact, since he'd been spending time with Gail, any signs of early Alzheimer's had greatly diminished. Before she knew it, it was past lunchtime.

"I have to get to my appointment, but I'll be back tomorrow."

Her father said, "What appointment? Are you sick?"

"Um, no. A hair appointment. I'm due for a trim."

"Thank you for helping. You're right. A little practice and I think we can get you up to speed. It's too bad that by the time you really get in the groove you'll be heading back home, hand good as new."

"I love your optimism, Dad." She kissed him and Grandpa.

"Things have a way of working out, honey."

She got to the hospital on time for her visit, but was told Travis was running late and not yet in his office.

"Should I wait or reschedule?"

The receptionist said, "I'd give him another half an hour or so. It's up to you. It's unlike him to be late."

"I know. I'll go get a cup of coffee and check back."

I could have stayed and helped at the shop had I known this. Travis's car was gone this morning. If he wasn't at work, where did he go? She wondered if he'd even been at home last night. Grandpa's tease about him having a mistress or a second wife might not be as far off the mark as she'd thought. She wished she didn't care.

She pushed the elevator button. When the door opened, Gail Capelli exited holding a small vase with roses.

"Mrs. Capelli, are you okay?"

"Yes, of course. I was visiting my friend. The one with the metal poisoning I told you about."

"That's right. She'd had the artificial hip joint put in. How's she doing?"

"Better. She's starting to get her energy back."

"What was the story again?"

"The company used artificial joints that hadn't been adequately tested. The combination of materials leached metal and made some patients extremely ill. My friend lost her hair, got rashes...I'm glad they figured it out, but now they have to re-operate to replace the joint."

"Can they do that?"

"As she told me, it can be complicated, especially if tissue has already grown around it. Plus, she's elderly and surgery always has risks."

"My mother mentioned someone at church who was losing her hair after a hip replacement. I wonder if it was for the same reason."

"Was it Pam Hanson? Poor thing wears a wig now. And not one of those made from real hair either. Everyone can tell."

"They recalled all the faulty joints, right? Grandpa may be needing that surgery sometime soon if his hip keeps hurting like it does."

"After the massive recall and the lawsuits, I'm sure the FDA is looking over their shoulder. Must have cost the company billions to trash all that inventory."

"And the company is based here? Did you remember the name of the company?"

"Yes, I did, after thinking about it last time we discussed this. Medivision. The Montagues own the office building and they manufacture over at a warehouse by Cusa Farms."

"Who is your friend's surgeon?" Sara had a feeling she already knew.

"Dr. Peters. Jailyn Peters."

"Was she implicated in the lawsuit?"

"Heavens, no. My friend tells me Dr. Peters was as angry as anyone. Had no idea the joints were faulty. She threatened to go after them herself."

The elevator doors opened again. "I'm going to grab a cup of coffee. Want to join me?"

"I'd love to but I've got plans. You know that neighbor your mother feeds?"

"Yeah. Jacob, right?"

"Yes. The poor man is having a hard time dealing

with his wife's death and of course I went through the same thing. Your mother brought me over to his place and introduced us. I'm going to go over and visit, perhaps take him out for a late lunch if he's up to it."

"That's so sweet. Is Grandpa going with you?"

"No, he has to work. He and your father have been putting in long hours trying to keep the business afloat. Frank says you've been a great help."

Nice to know I'm doing something useful with my time. "Okay, well, have fun. That's very sweet of you to care enough to help him out."

"You can't really understand unless you've gone through it yourself."

"Grandpa was devastated when Grandma died. It took him a long time to even get out of bed. We were afraid we were going to lose him too. He's been much happier since the two of you have been spending time together."

Gail's cheeks blushed. "Yes, we've spent long hours sharing stories. I'd better get going."

Sara headed to the cafeteria and sat down with coffee and her phone. She searched for information about the lawsuit and checked patient comments about Jailyn Peters.

Jailyn Peters had a mixed bag of reviews. Some praised her for giving them their lives back thanks to her surgical skill. A few commented on her businesslike demeanor and lack of bedside manner. *Here's an interesting one. A patient's daughter writes that Dr. Peters killed her mother by implanting a recalled hip joint. How can she prove that?*

Sara searched through medical malpractice cases and lawsuits. While not easy to sift through, she found three different lawsuits naming both Dr. Peters and Medivision. The suits claimed defective hip and knee joints contained metals that leached into the blood stream making the patients sick—just as Mrs. Capelli said. The implication was that Dr. Jailyn Peters implanted them knowing they were defective, or at the least that it was her responsibility as a doctor to have picked up that they were defective. *A class action lawsuit against Medivision is pending.*

Medivision is right here in Hudsonville. I wonder how many other patients were affected and don't even realize it? She found the recall notice and noted the model numbers of the affected joints. Looking at the wall clock, she realized it had been more than thirty minutes. If she hoped to get her appointment in with Travis, she had to get moving.

When she got to his office, the receptionist told her to go right in.

"Sara, I'm sorry about being so late. I had to cancel my other appointments, but I wanted to be sure you'd get in a session."

"Where were you?"

"Business."

"What sort of business?"

"Sara, it's private. You need to respect that. Now, give me your hand."

She complied, but wasn't happy about his evasive answer. "It's getting worse. I don't know what to do."

"I'm going to schedule an appointment with a neurologist to rule out underlying conditions. This isn't simply a hand problem. Unlike carpal tunnel or tendonitis, focal dystonia is a glitch in the signal from your brain to your hand."

"So you can't help me?"

"I didn't say that. I want to try medication. I work closely with the internist down the hall. I'd like you to schedule an appointment with him. If that doesn't work, Botox injections have been somewhat successful, but it'd be hard to confine the target area."

"Medication?"

"There are also neurological retraining exercises to try. I have to research them further. And we can consider changing how you play the instrument. Perhaps adjusting how you hold it."

"It's worth a shot. I read about an oboist with this problem who had the thumb rest repositioned. Is this going to get worse?"

"Typically it stabilizes. I'm confident we can make progress."

"What about acupuncture."

"You can try that as well. Complementary treatments have their place alongside traditional medicine."

"On another note, I did some research. Jailyn Peters has been named in several lawsuits involving Medivision devices."

"I remember when that whole scandal came out, shortly after I moved here."

"Do you think it's possible Dr. Peters still uses those faulty joints?"

"I can't imagine it. Besides, they're no longer on the market."

"What happens to the recalled joints?"

"Well, I imagine they are destroyed or melted down. I never thought about it really."

"What if the devices weren't destroyed? I mean, that's a ton of revenue going to trash."

"The FDA is all over Medivision since the recall. They're constantly being inspected, and it's a good thing. It reassures the public that it's safe to use their products again. Otherwise, they'd be out of business, even after cleaning up their act."

"Gail's friend had hip surgery less than a year ago. Dr. Peters was her surgeon. She's in the hospital now receiving treatment for metal poisoning. Wasn't that after the recall?"

"Let me check the data base."

"Can you do that?"

"I can see who had hip and knee replacements. They are all assigned initially to me post op." He sat at his desk. "I can only go back a year. I'm not sure how helpful this will be." He scrolled down the list on the computer, Sara reading over his shoulder. "Here's one of Jailyn's patients. Jot down the name."

Sara grabbed a note pad and started writing.

"Here are two more. One is Jailyn's patient. The other is Dr. Arnold's."

He continued. "Arnold, Arnold, Arnold…Here's Peters."

By the time they finished, they had five names on the list.

"Where should we start?"

"I have to respect their privacy, legally. If I currently am seeing them, I'll ask a few questions next time they come to the office. Frankly, I haven't heard any complaints since the recall."

"Why don't you call them?"

"Sara, I can't push this or I can get into hot water. Last thing I need is to get sued. Be patient."

"What about taking a ride to the Medivision factory?"

"And do what? Sneak in? Look how well that worked when you went to the cabin to spy on Preston."

"You're a physical therapist. Can't you claim to have interest in their new products or something?"

"Let me work on it. What are your plans for the afternoon?"

"Actually, I have to get a birthday present for Grandpa. There's a mall less than half an hour's ride from here. Do you want to come?"

"Have you ever met a man who voluntarily goes to a

mall? Unless, of course, he's trying to win someone over."

Her pulse quickened. Did he mean he had thoughts of winning her over? *Stop acting like a school girl. That's what happens when you aren't working and have too much time on your hands. Besides, he's a jerk. Remember the accident?*

"Or, if he needs to buy a present as well. It's my one-year anniversary working at the hospital next week and I wanted to pick up a little something for the nurses and receptionist in my office."

"That's very sweet of you. Let's go."

Chapter 25

The mall was small by San Francisco standards. Sara remembered how huge it seemed growing up when she and her Mom spent entire days shopping, eating lunch at the deli in the food court, getting cinnamon pretzels from the booth near Sears…*I always imagined having my own daughter to shop with. That window is closing. I'll wind up without a career and without a family.*

They circled the parking area three times before finding a space. Not unusual, she supposed, as it was almost holiday season.

Travis said, "I don't know what to get."

"There's a Yankee Candle store if I remember correctly. You can buy hand lotion. Nurses wash their hands a lot, right? Or gourmet coffee. I'll bet they get pretty bored working alongside you all day." She gave him a coy smile.

"Very funny. How about a gift certificate?" said Travis.

"Nah. Show some thought went into this."

"I'm willing to try the candle store. Lotion seems too personal." Travis followed her into Yankee Candle. Sara loved the smell of candles, though she seldom— make that never—burned them. Wait. There was that time the electric went out and she ran out of batteries for the flashlight…

Travis held a candle to his nose. "This makes me want to sneeze."

"Try this. Smells like a pine forest. Or here's one that reminds me of a tropical beach."

He took the two options from her hands. "Sold. One of each. Can we go home now?"

"Very funny. I haven't even started yet."

Travis grabbed the package and they headed back into the mall. Sara wasn't watching where she was going and bumped into another shopper. "I'm so sorry."

"Sara? Sara Baron?"

"Hunter Griffith? I haven't seen you since high school. I thought you moved overseas."

"I did for a while. Got married and we decided this was a better place to raise a child than where we were living. How have you been?"

"Good. I live out in San Francisco and play in the orchestra." *For now, anyway.*

"You kept up the music all these years."

That might be coming to an abrupt end. She smiled. "Yes, still playing the oboe. You said you came back to raise a child. How many kids do you have?"

His eyes narrowed. "Two. I mean, one that's still living."

"Oh, I'm sorry. That's awful."

"Boating accident out on the lake. Not really an accident. A drunk went slamming into our boat. Jordan was killed instantly."

"I'm sorry for your loss."

"Kicker is, the killer got off with not even a hand slap. Jury found her innocent. And you know who killed him? She went to school with us. As a matter of fact, you were friends if I remember."

Sara had a sinking feeling. "Who?"

"Ellie Rossi."

Travis touched her arm as if to say he understood how hard it was to absorb the comment. "I'm sure it was an accident."

"Going 70 miles an hour under the influence is hardly an accident. Do you know what it's like to lose a child? Do you know how awful it is to suppress your own tears so you can comfort your wife who can't stop sobbing, can't eat, can't sleep?"

"That's so awful. I'm so sorry."

"To top it off the court exonerates her." His lips curled into a sinister grin. "She wound up paying though."

"You mean because she was murdered?"

"What goes around comes around. I've gotta meet my wife at the food court. The last thing I want to do is shop, but we're trying to make things more normal for Noah, our other son. His homecoming dance is next week and he needs a suit. Nice running into you."

After he got on the escalator, Sara said, "Did you hear that? He had venom in his voice."

"You would too if you thought someone got away with murdering your child."

"He was a little off back in high school. It's the first time I'd heard the term bi-polar. Do you think he snapped and killed her?"

"Hard to imagine. Did Ellie drink?"

"Yeah. I wondered in the past if she enjoyed it a little too much. I mean, from the few dealings I had with her. But to speed in a boat that recklessly? And what was she doing all by herself in a boat anyway? She didn't even own a boat last I knew. I mean I never saw a boat trailer in the driveway or anything."

"Maybe it belonged to her parents. It's worth looking into, don't you think?"

"I'll ask Phil about it. I'm surprised no one brought this up."

Travis said, "Where are we going?"

"Mom's birthday is coming up too and she loves clothes. Let's go in here." She could swear he rolled his eyes when she said that. She found the petite section and browsed through the sweaters. "What do you think?

Mom likes bright colors."

"It's fine."

"Or look at this. It's cashmere." She had second thoughts looking at the price. As if he understood, Travis said, "I like the first one."

"Done. You know, Dad could use another sweatshirt to wear around the shop. The one he's wearing has a hole in it."

"The one that says San Francisco Philharmonic?"

"Yeah. I sent it to him when I first got the job. He was so proud."

"Isn't it a little early for Christmas shopping?"

"Yeah, but I like to beat the crowds. I usually put things away all year when I find something that catches my eye."

They found a thick sweatshirt for her father, and she couldn't resist buying a hardcover bestseller for Mrs. Capelli. After all, she'd been putting up with Grandpa and that deserved a reward. She made Grandpa happy and he was infinitely easier to deal with when he was happy.

"I don't know what to get Grandpa."

"How about a replacement scent for the cologne he wears?"

"Wears? You mean bathes himself in?" They both laughed. "Great idea. Any favorites?"

"I've got a few ideas. Come on."

She followed him to the counter, where they spritzed so many samples, her nose became numb. "You pick one."

"Here. This is one I've always liked." He sprayed it all over her coat sleeve.

"Sold. You've been so patient. How about I buy you dinner on the way home?"

"I can't. I have plans."

"Plans?"

"Yeah. Maybe another time."

She was sure he was seeing someone. Maybe the mysterious Cameron of prescription bottle fame. Her heart sank a little, thinking about eating a frozen dinner with Panther in front of the TV. *Stop the pity party. At least you have Panther.*

She couldn't help herself. "I thought we were becoming friends. Why don't you open up to me? If you have a date, say so. And why are you lying about your relationship with Ellie."

"Lying? I haven't lied."

"You said you barely knew her, yet you knew she didn't have a boat and you knew your way to the master bedroom the night she was murdered."

"Where's this coming from? None of that is your business."

"What are you hiding, really? I found Ellie's earring in your sofa and a notebook in her handwriting in your coffee table next to the remotes."

"You're a snoop and I wish I'd never extended my hospitality to you."

"I think you know more about her murder than you're saying. Why wouldn't you let the police take a mold of your tire track? And how is it that you're always right around the corner when I get a threat?"

"I was with you at your parents' house last time."

"And you stepped out to take a phone call earlier— when the tires were punctured."

"You're a whiny, ungrateful snoop. Did I mention nosy? Think about all the threats you received and you'll see I have an alibi for all of them."

"An alibi? Interesting terminology."

"Why don't you get on a plane and go back to San Francisco. Oh, I forgot. You might not have a job there anymore."

"That's hitting below the belt. I hate you. I hope I

never see you again."

"Get in the truck. I know you don't have money for a taxi." He was silent the whole way back to Hudsonville. She was fuming and hurt all at once. How did she let herself care at all about him?

Travis dropped her off at Ellie's. This time he didn't even get out and make sure she was safe. *He's in a hurry to get ready for his date.*

She opened the door to the dark house, flipped on the lights, and jacked up the temperature on the thermostat. A fire would be nice, but just for her? It didn't seem worth the effort. *After dinner I'll try practicing, maybe fix up a few reeds.* If she stayed much longer, she'd need to set up a work desk. *I won't let myself cry over Travis. No one will hurt me again like Brandon did.*

She took a Lean Cuisine out of the box and was about to pop it in the oven, when her phone rang.

"Phil? Yes, I'm home."

"I was wondering if you'd like to go out to dinner."

She didn't need to think about it. The loneliness here was already gnawing at her. "I'd love to."

Sara took a hot shower, reveling in the scent of the new shower gel she just bought at the mall. Not having not discussed the venue, she pulled on stretchy black pants, stylish boots, and an off the shoulder fine-knit sweater. Not too fancy, not too casual. Phil arrived exactly on time. He opened the car door like a gentleman.

"Did you hang out at the music store today?"

"You mean the oboe shop? For a while. With three of us working, we're beginning to make a dent in the back orders. Then we took a ride to the mall. I had to get Grandpa a birthday present. The big party's coming up and so far, I don't think he's caught on that we're planning it."

"We? You talked your father into going to the

mall?"

"No. Travis and I. He wanted to pick up some gifts for the nurses in his office."

"I'd have gone with you, except I had to work. Must be nice to take off in the middle of the day to go shopping."

Her first reaction would have been to jump to Travis's defense, but not anymore. She chose not to react to the comment. "The mall was crowded. Guess who I ran into?"

"I could try guessing, but it'd be easier if you just tell me."

"Hunter Griffith, from high school. You must know the name."

"No, why should I know who that is?"

"His son, Jordan, was killed in a boating accident. Actually, he claims Ellie was driving drunk, 70 miles an hour on the lake, and crashed into their boat, killing their son. Last summer. You don't remember the case?"

"Now that you bring it up I do. It was determined to be an accident."

"Did you know Ellie was the one driving the boat?"

"I did."

"Why didn't you mention that?"

"She was found innocent so it was irrelevant. Why tarnish her memory? Besides, although alcohol was found in the boat, by the time they got to Ellie, her blood levels were normal. She said it was an accident—she hadn't realized she'd harmed anyone."

"But Jordan's father thought differently."

"Yes, he claims she was speeding and reckless but that was hard to prove. The one witness who came forward had been drinking himself and wasn't credible in court."

"But there had to have been other witnesses."

"Like I said, no one else came forward and the

evidence left reasonable doubt. Why are you bringing this up now?"

"The civil suit was recently concluded, also clearing Ellie of blame. When I spoke to Hunter, he made a comment about Ellie getting what was coming to her."

He pulled into the Canton Palace parking lot. "I hope you like Chinese."

The dimly lit restaurant had a mural of a red dragon on one wall and a large fish tank in front of another. They were seated in front of a brass gong.

"Phil, can you reopen the file and take another look?"

"Look at what?"

"See if there is anything that was missed. Does Hunter Griffith have an arrest record or did he threaten Ellie?"

The waiter stood, pad in hand. "I'll have the wonton soup and Mongolian Beef. What about you, Sara?"

Hot and sour or egg drop? Heads hot and sour, tails egg drop. "I'll have the hot and sour soup."

"Egg roll or spring roll?"

"Ummm, Egg roll, and for the main course…"

Phil said, "We'll both take the Mongolian Beef."

As soon as she handed back the menu, she continued pushing Phil.

"Why don't you see if he has an alibi for the night Ellie died?"

"I have no reason to do that."

"I just gave you a reason. And let me ask you this. Do you think Travis Jennings could be Ellie's killer? He may be working with a partner. He has this second phone, and I saw a man in a trench coat talking to him in his driveway. They were arguing."

"Look, if I wanted to talk shop, I'd have stayed at the station. Can we change the subject? What's the best movie you've seen recently?"

"I haven't seen a movie in ages." *Not since I broke up with Brandon, as a matter of fact.*

"Who's your favorite band?"

"It's a toss-up between the Chicago Symphony and the Berlin Philharmonic. You?"

"Green Day."

"Green who? Never heard of them."

"Who are you rooting for in the Orange Bowl?"

"I hate football."

The evening dragged on. When they'd finished their meal, the waiter brought them fortune cookies. Phil read his aloud. "Measure twice, cut once. Not sure I get it."

"It means if you do something carefully and thoroughly the first time, you don't go back and redo it." *Like if you'd interviewed Hunter Griffin and asked for an alibi right after Ellie died, you wouldn't have to rule him out as Ellie's murderer now. Or if you'd stuck to your first impression of Travis instead of getting sucked into his charm, you wouldn't feel so hurt inside.*

"Open yours."

She reluctantly smashed the cookie. "This is your lucky year."

"I can see that," said Phil.

She was feeling anything but lucky and it was hard to imagine anything but darkness ahead. "I'm kinda tired. Do you mind if we go?"

"No problem, but I was hoping you might come over for a drink."

"I'll take a rain check." *I'd prefer to snuggle up with Panther and watch the late show.*

"I'll tell you what. Stop by the station tomorrow and I'll go through the case file so you can see for yourself the details of the Griffith case."

Chapter 26

The next morning, Travis's driveway was empty. Sara pictured him eating breakfast with this Cameron woman. *Why do you care? He's a jerk with a capital J, just like you thought. You have enough on your plate anyway.*

The house was too quiet. She turned on the TV for background noise, then went into the kitchen. "Panther, get down from the counter. You don't have to try to drink from the sink. I'll give you fresh water, and how about breakfast?"

She strained her memory. *Did Ellie's parents ever own a boat? Did Ellie ever mention boating?* She didn't think so. Surely if Ellie's family had a boat they'd have invited her to go along with them at some point when she was growing up. She and Ellie were inseparable back then. *What about Ellie's coworker, Camaya? They seem like they were close. She'd know if Ellie had taken up boating. Think I'll make a few stops before going to the station.*

She hoped her recollection of Ellie's parents being early risers was still correct. It was. Mrs. Rossi picked up on the first ring. Her voice sounded flat. Was she tired, or had she been taking medication to help her cope? If it helped, Sara was all in favor. She could use some herself.

"Mrs. Rossi? It's Sara. Do you mind if I stop by the condo? I have a few questions about Ellie."

"Do you think you found her killer?"

"Not yet, but I have a potential lead."

"Please, come on over. I haven't slept since Ellie's murder and I won't rest as long as I think of Ellie's killer going unpunished."

Sara stopped by the bakery to pick up donuts and take-out coffee, then headed to the condo where Ellie's parents lived.

The sleepy neighborhood was waking up when Sara pulled in. She passed a parka-clad couple walking hand in hand, a paper carrier on a bike, and a woman walking a terrier wearing a ridiculously bright doggie sweater and matching booties. *Panther wouldn't stand for that. Cats have more dignity than to be seen in public wearing silly outfits.* She felt the warmth of the donuts through the bag as she rang the doorbell.

"Sara, come in. It's freezing out there." Mrs. Rossi wore sweats and plaid slippers. Mr. Rossi, in a flannel shirt, stood behind her and took the donuts from Sara. "Take off your coat and come inside."

"I brought coffee, too."

"Thanks. I was just about to make another pot. Do you know something more about Ellie's case?"

"It's more of a lead I want to check. I was at the mall yesterday and ran into Hunter Griffith, from high school. You must know who I'm talking about."

Mr. Rossi said, "The one who dragged Ellie to court. He claimed she was drunk and speeding out on the lake and killed their son."

"Yes. I'm surprised I hadn't heard about it."

"Pure hogwash. He was out to make money from an unfortunate accident."

"Did Ellie own a boat? Or do you? I never heard her mention it before."

"No. We don't, and neither did Ellie. She said she was borrowing it from a friend."

"Why was she alone on the lake? And speeding like that."

"She didn't want to divulge much. She told us she was afraid and was speeding to get away from trouble. That's all she'd say."

"Trouble? Like with a boyfriend?"

"I don't know. We were in and out of the country on church business. Maybe if we'd been here... I suppose she could have been dating someone."

"Why keep that a secret? And was she running from him? Was he abusive?"

"Your guess is as good as mine. You know she was always very private about who she was dating—ever since she was a teenager."

"I'd forgotten, but you're right. She'd never tell me, her best friend, who she was seeing. The only one I knew about was Kyle, and that's because they dated her entire senior year." *Maybe not telling me she was engaged wasn't as odd as it seemed.* She was consoled by that thought.

Her mother said, "Wait! There was a time around then when I called and I heard a man's voice in the background. It was after dinner and he sounded like he was trying to get her to hang up. Like they were going somewhere. I asked her if she was alone and she said it was just the TV. Ellie never watched TV."

Mr. Rossi said, "I know Ellie liked to drink with her friends after work sometimes, but to get drunk and go on the lake? That wasn't her. Ellie swore up and down she was sober, and when she was tested, there was no sign of alcohol in her blood."

"Unfortunately, they didn't test her until hours later. The prosecutor tried to make a case that she'd had time to get it out of her system before being tested."

Sara said, "Hunter Griffith told me they found alcohol on the boat."

"Yeah. The prosecutor said in court that forensics found her fingerprints on a beer bottle in the boat, and that the boat was reeking of alcohol when it was recovered."

"How did Ellie explain that?"

"She said she was set up. Someone wanted her locked up where she'd keep her mouth shut."

Why on Earth didn't they mention this before? There was someone out there who was after Ellie months before she was murdered and her parents didn't say anything?

Mr. Rossi cleared his throat. "I know what you're thinking. In fact, we did go to the police last summer after it happened."

"And?"

"And they treated us like naïve parents making excuses for our daughter. Even went to the defense lawyer with it. She said her investigator turned up nothing as far as a boyfriend or any threats to Ellie."

"And that was behind Ellie's back. She begged us not to get involved," said Mrs. Rossi.

"Did you ever notice bruises, or signs she'd been abused?"

"No, never. Then again, there were periods of time where we were gone, sometimes weeks at a time."

"Had she received threats from Hunter Griffith after she was cleared in criminal court?"

"I don't know of any. He turned around and started a civil suit. Seemed confident of winning, at least that's what he said in interviews."

"But he lost."

"Yes. Just a few weeks before Ellie was killed."

"Would he have any reason to break into Ellie's house? Anything that would have proven his case?"

"I don't know."

"Thanks for talking to me. I'm going to look into this. Here was a clear threat that seemed to be pushed aside for whatever reason. I'll let you know if I find out anything."

Next, she stopped at Medivision to talk to Camaya.

When she arrived, two interviewees dressed in suits, studying notes, sat outside the boss's door. Craig Danalchek ushered him in and ushered the one he'd been interviewing out.

"We'll let you know. Next."

More like an assembly line than a job interview. Sara interpreted the interaction. *Don't call us, we'll call you. How many times did I hear that while I was auditioning—before I got San Francisco?* She rubbed her hand. *I can't go through that again.*

"Hi, come over here." Sara made her way over to Camaya's desk.

"Hey, looks like he's replacing Ellie already."

"He's already forgotten she ever was part of this company. He's replacing her and then some. The company is growing fast. He has two new positions to fill. Have a seat. You said you wanted to ask me more about Ellie."

"Yes. I just found out Ellie was involved in a boating accident. Did you know about it, and do you have any idea where she got a boat? Her parents say she didn't own one."

"I'm afraid it was my boat. When my Dad bought a bigger one, he let me have his old one."

"Did Ellie go boating often? I don't ever remember her mentioning boating."

"Oh, no. It was strange. The day of the accident, it was a Friday afternoon. Ellie was upset and asked if she could borrow the boat. She said it was urgent."

"Urgent?"

"She didn't elaborate, but clearly she had a problem to deal with and was desperate, so I said yes."

"And you have no idea what the problem could have been?"

"Honestly, no. I told you she'd been acting strangely. It was early afternoon and she planned to sneak out. Asked me to cover for her, which was unnecessary since our boss was already gone for the day and our co-workers certainly didn't care if she snuck out. She went out to leave, then came back and asked about the boat. Later, I saw her car still parked in the company lot. She must have taken a cab or walked to the marina."

"I have to ask. Had she been drinking?"

"No, of course not. At work?"

"I guess you're right." She felt embarrassed for sounding so insensitive. "Was she seeing anyone?"

"I don't think so. Then again, she may not have told me if she was. I didn't know about Preston right away."

"She *never* told me about Preston. Never mentioned she was engaged, or that the wedding was consequently called off. Can't say I wasn't hurt by that."

"That was her. Open about almost anything else, but kept her private life guarded. Don't take it personally. She told me about you. Told me stories about sleepovers and camp-outs with her best friend, Sara. She even kept a picture of the two of you in her desk." She fished the framed photo out of a drawer in Ellie's desk. "You should keep this."

Sara wiped tears from her eyes, fighting the urge to start sobbing. If she started, she didn't know if she'd be able to stop. *Breathe in, breath out.* When she was sure her voice wouldn't crack, she said, "The police found the boat. Why didn't she return it to you?"

"She called me crying after the accident. She said she was scared. I could hear it in her voice. She said she'd get the boat back to me the next day, if that was okay. I told her there was no rush. It wasn't like I planned on fly-fishing at sunrise or anything. The police intercepted it before she could return it."

"She was scared? Why? Because she'd hit the other boat?"

"I don't think that was it. It's more like she was scared someone was after her."

Craig Danalchek had stepped out of his office to usher in the next number in the interview cattle call. Camaya whispered, "I have to get back to work or there'll be another open position. Keep me posted, please."

"I will."

Interesting. Ellie borrows the boat to do something urgent. Where was she going? Why not take her car? Camaya senses she's scared of something or someone. Hunter Griffith is sure it was her fault her son died because she was drunk and speeding, yet Camaya says she hadn't been drinking, and Ellie's blood alcohol levels were fine—although time had passed before she was checked. And what about the beer bottle in the boat with Ellie's prints?

She looked at her watch and decided to head to the police station. She hoped she hadn't been too cold to Phil. She needed his help. Having her mother working at the station was an advantage as far as gathering information she might not otherwise be able to access.

When she arrived, her mother was busy at her desk, looking professional in her gray skirt and matching sweater. A hand painted nameplate on the desk said, *Patty Baron, Manager.* She wondered if her father bought it for her, or if her mother picked it up herself at one of the craft fairs she had a habit of, make that an obsession with, frequenting.

"Hi, honey. Are you here to see Detective Lambert?" Sara hated that twinkle in her mother's eyes whenever she smelled a potential son-in-law.

"Yes, is he in?"

"He's there. His door is open for you."

Sara walked in. Smoothing things over, she said, "I had a nice time last night."

"Me too. We'll have to go back. Did you get a good night's sleep?"

He doesn't seem to be mad or anything. I like that he's so even keeled. Unlike Travis, whose mood changed with each new wave. "I did. Did you get a chance to review the interview notes?"

"I've got them right here. The damage on the boat Ellie was driving matched the damage to the Griffith boat. A witness who was fishing at the pier says all three boats were speeding."

"All three? There was a third boat?"

"Griffith says there wasn't. Ellie said she couldn't remember if there was a third boat. If there was, it wasn't involved in the accident so it's irrelevant."

"Ellie told her parents she was trying to get away from trouble. The driver may have seen something. Didn't you want to interview a potential witness?" *Phil looks annoyed, better tread carefully or he'll shut down.*

"The witness on the pier had been drinking. Didn't know if he'd seen a third boat, or if he saw Hunter's boat twice. Couldn't tell us the size, the model, how many people were on board—nothing. At one point he wasn't sure if it might have been a sailboat. The information was too unreliable and vague. It'd have been like looking for a particular grain of sand in the desert."

"Did Ellie ever make a report over being abused or stalked?"

"No, I checked."

"Does Hunter Griffith have a record?"

"A parking ticket, which he paid. On time. Nothing else." The desk phone rang. "Detective Lambert. I'll be right there."

"An emergency?" *Stop it Sara. Physical therapist having an emergency—shady. A police detective having an emergency? Completely plausible.*

"I've got to go. I'll call you later." He caught her by surprise when he gave her a peck on the cheek before leaving.

Sara was hoping for more information, though it was the first time she heard mention of a third boat. *How could there be only one witness? It was a summer Friday afternoon. No one else in the entire town happened to be out fishing, swimming, or boating? Someone else must have seen the third boat.* She had an idea. She called Mrs. Rossi..

"Sorry to bother you again, Mrs. Rossi, but do you happen to know the name of Ellie's defense attorney? Thanks. Great. I'll let you know."

Sara drove down the street. The attorney's office was so close she could have walked over. She stared at a brick office building with newly painted white trim around the windows. The shingle at the entrance read *Claire LeBlanc, Attorney at Law.*

When she walked in, a woman about her mother's age was typing behind the front desk. "Hello, I was wondering if I could speak to Ms. LeBlanc. I don't have an appointment, but I just need a few minutes of her time."

"That would be me. Good help is hard to find. It's a one-woman show around here. Are you in need of an attorney?"

"No, I'm a friend, *was* a friend of Ellie Rossi. I'm the one who found the body."

"I'm so sorry. Tragic, simply tragic what happened to her. How can I help you?"

"I'm trying to find out if you had anything on Hunter Griffith, the man whose son died in the boating accident. Do you have any, forgive my bluntness, dirt on him? The police say they have nothing but I know being Ellie's attorney you must have done some thorough digging."

"Hunter Griffith didn't have any formal complaints against him, but he stood up and openly threatened Ellie when the verdict was read. He said in front of the entire courtroom that he was going to kill her like she killed his son."

"And he wasn't arrested?"

"It was only a threat, and he had just lost his son. I don't think anyone took it seriously. The car, however..."

"What do you mean? What car?"

"Ellie's car was vandalized not long after that. I told her to report it and she was set to do that, only she changed her mind."

"Changed her mind?"

"She told me the insurance would take care of it and she was determined to drop the whole thing. I thought it was strange, but then again, she'd just been through a lot and I assumed she wanted to put it all behind her."

"What do you make of the police finding the beer bottle with Ellie's prints in the boat?" "Ellie swears it was planted. She didn't bring beer with her, nor did she see any on the boat when she got in. You know, I might have something for you. Jordan Griffith, the boy who was killed, had a history of reckless driving and underage drinking. He was a minor, so all this wasn't brought out in court. To top it off, our sole witness thought it might have been a younger man driving the boat. That was our reasonable doubt. What if Jordan was drinking and was responsible for the crash, not Ellie?"

"What about a third boat? Didn't the witness say there was a third boat?" *Phil said the witness didn't know if there'd been a third boat.*

"He did. He even gave me a description, then called the next day and said he was wrong. There wasn't another boat. I dropped by his place of employment later that day to sign his statement and…"

"And what?"

"He was wearing sunglasses inside the store where he worked. The lighting was super dull, too. And there's more."

"What?"

"It was very warm that day, but he was wearing a long sleeved shirt. His finger had a splint on it."

"Like he'd been in a fight?"

"Or was beaten up. It crossed my mind that he may have had help deciding to take back his account of seeing a third boat, but there was nothing I could do."

"You've been really helpful. Do you suppose the witness would be willing to talk to me?"

"I'll call him and give him your number. It's up to him. Hope you find justice for your friend."

When Sara got into the car, she called Camaya. The prints on the beer bottle still troubled her.

"Camaya, can you think of any way that beer bottle could have gotten into the boat and why Ellie's prints were on it? Did she drink that brand of beer? I saw on the evidence report that it was a local apple-flavored craft beer."

"Oh, that was her favorite. As a matter of fact, we all went to happy hour Thursday night at Ralph's. It's kind of an office tradition. She hadn't been joining us much lately, but that night I convinced her to come. I suppose if someone was sly enough, they could have taken a bottle she drank from, though I know that sounds far-fetched."

"Maybe not. Who was at that happy hour? Can you make a list?"

"It was months ago and they all kind of run

together, but I'll try. Oops. Boss on deck. Gotta go."

Chapter 27

Sara told her father she would help out this afternoon so she made her way to the oboe shop.

"Grandpa, you've made a lot of progress on that oboe. Didn't you start it yesterday?"

"Yeah, yeah. I could do this in my sleep."

She took out the wood she had started shaping yesterday. "How are things with Gail?"

"Ah, good. We're getting together to play cards tonight at our place. Jacob's coming, too."

"That's good. I know Jacob has been having a hard time since he lost his wife."

Bob said, "Less yacking, more hacking. We're making progress on our list. Need help, Sara?"

"Can you check this before I continue, just to be sure?"

Her father measured the work she'd done, comparing it to a graph he was holding.

"Dad! I think I got it." She grabbed the logbook from the drawer and opened to great grandfather's numbers. "This has to be measurements, like we said. Just the darker numbers."

"Yeah, but I told you, the numbers don't make sense."

"What about the proportions?"

Her father held it under the lamp. "The proportions are a little funky, but could work if the numbers are correct."

Her grandfather said, "My father loved codes, especially the ones where you have to transpose the numbers or letters. Is there anything else on the page?"

She looked carefully. "All these other lighter numbers. Wait, there's a few letters. Give me that pad of paper and a pencil."

She jotted down the few letters she found. I E O R S E A C M N I J O R. She played around with the order.

"Let me see that," said Grandpa. As he got up, he grabbed his side. "Ow. My hip."

"Are you okay, Grandpa?"

"Yeah. I'll live. Give me that."

She handed him the paper. He fiddled with the letters. "I know this means something, I need time to work on it." He got up to show Sara. Bob said, "How about working on what's in front of us. We're on a roll. For the first time in a long time I have a glimmer of hope that we can catch up. Sara, this looks good so far." He handed her back the slab of wood she'd started carving.

She continued working until her father was ready to quit. She'd kept her phone beside her all day hoping for a call from the witness the defense lawyer was going to contact on her behalf. Nothing. No calls from the witness; no apology calls from…the idiot next door.

It was past dinner-time when she drove back to her place. She saw Travis's car in his driveway. He hadn't had the courtesy of telling her when or where he was going and after their argument? *He'd better not be expecting a ticker tape parade from me, that's for sure.*

She turned off the alarm, took off her jacket, and shivered in the icy house. She turned on the lights and jacked up the thermostat.

"Panther, come here." The cat ran to her. "At least someone cares if I'm here or not." She opened the freezer and took out a frozen lasagna. While it heated in the microwave, she tore open the bag of peanut M&Ms she'd stashed in the pantry. A knock on the door made her jump. Chomping the mouthful of candy, she checked the security camera.

"Travis?" She unlocked the door.

"Yeah. Why do you sound so surprised?"

"We had a fight, remember?"

"Did we?"

She clenched her fists. "You vanish without a word and reappear like a lost puppy. Then you have the nerve to show up on my doorstep?"

"I told you I'm very private. I was hoping to share a pizza, but if you're mad, I'll leave." He swiped the pizza box under her nose. *He's not going to win me back with a pizza.*

She wanted to tell him to get lost. She wanted to say friends treat each other better than that. Instead, she said, "No, come in." *If he killed Ellie or knows who did, I need to keep him close.* The microwave beeped. "I made dinner. But I can be talked into sharing a pizza. Want half a lasagna for an appetizer?"

"As much as I love frozen dinners, I'll pass, but you go ahead."

"Okay, your loss."

"Your mom is an Italian super cook. How can you stand that?"

"You get used to frozen dinners when you live alone. I've seen your kitchen. I know you don't cook, so what do you live on?"

"Mostly takeout. Lots of pizza."

"Ellie has a bottle of wine in the fridge. Want some?" She took his nod as a yes, and tried opening the wine. "I need a cork screw." She searched through the kitchen drawers. "If she has wine, she has to have a cork screw."

"Let's take a look." Travis searched the remaining drawers.

"I saw a box of kitchen stuff out in the garage. Looks like she had too much to fit in the kitchen. Ellie always loved cooking and bought every gadget on the market."

"Garage it is. Come on."

She followed Travis through the kitchen door into the garage. "Maybe in one of the boxes above the washer and dryer?" She grabbed a step stool and tried to peek inside.

"Just hand it to me. It'll be easier to see down here."

When they had a handful of boxes on the floor, they opened them. "This is a box of high school memorabilia. Yearbooks, track medals…here's a photo of you and Ellie!"

"Let me see that." She held the picture in her hand, remembering the day vividly. They'd taken their last final exam and posed for silly pictures in front of the school with two of their friends. Tears streamed down her cheeks. "I don't think anyone would mind if I keep this. I'll take the rest to her parents. I wonder if they plan on selling the house now that Ellie doesn't need it."

"Maybe they'd rent it to you—if you wind up staying, I mean."

"Maybe." *We'd be neighbors. If I don't get over this stupid crush that's brewing it'll be hard watching him bring dates to his house. Besides, his behavior is hot and cold. I can't deal with that sort of stress with all that's on my plate.*

"Here. I actually found a cork screw under the Magic Bullet and Slice'o'Matic."

"Let me do the honors." She followed him into the kitchen where he deftly managed to open the bottle. "What about wine glasses?"

"I'll bet they're up there in the cabinet over the sink I can't reach." She pulled over a kitchen chair and climbed up.

"Careful there." He wrapped his hands around her waist, steadying her. An involuntary tingle ran through her body. *Stop acting like a silly school girl.* She took a breath, found the glasses, and stepped down. She caught a whiff of his Irish Spring.

"While you were away, I researched the boating accident that Hunter Griffith mentioned. Had you heard about it, before we ran into him at the mall?"

"Vaguely."

"Why didn't you mention it before?"

"It wasn't relevant. Frankly, I hadn't even thought about it until we ran into him."

"Hunter Griffith, was convinced it was Ellie's fault. I found out he threatened her in court and did you know Ellie's car was vandalized?"

"You think Hunter Griffith killed Ellie?"

"Did she ever say she thought he was after her? It would explain the safe room and new alarm system."

"She *was* scared of someone. I asked her about it when I saw her outside the next morning. She said it was nothing."

"We knew Hunter from high school. He was a strange bird. During senior year he was Baker-acted, taken to a mental ward without his consent because he threatened to kill himself. That's what we got from the rumor mill. Later we heard he was diagnosed bi-polar."

"Bi-polar doesn't mean violent, even if he was off his meds. I'm not saying he wasn't an angry father who flipped out and wanted revenge, just that it can't be blamed on that diagnosis."

"Phil didn't think he was involved. Wouldn't even check on an alibi for Hunter for the night of Ellie's murder."

"Since they have so few leads, I don't know why he wouldn't check it out. Of course, he may have already done so. He's under no obligation to disclose police business to you. Are you ready to eat? The pizza's getting cold."

As they ate, Sara tried to think of a way to verify Hunter's alibi, but was at a loss. Was she bold enough to ask him outright? Travis seemed to read her thoughts.

"Without police help, the best we can do is maybe ask the neighbors if they saw anything that night. It was months ago, however. And the police must have thought to interview neighbors."

"It won't hurt. I've met the lady next door, but that's about it. You?"

"I've at least said hello to everyone on our street. We can go for a walk tomorrow and try. Now, let's finish dinner. Want to watch a movie?"

"Sure, why not. Drama, mystery, or romantic comedy?"

"Rom-com? Seriously? I vote for mystery."

"How are your parents liking North Carolina?"

"I haven't spoken to them in a while. They've been traveling. They've gotten into cruising."

"Why haven't you talked to them? Did you have a falling out?" She knew she was being too nosy and didn't expect an answer.

"No, we just haven't talked. It's complicated. I don't want to talk about it." He turned up the volume on the TV. "Got anything to go with the pizza?"

"Pause the movie. I have an idea. Come on." He followed her into the kitchen. "I know I saw some somewhere. Here! Popcorn kernels. Wasn't there a popper in that box where we found the cork screw?"

"You're right. Why don't you start a fire and I'll get it?" She came back with the popper but it was missing the plug. *Maybe it's still in the drawers?* She grabbed another slice of pizza while she searched. *There has to be a corn popper plug somewhere in here.* "Got it."

Travis had started a fire and turned off the living room lights. When Sara came in toting a bowl of popcorn, Panther was snuggled next to Travis on the sofa.

"Unpause?"

"Sure." She handed him the remote. Travis covered her hand with his.

I know the fire is making it warm, but so is being so close to Travis. The hair on her arms stood up and she had all she could do to stop herself from turning around and embracing him. *Stop. He doesn't want this and you shouldn't either.* Self-control gone, she turned to him.

Travis's arms tightened around her. She felt her heart beating faster. He looked into her eyes, then moved his mouth closer to hers. Their lips touched. She'd never felt this kind of chemistry with Brandon or anyone else for that matter. She melted into his embrace and he kissed her. He had to have felt the spark.

Travis pushed away with a sudden jerk. "No, I can't do this. I'm sorry. I should go."

The fire crackled. Letting go of the moment was difficult. "If that's how you feel."

"It's not…I mean…"

"You don't have to explain." She stood up and flicked on the lights. "Thanks for the pizza."

Travis put on his coat. "I wish…Anyway. Do you want to take that walk tomorrow and see if we can find anyone who saw Hunter the night of the murder?"

She was disappointed as well as hurt. If she said no, she might be cutting out an opportunity to gather more information. *Can I risk putting my feelings on the line to help my best friend? There's not a real choice here.*

"Sure. I'm helping at the shop tomorrow. I'll be home dinner-time." She closed the door behind him, resisting the urge to slam it. What was his problem? He seemed to be attracted to her, but maybe he wasn't. Did the interracial aspect bother him? Was he still involved with Cameron? Or married like Grandpa suggested? She scooped up Panther and went to bed. *I should have known better and not allowed myself to be vulnerable. Again.*

Chapter 28

The next morning, Sara bolted upright in bed, terrified. In her sleep, she'd been falling—rolling down a rocky hill. She was dragged into a thick forest, calling for help, but no one came. She fell into a hole. Down, down, darker and darker, no handsome prince rescuing her. *It's a message. No one will rescue me. I have to rescue myself.*

Sara resisted the urge to look out the window at Travis's driveway. *I don't care if he's home or not. I won't let my emotions be held hostage.* She guzzled down two cups of coffee, then put together her oboe.

It almost felt foreign in her hands. She'd been used to playing hours a day and now she'd barely touched it since arriving in Hudsonville. She popped a reed into her mouth to moisten it and rummaged through her Barret Etudes. *Here goes nothing.*

The reed she'd soaked sounded horrible. Instead of trying to scrape it into shape, she threw it against the wall. Lacking the patience to try another one, she got dressed and headed to the shop. On the way, she went into the bakery and picked up a dozen donuts, wishing there was a drive-thru like there was back home.

Her impulse was to stuff down her feelings about Travis by gobbling down a few in the car, but she arrived at the shop with a full dozen. *Maybe I have more self-control than I thought. After I broke up with Brandon, I gained five pounds.* Her father and Grandpa were already working when she entered the chilly shop.

"Grandpa, how was the card party?"

"A lot of fun. We're going to make it a weekly thing. Gail has a few more friends she'd like to include. She even mentioned starting a club of sorts that gets together by day to do activities. Transportation is a problem, though. Most folks our age around here don't drive anymore, especially when the weather gets bad."

"Too bad Hudsonville doesn't have public transportation."

"You mean like your silly cable cars back home?"

Ignoring the comment, Sara started working on the oboe she was making. "Grandpa, did you come up with anything regarding the code we found?"

"I see the name Rosie, but I don't understand what the other letters mean. I'll keep working on it."

"Maybe he meant a rosewood oboe," said her father. "We basically ruled out the idea of him having a girlfriend."

"If so, maybe he was planning on making a rosewood oboe, using the proportions of the numbers, somehow transposed. We need to look at the remaining letters." Sara continued working.

"Sara, what's on the symphony programs this spring?"

Her throat tightened. "*Beethoven Symphony #3, Daphnis and Chloe*, A couple of concertos. The usual fare."

"Maybe Mom and I can come out for a concert this spring." He glanced at Grandpa. "If everything is well."

"I don't need a babysitter. If you don't go out to visit Sara, don't go blaming me."

"Dad, thanks for your optimism. Grandpa, you should come, too. Cable cars aside, you like San Francisco. Remember that restaurant in Chinatown you loved?"

"Now that's incentive, but I won't be much good going up and down those hills with this hip."

"Pops, you should have that replacement surgery soon. You could be up and around before spring hits."

"And you can even invite Gail to come along," said Sara. *It would be kinda neat having my old music teacher in the audience.* Then she remembered. There was a good chance she'd still be on leave this spring. Unless things dramatically improved, she was out through May.

Sara's phone vibrated. She put the work in progress on the desk and answered.

"Hi, Camaya. Yeah. Yes, they said her prints were on the beer bottle. The day before? I'll let the detective know. Thanks."

"Who was that?" asked Grandpa.

"Ellie's co-worker. She told me that Ellie and a bunch of them were at Happy Hour the evening before the boat crash. And, she just remembered a case of craft beer had been delivered to the breakroom a few days earlier with a thank-you card. It was the apple craft beer that Ellie, and few others, drank. Camaya thought it was from a client. It could explain how Ellie's prints got on the bottle in the boat. If someone wanted to frame Ellie, they could have easily grabbed one of her empty beer bottles out of the recycling bin."

"Really?" said her father. "That means it had to be someone who worked with her or someone who visited the building. They'd have to have known Ellie drank that type of beer and know which bottles she drank from. Unless he had the knowledge to transfer prints."

Grandpa said, "I saw on YouTube where you can transfer prints. Especially onto a surface like glass."

YouTube? I didn't know he knew how to answer a cellphone let alone get to YouTube.

"Thanks, Grandpa. The boat wasn't found until the next morning. There was a window of opportunity."

She called Phil to tell him her new theory.

"Sara, that sounds like a spy novel. Yes, it's possible, but the person framing her would have had to know about the beer being delivered to Medivision, and how to transfer prints. They'd have to have had access to the breakroom."

"Exactly. Can't you question her coworkers? See if anyone spotted someone going into the breakroom?"

"And coming back out holding a beer bottle? If one of her coworkers wanted to hurt Ellie they had easier ways. And an outsider is unlikely. The building has security."

"You can check the security tapes!"

"Yeah. I have another call. We'll talk soon."

Sara continued working. If it didn't happen at work, then who had access to Ellie's house to get her prints? Preston's prints were on the lamp, but it makes sense he'd have been in the house. They were engaged, after all. But who else was there? *Travis was there. They found his prints. No, I can't think that way just because I'm mad at him.* It nagged at her. She was beginning to suspect him before she got mad at him.

Grandpa said, "If that wet behind the ears detective won't take you seriously, why don't you talk to Jacob."

"Our neighbor Jacob?"

"He's a retired detective. Just cause he's old don't mean he can't help. And he's always home."

"Grandpa, that's brilliant." She put down her tools and kissed him on the cheek. "I'll be right back."

She knocked on Jacob's door.

"Sara? Can I help you?" He seemed surprised to have a visitor.

"I hope so. Grandpa reminded me you were a detective. As you probably know, Elle Rossi's murder case is still open."

"Come in. It's cold out. What can I do to help?"

"How hard is it to lift prints from someone's house and transfer them to a glass bottle?"

"Not general knowledge, but not hard to look up how to do it. If the first set of prints came from a clean surface, they could easily be transferred to glass."

"Ellie's prints were found on a craft beer bottle in the boat which killed Hunter Griffith's son. I think she was framed. Someone had delivered her favorite beer to the breakroom at her workplace. And she'd been to a bar the night before the accident. It wouldn't be hard to plant the bottle or transfer prints to it, then put the bottle in the boat so it'd look like Ellie had been drinking."

"You're right. It could have happened that way."

"The detective on the case dismissed the idea. I thought he should check the security tapes to see who left the beer."

"Did you check the stores that sell it? You said it was a craft beer."

"That's a good idea."

"Do you think the boat 'accident' was preplanned?"

"Not really. Camaya, Ellie's coworker, said Ellie frantically asked to borrow her boat on the Friday afternoon of the accident. A witness on the water says she was in a big hurry. It didn't sound planned." *If it wasn't planned, what was the person framing Ellie planning on doing with the prints?*

"It may have been a convenient coincidence. It doesn't preclude someone having the idea to use her prints to frame her in some capacity. Let's see who sells that beer around here." He opened his laptop. "What's it called again?"

"Apple craft beer? I don't know an exact name."

Jacob searched and within minutes came up with the name of the brewery. "When was it sent to the break room?"

Sara looked at the calendar. "This week, here."

Jacob grabbed his phone. "Hello, I'm trying to find out if a case of apple craft beer was sent to…"

Sara whispered, "Medivision."

Jacob nodded and jotted information on a notepad. "Thanks."

"Well?"

"The only case of locally delivered beer that week was sent to Medivision. It was paid for with a company credit card."

"So it was someone high up enough in the company to have access to a company card?"

"Unless someone stole the card, but in that case I'm sure it would have been reported and canceled rather promptly."

"Thank you!"

"If someone wanted to kill your friend, why wouldn't they simply poison the beer and send it directly to your friend? Why go through all the trouble of framing her?"

"I don't know. Maybe they wanted her out of the way, but not dead."

"Any time you need help, let me know," said Jacob.

"You bet I will. See you soon."

She returned to the shop, but had a hard time concentrating. When she got home, she whipped up a quick dinner. Travis was going to drop by after he got home from work so they could take a walk and ask the neighbors if they saw Hunter the night of Ellie's murder. She'd just finished her burger when he knocked.

"Ready? This is the time of day you see the neighbors walking their dogs, checking the mail, taking walks. Bundle up. It's especially cold tonight."

That's it. Act like you care about my comfort. She tried not to sound annoyed. "Did you ever see anyone over here visiting Ellie?"

"Honestly, no, but I'm in and out all the time. Wait. I did see Preston Montague over there back when they were engaged."

Convenient. He never mentioned seeing Preston until now. Just like he didn't remember the boating accident until after they ran into Hunter Griffith. She grabbed her jacket and locked up.

"Where do we start?"

They'd barely gotten out of the driveway when they saw an elderly couple walking hand in hand. Travis seemed to know them. "We'll start right here."

He approached the couple. "How are you today? Still fitness walking, I see."

"Since George had that stent put in last year, we've been diligent. Rain or shine, hot or cold. I can't lose my better half."

George grumbled. "I ain't going nowhere. Best shape ever. I've lost ten pounds since we started our walks."

"A friend of ours has been bedridden since her surgery. His wife is playing nursemaid. I'm not spending our golden years giving bed baths."

"She doesn't give me much of a choice," said the hubby. "She leaves my sneakers right at the front door."

Travis said, "Since you are regulars, I want to ask you something. Do you remember the night Ellie was murdered?"

"Of course. George and I heard sirens and saw all sorts of police cars and an ambulance pass our house.

The next day we read about it in the paper. Poor girl. Such a sweet young thing. Always a smile and a friendly wave."

"Earlier that night, did you see anything out of the ordinary? Anyone in the area that you found suspicious?"

"Like we told the police, no one." George jogged in place.

"George, remember later we thought about those sneaky teenagers from down the block. Two brothers—the Howards' kids, and the boy on the other side of our house. Brayden Carlisle. Every weekend they blast the music and park over by the woods."

Sara said, "Why didn't you call the police back?"

"Didn't want to get them in trouble with their parents," said George. "We watched those boys grow up."

"George, Nancy down the road says the music makes her crazy. She lives near the opening in the woods and even says she can smell the marijuana from her back porch when they are out there."

"Do you think it's possible those boys saw something?" Sara was talking more to Travis than the couple at this point.

"The police interviewed everyone on the block, but I doubt those boys would have admitted they were partying and smoking. Partying is a verb, you know. Means they were drinking. I'll bet they claimed they were home and their parents probably thought they were in their rooms playing those video games or talking on the phone."

Sara said, "I'll tell my friend the detective. They very well might have seen something if they were out in the woods that night."

George shivered. "I'm getting cold standing in one spot and can't jog in place any longer."

"Of course. Keep going. Enjoy the rest of your walk."

"What now?" said Travis. "Want to keep going?"

"I'd like to go knock on the Howards' door, but, of course, that would be awkward. I guess the best thing to do is to notify Phil."

"Wait a minute. The kid on the bike. Across the street. That's Brayden Carlisle. He comes around offering to shovel driveways when it snows. For money, of course."

"Probably to fund his habit. Does he know you?"

"Yeah. He knocked on my door more than once. Come on."

Travis hustled and waved to Brayden Carlisle. "Brayden, can we talk for a minute?"

Brayden hopped off his bike. "Yeah. Need your driveway shoveled?"

"No. This is Sara Baron. She's staying at Ellie's house. She was a close friend and she's the one who found the body."

"Oh, man. That's a bummer."

"Brayden, we're trying to help the police find out who killed Sara's friend. Did you see anyone go in or out of Ellie's house that night?"

"No, man. The police already asked me and my parents. I was upstairs in my room."

"Look, we aren't the police and don't care if you were engaged in underage drinking or dabbling in recreational drugs. Our only concern is finding Ellie's killer and if you saw something, we won't drag you into it. Honest."

Sara said, "You're loyal to your friends, right? Put yourself in my shoes. What if your best friend was murdered? I have to know who killed mine. Please, if you know anything…" Playing the empathy card with a teenager was like convincing a tiger to become vegetarian, but she had to try.

"You swear you won't tell my parents or the police?"

"If you know something, we'll relay the information to the detective. We won't say where we got it."

"Well, the night that lady died, I drove my bike past her house. On the way to the woods, I saw a man come out of the front door of her house. On the way back from the woods, hours later, there was a different man leaving her house. He went out the back door. I ain't judging or anything."

"Go on," said Sara. "Can you describe them?"

"The first man was short and heavier than the other guy. He was wearing like a dress coat and a cap with a brim."

That could describe Hunter Griffith. Sara said, "Like a baseball cap?"

"Kinda."

"Where did he go when he left Ellie's? What direction?"

"Towards the woods. I heard a car start up right afterwards. He must have parked it there."

"What time was it?" asked Sara.

"I guess around 7 or 7:30."

"And the second man?" asked Travis.

"The second one was wearing a parka, like his." He pointed at Travis. "He was wearing an orange ski cap. Real bright, like the roadmen wear when they're doing repairs."

"Young or old? Tall? Short?"

"I guess he was average height. Not too tall or too short. That's all I could see. He was on foot going the opposite direction that I was."

Travis said, "He was an older man?"

"Younger than the first from what I could tell. Now this guy ran towards the woods. He was on foot."

Sara said, "That could be his son, Noah. Maybe he went back to clean up his father's prints or to make sure Ellie was dead. What if Noah avenged his sister's death by killing Ellie?"

"Do you know what time it was?" said Travis.

"I snuck in before midnight. Must have been sometime around 11 or 11:30. You think he killed your friend?"

"It's a lead for sure. Thank you."

Travis had a business card in his pocket. "Call me or knock on my door if you remember anything else."

"You promised not to tell my parents, right?"

"We won't tell your parents."

He sped off on his bike. "Travis, neither of those descriptions sounds like Hunter do you think?"

"Average height wearing a parka? Could be anyone. The old guy with the baseball cap? Don't think that was him," said Travis.

"We have to see if Hunter and his son had alibis. Maybe the defense attorney can point us in the right direction."

"She was done working with Ellie's case by the time of the murder. I doubt she'd be of help."

"How am I going to relay the information we learned tonight to the police without disclosing where we got it. We promised Brayden."

"An anonymous letter? Wait, isn't there a police tip line?"

"Yeah. Let's go inside and give it a call."

Chapter 29

The next evening, Sara's mother called after work to tell her about the call to the tip line. "Detective Lambert was on the phone all morning talking to the lab. In the afternoon. Guess what? He had Hunter Griffith at the station. I thought he was going to arrest him or something."

"Did they arrest him?"

"He was still being questioned when I left. I think this might be it. I think they may have found Ellie's killer."

"I sure hope so." She doubted it would have been so easy to get a confession.

"What time are you coming over tomorrow night?"

"Tomorrow night?"

"Dinner. Seriously, tell me you didn't forget."

"Okay. I won't tell you. I'll be there around 6. Travis is still invited, right?" *I almost wish he wasn't. Maybe he'll have another emergency and bail out.*

"Of course. And Detective Lambert will be there too."

At least I can hear what happened when Phil questioned Hunter. I have to act surprised, like I only know because my mother said something.

She went upstairs and looked at the gifts she'd purchased. She'd better get wrapping. She had picked up a wallet for Travis on a whim. *Should I still give it to him, or wrap it up for Grandpa?*

The next morning, she went by the shop. They'd agreed to put in a few hours since they were getting close to catching up on orders.

"Sara, I think I solved part of the code. I deciphered the words *a minor* and *c major*. I think the numbers on the graph have to be transposed."

"That's brilliant. Does it work?"

"If we transpose each number using the proportion, the graph makes sense. I haven't seen an oboe made following these specs, but the more I think about it, he could have been on to something."

Sara's father said, "The subtleties in the measurements are just enough to really improve the integrity of the scale. I told Pops we'd take that hunk of rosewood you started and try it."

"But if it doesn't work, you'll have wasted a lot of time. Shouldn't we focus on the orders until we're caught up?"

"I have a feeling about this. If it works, we could have the next best thing to sliced bread and we'll triple our orders."

She hadn't seen her father or grandfather this excited in an awfully long time.

"Let me see that new graph."

Sara worked on the wood, anxious to get it to the point where the body could be completed and the tone holes drilled. It wasn't happening overnight, but maybe by the time she went back home they'd have something. *Or, I'll be here carving oboes for the rest of my life. Time will tell.*

Sara went home, had lunch, and took a nap. When she woke up, she had just enough time to take a shower and get ready to go to her parents' for dinner. *Why can't I sleep that soundly at night?* She pulled on her jeans and a blue sweater that matched her eyes. She stared at the bag of party favors in the corner. *I have a lot to do to help get ready for Grandpa's party. He's going to be so surprised. I hope he keeps his Barack comments to a minimum; it's embarrassing.*

Travis picked her up, looking handsome in a fisherman's sweater and new jeans.

"I hope they arrested Hunter Griffith and this is all solved and behind us," said Sara.

"Would be nice to have closure, but hope we don't spend the evening talking about murder."

"It's going to be hard not to slip about the party in front of Grandpa now that it's so near. He thinks we're taking him out to dinner, end of story."

"I hope he likes surprises."

"He'll grumble, but in the end he'll love it. He secretly loves attention. How about you? Do you like surprise parties?"

"I don't like surprises, period. My idea of a birthday is a good dinner and a big, chocolate birthday cake. With ice cream. Gotta have ice cream."

"Mom always baked our birthday cakes when Scott and I were growing up. And we always had the store brand Neapolitan ice cream. No one ever ate the strawberry. I always wondered why they didn't make just a chocolate and vanilla combo." *I miss Scott.*

"Just pull in behind Gail's car." Her mother was already waiting on the stoop.

"Sara, Travis, come on in. It's freezing out."

"Especially when you aren't wearing a coat, Mom."

Travis handed her a bottle of wine. A fire crackled in the fireplace and Grandpa and Gail sat in front of it sipping cider. At least it smelled like cider. Sara had barely taken off her coat when the doorbell rang.

Phil came in holding a healthy African Violet which he handed to Sara's mother. "Thanks for inviting me."

"You're welcome anytime, Detective. Come, do you want hot cider or wine?"

"I'll take wine."

"How was work?" said Sara.

"Good. Spent the day questioning Hunter Griffith. We'd received a call on the tip line that a man fitting his description was seen at Ellie's the night of the murder. Came right out of the blue." He looked at Sara in such a way it was obvious he knew it was her who called in the tip.

"So, what happened? Did he confess? Is he in jail?"

"Not so fast. He swore he was nowhere near Ellie's the night of the murder. He wasn't even in town."

"Where was he?"

"New York City meeting with a lawyer."

"So he knew he had to line up a defense."

"No, he was setting up a scholarship program in his son's name. The lawyer was drawing up the paperwork. He had an alibi. I spoke to the attorney myself."

Sara's heart dropped. She'd been sure Hunter was guilty.

"What about his son?"

"His son is dead. That's what started the whole business with Ellie being dragged to court."

"Not Jordan, Noah. I saw Hunter at the mall. He has another son who's a senior in high school."

Hopefully Noah doesn't have an alibi. If neither of the men at Ellie's house the night of the murder was Hunter or Noah, then who were they?"

"Come, dinner is ready." Patty led the way into the dining room.

Travis said, "Gail, weren't you bringing Jacob over?"

"He's going to the cemetery. Poor man misses his wife so much. I know how he feels."

They'd just sat down when the doorbell rang.

Patty said, "We aren't expecting anyone. Maybe Jacob changed his mind." She went to the door and screamed.

Sara and the rest of the house ran to the door. Sara threw her hands up to her face and tears streamed down. "Scott!"

A handsome man in uniform grabbed his mother in a bear hug. "I'm home."

"Scott! This is the best surprise ever. Why didn't you tell us you were coming home? Oh, it doesn't matter. I'm so happy to see you."

Bob gave his son a hug. "You must be exhausted. Long plane ride from Iraq."

"Yeah, but I'm running on adrenaline. Sara!" He hugged her so hard she could barely breathe but she didn't want him to let go. "I had some leave coming and was fortunate enough to make it home in time for, um...in time to get a home cooked meal. Hey Gramps!"

"Gail, my son is an officer. He graduated West Point."

"Frank told me all about him. You must be very proud."

Patty made the remaining introductions, while Bob found a folding chair. Sara couldn't believe her brother was standing here in front of her.

"Mom, is this lasagna? Do you know how many times I've craved your lasagna since I've been deployed?" Scott sat down and grabbed the spatula.

"I'll make you lasagna every night you're here. Now eat before it gets cold."

Sara sat sandwiched between Travis and Phil.

Scott leaned across the table. "Travis, what brings you to town?"

"My job. I'm a physical therapist over at Hudsonville Community. I wanted a change from big city life."

"Where are you from?"

"Chicago."

"If I were moving from Chicago I think I'd have gone somewhere warmer. A little town in Florida, maybe? Then again, after being stationed in the desert, Antarctica's looking attractive to me."

"This opportunity came across my desk and the dollar stretches a lot farther than it did in the city. Besides, I never minded the snow. I rather enjoy skiing."

"Me too. We'll have to hit the slopes one day. Sara skis, too. Sort of. What about you, Phil?"

"I'd rather spend my days off watching football with a pizza in front of me."

Grandpa said, "No one's asked me."

"Pops, with that hip of yours I think you'd be best off joining Phil."

Travis said, "How much longer do you have to be in Iraq?"

"My tour is up in a few months. I'll have to decide whether or not to reenlist. I've been offered jobs already as a civilian in the IT business."

"My boy is quite the computer expert," said Patty. "He does intelligence for the army, right, honey?"

"Yeah, but I can't talk about it or I'll have to kill you." Sara watched the change in expression on Gail's face. Scott broke into a smile. "That was a joke. A bad one at that. Pass the garlic bread."

Sara said, "Phil, what's your next move now that Hunter Griffith has been cleared?"

"I don't have one, really."

"What about the men who were seen at Ellie's the night of the murder?"

"And how do you … Never mind. I knew it was you who made that anonymous tip."

She neither confirmed nor denied the accusation. "The boy who told us doesn't want his parents to know he was partying out in the woods with his buddies instead of in his room playing video games like they thought."

"What if the boy himself is the murderer? You'd have tipped him off and you'd be next on the list. I asked you to trust me on this." Phil took a sip of wine.

"Then you've already looked into the two men?"

"No, not yet. We interviewed all the neighbors, no one mentioned seeing either one."

Sara said, "There was a younger man. Could have been Noah, Hunter Griffith's other son. And then again, there could be witnesses you didn't question. Like the one Travis and I found."

"Travis, you encouraged her?"

"I supported her. I trust her instincts. Besides, it would've been like trying to stop Niagara Falls with a catcher's mitt."

Scott said, "Woah. I'm lost here."

Sara poured herself another glass of wine. "I came here to house sit for Ellie while she went to Europe. When I walked in, I found the house ransacked, and Ellie was dead on the bedroom floor. We've been trying to solve the murder but keep hitting dead ends."

Phil cleared his throat. "She means *the police* are trying to solve the murder. She's playing amateur detective."

Sara took offense to being called amateur. *I think I'm rather good at this.*

"Ellie Rossi? Jelly Belly Ellie?"

"She hated it when you called her that."

"I know. But seriously, Ellie's dead?"

"Yes. First we thought it might have been her ex fiancé, Preston Montague. He had given her an heirloom ring that she supposedly refused to return when she broke it off. Also, she caused great embarrassment to his family in doing so."

Travis added, "But they found the ring. The mother was trying to pull an insurance scam."

"And then Preston turned up dead, so we crossed him off the list."

"So we began to suspect Preston's ex. The one he dated and broke up with when he met Ellie. She's a doctor at the hospital and we found out she has a history of jealousy related incidents."

"She popped Preston's tires back in med school." Travis poured more wine.

"And she was charged with battery by a former boyfriend. Oh, and she was overheard threatening Ellie in the hospital cafeteria."

Phil said, "Only there's a small problem." He raised his voice, not to the level of yelling, but certainly to the level of emphasis. "She has an alibi for the night of the murder."

"She claims she was working at a clinic across town. The police have the sign in sheet but it's possible she slipped out and came back."

"Who said that was a possibility?" said Phil. "We have no inkling of proof that she left the clinic that night. As a matter of fact, we interviewed a patient who was being treated by her exactly during the window of time we think the murder occurred."

He never told me that, and I'm still not convinced. "Then we suspected Hunter Griffith. Ellie crashed into their boat and killed his son while allegedly speeding and under the influence. She was cleared by the court, and Griffith recently lost a civil suit against her. Her blood alcohol levels were normal, and a witness says both boats were speeding."

Travis said, "Don't forget, a witness saw a third boat which appeared to be chasing Ellie's."

"But we discovered Ellie's prints on a beer bottle we found in the boat the next morning," said Phil. "Be that as it may, Hunter Griffith has an airtight alibi for the night of Ellie's murder, like we were discussing. And there's no reliable evidence of a third boat."

"That shows someone wanted to frame Ellie. Get her out of the picture. Also, Ellie had a safe room and a security system put in her house. Plus, her coworker as well as her mother say she was afraid of someone. She'd been acting differently."

Scott said, "If Preston and the doctor are eliminated, who's left?"

"The two men the teenage witness saw," said Sara. "A man in a dress coat going into Ellie's around 7 or 7:30, and later, a man in a parka leaving the scene. It occurred to me one of them could be Noah Griffith, Hunter's son."

"Reported by a teenage witness who was drinking and smoking weed," said Phil. "Hardly reliable. And don't forget we found prints and a tire track. They belong to that guy sitting there." He pointed at Travis. "And at least one of the descriptions from the teenager fits his, if we're going there."

Sara said, "You can't be serious."

"Just pointing out the facts. That's what detective work's about. Objective facts and logical conclusions. It's hard to keep emotions from interfering when it's a friend or loved one you're talking about."

That's for my benefit. I can keep my emotions at bay and look at a situation logically. She glanced at Travis. *Most of the time.*

Grandpa said, "Is this proper talk for a homecoming dinner?"

"No, Pops, it isn't. Scott, Sara found your great grandfather's logbook in the shop. Looks like he came up with a unique set of oboe measurements. We're replicating them."

"Could be the next best thing since sliced bread," said Grandpa. "Could be the holy grail that'll save the business."

"Save the business? When I left for Iraq things were going strong."

"We were running behind, but now that Sara's been helping out, and Grandpa's got his mojo back thanks to Gail, we're almost caught up. Too bad Sara can't stay longer."

"I've missed a lot while I was gone."

Patty said, "If you are all full, let's go inside and watch a movie."

Sara sat between Travis and Phil on the sofa. She must have nodded off, because she woke up with her head on Travis's shoulder. The warmth of the fire, the glow of the TV, her brother here in the flesh…things felt kind of perfect.

Chapter 30

Another nightmare. Sara found herself in the middle of the dark lake that'd been a recurring part of her recent nightmares. She kicked until she couldn't feel her legs and flailed her arms about until she no longer had the energy to lift them. It was pitch black and she felt herself sinking toward the bottom of the lake. When she tried to breathe, she swallowed icy cold water and sank further down. Then, she felt strong arms around her, pulling her to the surface. When they broke through the water, she felt the glow of warmth on her face and peace rippled through to her toes.

Sara woke up with a start. *I'm not ready to die. I hope that's not what the nightmare was trying to tell me. Mom reminded me death comes in threes...* She shook it off, and realized it was a new day. Scott was home, that part hadn't been a dream, and she was excited about spending time with him.

She told Travis she'd pick him up this morning, though she still kind of hated him for the distance he'd created between them. He'd volunteered to help get the Elks' Hall ready for Grandpa's party later. She fished through the dresser drawers and chose a long red sweater and black leggings. She'd come back and change before the party.

She locked up and went over to Travis's. *His lights aren't on yet. I hope he didn't oversleep.* She knew it was unlikely. He was an early riser. His car was in the driveway.

She beeped the horn, then texted him. No response. She got out and knocked on the door. Not there. Where would he be? She was clear on the time she was coming by and Travis said he'd be up and ready. This wasn't like him. Then again, how well did she know him after all?

"Travis, open up!" She pounded on the door, then tried calling him. Nothing. *Desperate times call for desperate measures.* She dug in her purse. *Got it!* She'd never given him back the key he gave her when she first arrived and stayed at his place.

When she opened the door, it was dark, and cold. His parka was hanging on the coat rack. She checked the kitchen. Clearly he hadn't eaten breakfast. She headed upstairs with a vague sense of déjà vu.

Travis wasn't in the bedroom. The bed hadn't been slept in. *Maybe he ran out to get muffins to bring over for breakfast. But then again, his car was in the driveway. Something doesn't feel right.*

She called the hospital to see if he'd been called in on an emergency. He hadn't. Nor had he been admitted as a patient. Her phone rang.

"Travis?"

"No, it's Mom. Where are you? We're about to leave for the Elks' Hall. I've got all the decorations and favors in the trunk."

"It's Travis. I told him I'd pick him up but he isn't home and... Never mind. I'll meet you there."

Why did Travis leave her high and dry? He could have at least texted or left her a note saying he had a change of plans. She was getting a little sick of his secrecy and guarded privacy. Served her right. She knew he wasn't interested in a relationship, yet she'd begun to hope it might happen.

She pulled into the parking lot and carried in the box of party favors Travis had helped her put together.

She'd brought the wallet just in case Travis showed up later.

"What's wrong, honey?"

"Mom, I don't know what happened to Travis. Why would he simply disappear without a word? *It wasn't the first time, either. Maybe Grandpa is right and he's spending time with his wife!*

"Maybe he had a family emergency. Did you call the hospital?"

"Yes. He isn't there."

"You can have Detective Lambert check for accidents if it'll put your mind at ease."

"I know. I'm sure he's fine. I'm not going to let him ruin Grandpa's party for me. What can I do?"

"Let's hang the balloons first."

Sara grabbed a folding chair and ribbon. Thankfully the balloons were prefilled with helium. She remembered blowing up balloons for parties when she was a kid. Took more air than oboe playing."

"I'm going to cover the tables. I got these tablecloths on clearance. They were exactly what I was looking for."

"Luck was on your side."

"Sara, you seem down. Travis will be back, you'll see."

"Why didn't he tell me he was leaving? He'd promised to help decorate; he was over last night so it's not like he forgot."

"Maybe he's afraid he's falling for you."

"Fat chance. He made it clear he doesn't want a relationship. We're just... I don't know what we are. Acquaintances."

"If it's meant to be things will work out."

Scott walked in with a large box. "Here's the cake Sara ordered. Where do you want it?"

"Over there next to the punch bowl. Did you remember the candles?"

"Gottem' right here. I can't believe he's turning 80."

She spent the afternoon catching up with Scott as they helped set the tables.

"Did you make the slide show? The projector's in the car."

"Yes, Mom. Told you I'd have it ready."

"You work fast. I can't believe you pulled it together on such short notice."

"All in a day's work." He fetched the projector and hooked it up to his laptop. "We're ready to roll. All set for tonight."

"He's going to be so surprised. I can't wait," said Patty. "Let's go home and get a little rest before the big event."

Scott walked Sara to the car.

"I can tell you're worried about Travis. Has he done this before?"

"Yeah, he's disappeared on occasion, usually with an abrupt heads-up, but we just talked about Christmas last night. What changed between then and this morning? Do you think he has a girlfriend?"

"Possibly, but maybe he's shying away because he's falling for you. I saw how he was looking at you last night."

"Really? That's what Mom said. He said he wasn't interested."

"I know I've done it before. Remember Donna? I was head over heels in love, or so I thought. Then when I was about to tell her this, I chickened out and pulled away. Broke up and never gave her an explanation."

"You were a real shmuck! She hated you after that."

"That's what I'm saying."

"Can you help me? You have all that army intelligence background, right? Some things haven't added up."

"Like what?"

"Like he says he's from Chicago, but he says 'soda' rather than pop. He isn't a Cubs fan. And he used the term 'sunbreak.' That sounds specific to a region and I don't think it's Chicago. And he's evasive about his family."

"Sunbreak. I heard that term when I was out in Seattle. Anything else?"

"His house is almost sterile. Just enough plates and silverware for one person. No family pictures, everything in the house looks brand new."

"Okay. I'll come by in the morning and see what I can do. For now, let's enjoy Grandpa's celebration. I'll come by and get you in a couple of hours."

As soon as she got home, she googled Noah Griffith and searched his social media. *Kids still haven't caught on about privacy settings. If I ever have a kid...*She scrolled through, checking for the date Ellie died.

Nothing on Facebook. Big surprise. Instagram? Bingo. She found pictures of him at high school football practice. *Maybe he still had time to clean up and go kill Ellie.* She continued searching and found a picture of him and his friends eating pizza at Antonio's. She checked the time stamp. *He has an alibi. And a ton of witnesses to verify it.*

She lay down with Panther and read for a while. Somewhere in there, she must have closed her eyes. When she awoke, she barely had time to get dressed and do her makeup before Scott honked.

"So you think Grandpa has no idea about the party?"

"If he did, he wouldn't have been able to resist telling us he knew."

They pulled behind the Elks' Hall and walked in through the back door. She immediately spotted Gail and Jacob. Gail wore a satin dress with pearls and high heels. *She looks younger every time I see her. As a matter of fact, so does Grandpa. Even Jacob seems to be doing okay.*

Patty Baron set out trays of canapes, pigs in a blanket, and an assortment of cheeses and crackers. "Bob, did you get the ice?"

"I already put it in the punch bowl. The rest is in the cooler. I'll go pick up Pops."

Friends from church and the Elks' hall gathered around, chatting. After a while, Patty said, "Hide. Dad just texted. They're right down the road."

Everyone scrambled to take cover behind the tables and behind the door.

Patty received a text and said, "One, two…" The door opened. Everyone shouted, "Surprise!"

Grandpa's mouth literally hung open. "What's this?"

Gail ran over and put her arm around him. "Happy 80th birthday! We're all here to celebrate."

"I don't like…" Gail gave him a discreet swat. Sara saw from behind. "I don't know what to say. Thank you, everyone. Patty, was this your idea?"

"You don't turn 80 every day."

"Just a heads up. When I turn 90 I'm expecting a family cruise to the Bahamas!"

"You got it, Pops."

Sara mingled and met some of Grandpa's friends. Friends she didn't know he had.

"Hello, I'm Carlos."

"Sara. I'm Frank's granddaughter."

"I know who you are. Your grandfather talks about you all the time. He's so proud of you, playing in the

Philharmonic and all. He's got your picture on the lock screen of his phone."

"I had no idea. How do you know Grandpa?"

"I'm a fellow Elk. Known him for years. We play cards." He took off his cardigan. "Getting warm in here. Never can get the thermostat to hold a steady temperature in this room. Either too hot or too cold. Dress in layers, that's the thing to do."

Sara noticed an oblong, gold pin on his shirt. It was identical to the two she'd found. "What's the pin for?"

He looked down at his shirt, twisting his neck to see. "This? It's from trivia. Ralph's runs a weekly trivia. If you collect five pins, you drink free for an evening. It's tough competition. I've just got the one." He pulled at it to show her, but it fell to the floor. "The clasp is awful. It's always falling off."

Trivia. That's a great lead. I'll have to look into it tomorrow.

Patty lit the candles on the cake. Grandpa blew them out in two breaths. *Still got his oboe lungs.*

The party was a big hit. After the guests left, Sara helped her parents clean up. Scott pulled the car around to the front.

Scott said, "I'm hoping longevity runs in our genes. Grandpa's looking good for 80."

"And he's got friends! Who knew?"

"Ready to go?"

"Yes. I'm exhausted."

When Scott dropped her in her driveway, she couldn't resist. *I'll try one more time to make sure Travis is okay. After that, I'm calling it a night."* She'd been texting him all day and gotten no response. *If he turns up dead and they go through his texts, they'll think I'm a stalker.* She banged on his door. "Travis? Are you in there? Open up."

She pulled the key from her purse and went inside the dark house. *You might not like what you find. Last time you went into a dark house at night you discovered Ellie's body.*

Nonetheless, her concern, rather her curiosity, won out. She flipped on the lights and called his name while she went in and out of the rooms. No sign of him anywhere.

She couldn't resist snooping in an effort to understand what was going on. She went through the drawers in the kitchen, again finding mostly empty space. She went into his bedroom and opened his drawers. She reached behind drawers and searched the few items on his pantry shelves. Nothing hidden in a cereal box. Nothing under the mattresses. Just those pills with the name Cameron Stokes in the medicine closet.

She checked the garage. *If I went out of town for any length of time, surely I'd park my car in the garage—especially if it wasn't cluttered with a bunch of junk. There's plenty of room in here.* Nothing in the washer or dryer. Nothing behind the rake or shovel.

She went back inside. His parka caught her eye. She wondered why he hadn't taken it seeing as it was the only coat she'd ever seen him wear—even to the funeral. Taking it off the hook, she felt in the outer pockets. *Just a pair of gloves.* She felt the lining and felt a lump. When she unzipped the lining, her mouth hung open. It was a ski cap. An orange ski cap. *Of course! He was wearing this cap the very first time I met him, when I skidded on the way to finding Ellie's body. So it was him Brayden Carlisle spotted going into Ellie's the night she was murdered! He fits the description.* She called Scott.

"Hey, I think I found something important in Travis's house."

"You went over there alone, in the dark? I told you I'd help you in the morning, Sis."

"I know, but I just had to check. I know you're still battling jet lag, but can you be here first thing in the morning?"

"I'll be there. Now get some sleep."

Chapter 31

Sara was awake before sunrise. Scott came by shortly after with leftover brownies from the birthday party. "I brought us breakfast. You got any coffee?"

"Sure do." She poured them each a mug.

"What's going on? You said you found something important."

She took the orange cap out of the drawer. "I found this hidden in Travis's parka. A neighbor said he saw a man with an orange ski cap enter Ellie's house the night she was killed and he was wearing an orange ski cap. I saw him wearing it earlier that evening, when I first met him."

"Orange ski caps aren't exactly one of a kind. Any other evidence he was there that night?"

"Police found a tire track in Ellie's driveway, this driveway, that matched his truck."

"So? He could've stopped by. They were neighbors."

"He said he hadn't seen her that night. And it snowed. Kinda. It was more like freezing rain. Anyhow, the tracks would've disappeared had he been there before that time."

"Anything else?"

"They found his prints in here."

"But he was her neighbor, so they'd expect to find those."

"In his medicine cabinet, there's an old prescription with the name Cameron Stokes. He never mentioned a girlfriend, but he's very private so it wouldn't surprise me."

"Anything else?"

She hesitated. "I found two oblong gold pins. Last night Grandpa's friend told me they give them to the monthly trivia winner at Ralph's. I don't know if he plays trivia, but it's worth checking out."

"Where's your laptop? I'll start by looking for a criminal record as well as a marriage certificate."

"You can do that?"

"I do it all the time for the good ol' USA. Let me have that." He typed and searched.

He's going to find a wife. Maybe a criminal record, too. I'll bet Travis is a fugitive. He fled the scene of the crime and started over here in Hudsonville.

"There's no record of a Travis Jennings. No birth certificate, social security card, driver's license. Nothing."

"How can that be?"

"He may be using a false name. What was the name on the medicine bottle?"

"Cameron Stokes."

He searched again. "There's a man by that name. Born in Seattle. Around your age."

"A man?" She was relieved it wasn't a woman after all who'd be storing her pills in his medicine closet. "Maybe that's him."

"I don't think so. Here's a death certificate from a little over a year ago."

"That's when he moved here—at least that's what he says. Is there a picture?"

Scott searched some more. "Here's his driver's license photo. It looks like him, if you lose the dreads and beard, right?"

"It's him." She felt her heart drop to her knees. "But how can he be dead? It'd be one thing if he was assuming this person's identity, but it's him and there's no record of a Travis Jennings. I'm confused."

"He's using an alias. Maybe he faked his death. Let's see." More clicking and typing. "He died in a car accident. The car burned up. They must have assumed it was him driving."

"But it wasn't. Travis has been lying about everything. Why?"

"My guess? He's a fugitive. Maybe he robbed a bank or jewelry store and made off with the goods. I don't know."

Great minds think alike. "Or he committed murder?"

"Let's check this out." He typed and clicked, fingers flying over the laptop keyboard.

I once thought I was a good judge of character. Ha. Serves me right for falling for a virtual stranger and trusting him even when the signs were clear.

"Nope, I was wrong. This Cameron Stokes doesn't have a criminal record."

"That's a relief, I guess."

"Seemed like a nice guy. What possible motive does he have for killing Ellie?" asked Scott.

"They were neighbors. Maybe she figured out who he really was and threatened to blow his cover."

"If he did something illegal and was hiding under this new identity, it had to be big."

"Scott, do you think they were romantically involved and had a falling out? I found her earring in his sofa. Maybe that's why she broke up with Preston Montague."

"My theory makes more sense. Lots of folks have relationship issues. Most don't kill over them. But secret criminal activity, even without a prior history...I've seen it before."

"Then let's figure out what he was hiding. Any ideas?"

Scott typed. "Cameron Stokes was an orthopedic surgeon. Let's see if there were any lawsuits or accusations against him." He searched and typed. "His record looks clean. Looks like his patients rated him highly."

"He gave up a career as an orthopedic surgeon, came here, changed his name, and became a physical therapist. Wouldn't he have had to prove who he was when he applied at Hudsonville Community?"

"Yeah. I'm a bit stumped on that one. He'd have to have shown qualifications as a physical therapist, medical training, college degrees..."

"Jailyn Peters, one of the other suspects in Ellie's murder, is an orthopedic surgeon. Could she have helped him fake it? Maybe they knew each other before he moved here."

"She could have vouched for him, but no hospital is going to hire a doctor or physical therapist without thoroughly checking the credentials. Imagine the lawsuits if they didn't?"

"Let's look at what they have in common. Both orthopedic surgeons. Jailyn Peters had connections with Preston Montague—she used to date him. The Montague family practically owns Medivision, the medical device company that supplies the hospital. Maybe they were both investors in the company..."

"But whatever sent him here happened *before* he arrived. I don't know. I would say to stay clear of the guy. Don't put yourself in danger."

It was hard for her to see Travis as a criminal, a dangerous one at that. A murderer, even. *How could my instincts be so terribly off?*

"Okay. You keep thinking. I'll bet he doesn't even come back here. The way he left it was like he was fleeing the scene. I'm going to go over to the shop and help out. Want to come with me?"

"You know I never liked that oboe making stuff. I'm all thumbs."

"But, you're a whiz when it comes to computers. They're still doing receipts and billing by hand. If you set up some kind of system that's easy to use, it would make things move much quicker over there."

He shrugged his shoulders. "Okay. I'm in."

"I'll drive," said Sara.

"What's the story with Grandpa? Mom's last letter said how bad he's gotten. She told me it was Alzheimer's and she was worried they'd have to find a nursing home in the not too distant future."

"Honestly, I think he'd been on a downhill slide since Grandma died. He was depressed in my not so expert opinion. Ever since he met Gail he's sharp as a tack. You should see him whiz through making an oboe."

"He seemed plenty upbeat to me. Good for him. I'm sure Mom and Dad are relieved to see him happy again."

Sara and Scott arrived at the oboe shop mid-morning.

"Scott, you changed your mind about being interested in the family business? A day late and a dollar short," said Grandpa.

Bob Baron said, "It's a little late now, son. It'd take years to train you. Unlike Sara here who hung out with us all the while growing up. She stepped right in and is making oboes like it's in her blood."

"Dad, I'm here to help, but not with oboe making. Sara says you're still doing billing by hand. I can set things up for you that will save you time. I can also help with the web site and mailing list."

Grandpa said, "Nah. It'll just be confusing."

"No, really. Let me give it a try and if you don't like it, keep doing what you've been doing."

"Dad, it couldn't hurt," said Sara. "You've got nothing to lose."

"Okay. Have a stab at it, Scott." He picked up a pile of receipts and the billing log and plopped it down on his desk. "You can use the computer. The password is on the sticky note next to it."

Scott sat down to work. Grandpa said, "I think we've solved my father's code. I unscrambled the rest of the message and it says 'a to c.' I figured, maybe it's not a numerical value, but a proportion, since oboes are a conical shape. If we use the proportion, A is 440 Hz, C is 526 Hz, and apply it to the numbers he listed on the graph, it makes sense. It looks like it could be a significantly more uniform scale."

"Let me see." Sara took the paper. "I think you've got it!"

"I took one of the partially finished oboes and started placing and sizing the tone holes using these numbers. I'm going to see how it turns out."

"Pops has still got it," said Bob. "If we come up with a better tuned scale, these things will sell like hotcakes. Meanwhile, Sara, let's keep plugging away on our list. I'll bet we can be caught up in no time."

They worked straight through lunch and into the late afternoon. By quitting time, Scott was well into converting the paperwork to computer files, and Grandpa had made a significant dent in the experimental oboe.

"This is really nice," said Bob. "Our family working together at the business my grandfather started. He'd be proud."

"Not if we wind up selling to Frazier Woodwinds," said Grandpa. His eyes twinkled. "But I've got a feeling we won't have to."

"This calls for a celebration. Want to go out for dinner? My treat." *It's not in my budget but I'm going to splurge. This can be the key to preserving the family legacy for generations. If Scott and I ever get our acts together and have our own families.*

"As much as I love the idea of being treated to dinner by my daughter, Mom's had stew brewing in the crock pot all day and she'd kill me."

"Gramps?"

"I've got a date with Gail."

Scott said, "I guess it's the two of us, but my treat. Pick the place."

Sara directed Scott to the Greek diner. It was snowing lightly and the twinkling lights on the diner window reflected onto the sidewalk. The waitress seated them at a booth near the door.

Scott said, "You have no idea how much I've missed good old American food."

"Hate to break it you, but this is a Greek diner."

"I use the term broadly. How's San Francisco treating you? Felt any earthquakes yet?"

"Just a couple of tremors, in more ways than one. I'm going to tell you something I recently shared with Mom and Dad."

"Sounds serious."

"I've been having trouble with my hand. My fingers on my left hand shake or clench up and freeze with no rhyme or reason while I'm in the middle of playing. At first I thought I had a touch of tendonitis, or at worst, carpal tunnel."

"But it isn't that?"

"No. It's a condition called focal dystonia. Not common, but more common amongst musicians than in the general population. I took a medical leave. I may have to give up my job."

"Sis, have you gone to a specialist?"

"I've done what I can afford to do. Travis has been helping me with physical therapy exercises and medication but it's not responding the way we hoped it would."

"I've got friends in the medical field. I'll see what I can turn up."

"Thanks, but I may have to accept it and find a new career. Like making oboes."

"Wouldn't your hand problem get in the way of that, too?"

"Weirdly, it's confined to my left hand. The one that's over taxed when I play."

"It's nice you're helping Dad out, but is that a career?"

"If this new-fangled design catches on it could be. Besides, maybe I'll settle down, get married, and have a couple of kids. This way we'd have someone to carry on the family legacy."

"I wasn't thinking of producing heirs, but I would like to settle down once I leave the army."

"Are you leaning toward retiring?"

"I'm undecided. We'll see how things go over the next few months. What did Mom and Dad say about your leave. I'm sure they're understanding."

"Mom's worried. I think Dad is too but he tries to hide it."

"Isn't that what parents do?"

When she pulled into the driveway, Travis's house was still dark. Once inside, she texted but he didn't respond. *No matter where he is, he could at least answer my text and tell me he's okay.* She tossed the phone on the sofa. Panther meowed at her feet, rubbing against her legs, then paced back and forth to the food bowl.

"You are one smart cat. I'm glad you're getting your appetite back." She went to the pantry. "Looks like we're getting to the bottom of the bag." She poured the food into the bowl. Something fell into the food bowl. *What on Earth? A thumb drive? Is this what Ellie wanted me to keep safe? Is it what she didn't want 'them' to get?* She immediately plugged it into her laptop and watched a series of numbers and dates populate the screen. She wasn't sure what she was looking at. There were photos included as well. *Are these metal contraptions artificial joints?* She called Scott and asked him to come over. She did a bit of research while waiting for him. When she heard a knock, she raced to the door.

"Scott, these look like photos of hip joints. See, I Googled it. Don't you think that's what they are?" She showed him the pictures from the thumb drive.

He squinted. "I think so. And are those serial numbers etched in there?"

"Yes. And look. Anecdotal evidence with dates. Patient numbers followed by doctor visits, symptoms, complaints…"

"This is very detailed."

"Ellie was collecting evidence. Here's more data. A list of patient numbers and complications. Look. Hair loss, fatigue, even death!"

"Ellie was a whistleblower!" said Scott. "Didn't you say she had a safe room installed? And a new home security system?"

"Yes. Plus, her co-worker saw her with files and said Ellie told her she felt as though she was being watched. Gail said Ellie kept looking over her shoulder at church." She gasped. "The boat! Camaya said Ellie needed to borrow her boat for something urgent. She was going to take her car, then changed her mind."

"Maybe she was delivering those files and knew she was being followed, or that her car was being tracked."

"Tracked? How?"

"Where's the car now?"

"In the garage. Why?"

"Show me."

Sara led him into the garage. "It's been here since the night I arrived. I've driven it a few times. What are you looking for?"

Scott swept his hand methodically under the bumpers and over the tires. "Is there a flashlight in here?"

Sara rummaged through a box of storm supplies. "Here."

Scott got on the ground and shone the light under the car's carriage.

"Do you see something? Be careful. What if Travis planted a bomb under there?"

Scott got up and opened his fist. He held a small metal disk. "Not a bomb, but potentially just as dangerous. We use these in the army. It's a tracking device. Whoever planted this knew every place this car went. If Ellie was suspicious and had evidence to deliver, she wouldn't have driven this car."

"She would have...borrowed a boat!"

"That would have been a clever move."

"Do you have to be in the military to get one of those devices?"

"No. This isn't military grade. I'll bet it was purchased on line from one of those spy stores."

"You mean like a site where you could order a spy camera?"

"Yeah. You can get all that stuff online. Not necessarily good quality, but this tracker appears to be working." He waved it back and forth. Sara saw a flashing red light when the device moved.

"A witness saw a third boat chasing Ellie's the night Hunter's son died. He was beaten up and denied it afterwards."

"She must have had enough evidence to sink the company and she had to be stopped."

"What if Travis moved here to keep an eye on Ellie? You said he was an orthopedic surgeon back in Seattle, right? Was it a coincidence that he happened to rent the house next to hers? What if he participated in the cover-up and knew Ellie was onto it? Medivision is publicly traded. In his position, if he owns shares of stock and refers his patients for surgery, he has the potential to make a killing. Only…"

"Only what?"

"Medivision stopped using the recalled parts."

"Who says they stopped using those parts? Must have had millions of dollars in inventory just sitting there."

"Wouldn't the FDA or some such agency be keeping careful watch?"

"I'm sure the serial numbers could have been changed, or the parts hidden. We're talking a big company and a lot of money."

Sara scanned the information on the thumb drive. "Many of these patient complications occurred in surgeries performed *after* the recall."

"It's possible the company hired him to move here and help keep an eye on things at the hospital, or help with the cover-up. And no, I don't think it was a coincidence that he happened to rent a house right next door to Ellie," said Scott.

"And I saw him huddled together, talking to Jailyn Peters once at the hospital. His prints were in this— Ellie's—house. I found one of Ellie's earrings stuck in Travis's sofa. There was a second cell phone, his truck tire track in this driveway the night of the murder, and now he's disappeared. I've been so stupid. I can't believe I didn't see this."

"He's a charmer. Picked that up right away first time I met him. You can't blame yourself. The police haven't caught on to him and they're the professionals."

In actuality, I think Phil had his suspicions. "Now the witness and the orange ski cap! Let's call the police. And wait."

"What?"

"When Preston died, he was clutching a gold pin. At the party, I found out there's a trivia contest at Ralph's every week and the winner gets the gold pin. Whoever killed him must have been at the contest."

"Did Travis ever mention trivia?"

"No, but that doesn't mean he didn't go. We should check. I'm sure he's the killer. And Medivision is still using the recalled parts."

"Whoa. You can't make an accusation like that without proof. Ellie's info doesn't show that Medivision is still using the recalled parts."

"How can we get proof?"

"You'd have to have one of the parts and show it's the same as the faulty ones. That'll be difficult."

"So, we'd have to sneak into the warehouse, in other words, and swipe one?"

"Yes, but that would be breaking and entering. Even if you got what we needed, it couldn't be used in court if it had been obtained illegally."

"What do we do?"

"Let's sleep on it. Maybe by morning I'll have an idea."

Chapter 32

The next morning, Sara woke up to the buzzing of her phone on the nightstand. "Hello?"

"Sorry I missed the big party. I was hoping I could take you out for breakfast to make up for it. I have a gift for your grandfather. Then we can work in a physical therapy session if you'd like. Has your hand gotten any better? Have you tried playing?"

"Travis? Are you kidding me? You disappear without a word and then show up and expect things to go on as normal? We were all expecting you for the party. It was rude of you not to show up without even calling."

"Sara, I'm so sorry. Truly. I had no choice. It was…"

"A family emergency? A work thing? I'm sick of excuses. I thought you wanted to stay friends, even if you aren't attracted to me."

"That's not…I'll make it up to you, I promise. There's a new treatment for your dystonia that I read about while I was away. It's an off-label use of an existing drug. They've had some early success."

She knew better. Look what happened with Brandon. She'd ignored all the little signs that he was about to dump her and was blindsided in the end. No. She couldn't let herself fall into that trap again. Besides, she was nearly convinced Travis was a murderer. Why was she even talking to him?"

"Just breakfast and a session. Besides, I have a gift for you. If this new drug works, you could be in remission in time for the season to start."

It's not like I'll be alone with him. First the diner, then the hospital. If he's telling the truth about that new treatment, I can't afford to ignore it. She had another thought as well. *We need proof before we bring our suspicions to the police that he killed Ellie. Maybe he'll slip and give himself away. I'll ask him about trivia.*

"Do you want me to beg? I can beg."

"Okay. But I'll meet you there so afterwards I can drive back from the hospital. You'll be working all day, right?"

"Okay. If I get there first, I'll order us coffee."

What am I doing? She called Scott and explained.

"Sara, are you crazy?"

"It's our best chance of nabbing him."

"You'd better not be alone with him. Not even in his office."

"The nurses are in and out. I'll be okay. I'm going to try to trip him up about Ellie's murder."

"He'll see right through that. Just act natural and keep your eyes open, that's all."

Sara put the thumb drive back in the cat food bag. It'd been safe there all along. Even with the new security system, she couldn't trust Travis wouldn't have access. She pulled on a turquoise sweater and jeans, brushed her hair into a ponytail now that it'd gotten just long enough to do so, and drove to the diner. Travis's present was still sitting on the passenger seat where she'd left it the other day.

Travis had gotten a haircut and his face was baby smooth, lacking the usual hint of rugged stubble. She hated that in spite of knowing he was likely a coldblooded killer, the physical attraction remained. *I need a shrink.* Her skin tingled when she looked into his chestnut eyes. *Is this attraction, or is it fear?*

"Hi, Sara. Coffee's here as promised. And I got you this. It's a peace offering." He handed her a beautifully wrapped box with a red bow. *He had to have paid to get this gift-wrapped.*

"Should I open it now?"

"Of course."

She unwrapped the box and pulled out a multicolored, knit scarf. "It's so soft."

"Cashmere. Like the sweater you were eyeing when we went shopping. I noticed the scarf you've been wearing is a little tattered."

She stroked the scarf that hung around her neck. "My Grandmother made this one when I left for college. It's seen better days." She wrapped the new one on top of it. *Did he have a tracker sewn into the seam?*

"Here. I got you this." She handed him the present she'd been toting around in the car.

"A wallet. And you had my initials engraved in it."

Too bad they aren't really your initials.

They ordered waffles and while they ate, Sara brought up the recalled hip joints.

"Travis, what do you think Medivision did with all those recalled hip and knee joints?"

"I'd expect they had them melted down. At least they'd have recouped a small percentage of what they'd invested, though I'm sure it was still a drop in the bucket. That's providing they followed the court order and destroyed them."

"You have your doubts?"

"It had to have cost them a ton of money. The FDA will have been all over them, though. At least at first. How are your waffles?"

"Delicious, but I'm pretty full. Are you ready to go?"

"I'll meet you back at the hospital."

Sara called Scott from the car on the way.

"Scott, I just saw Travis. We had breakfast and I am on the way to the hospital. He has a new treatment he wants me to try. For my dystonia. I'll explain later."

"Be careful, Sis. Don't be alone with him. Ever."

She pulled into the parking garage just behind the blue truck. She lagged behind until they were safely inside the hospital, then followed him into his office.

"Has it gotten worse? Have you noticed having trouble in any other activities besides oboe playing?"

"Not really. Still occasionally dropping a glass or my keys, but it's been isolated to my left hand, thank goodness. I'm still able to make oboes."

He examined her hand, had her grip a rubber ball, and tested her reflexes. "The new drug needs to be taken with food twice a day. In the study, the subjects saw lessening of their symptoms after 4-6 weeks."

"Are there any side effects?"

"Headaches, nausea. That's why they say take it with food. I have samples for you to try. Got them from the internist I work with. They're in the other room, I'll be right back."

She saw his phone vibrate through his thin white coat. He shut the door behind him, but she opened it a crack and moved closer when she heard Travis talking.

"Yes, Medivision factory. Orchard Road. Noon. I'll be there."

Several minutes later, he returned with the samples. "Here you go. If you tolerate it well, we'll get you a prescription. Here's hoping."

"Thank you."

"I'll drop by tonight. Will you be home?"

She didn't want to be alone with him after what they'd discovered. "I'm having dinner with my parents. Gotta go."

Noon at the Medivision factory. She called Scott and arranged to meet him there. She hoped he had a plan. She knew spying would be involved and wasn't at all sure how she'd go unnoticed. *I hope Scott's army training comes in handy.*

Her heart beat quickly on the way to the Medivision factory. If she and Scott could get proof that Medivision continued using the recalled parts and that Travis was involved in the cover-up, she was sure they could nail him for Ellie's murder. *How could I be so wrong about Travis?* It'd be a long while before she'd trust her judgment in men again. If ever. She turned down Orchard Road to the Medivision factory. She looked for Scott's car but he hadn't yet arrived. She saw Travis's truck and parked at the opposite end of the lot. *He's here, just like he said he'd be.* She turned off the engine and waited.

Where is he? It's already 12:20 and Scott is always on time, even before the army. I'm freezing in here. She stroked the soft, new scarf around her neck. She called and texted but got no response from Scott. *We are going to miss the entire transaction if he doesn't show up soon.* Another ten minutes passed. *That's it. I'm going to see if it's possible to look in the window.*

She locked the car and jogged up to the building. She crept along the outside, hunting for a window, like she'd done at the cabin when they were searching for Preston Montague. *That turned out well.* Even if she spotted Travis speaking to the higher-ups at Medivision, she wouldn't be able to hear the conversation. Without Scott's help, she had no idea what she was doing. *I'll go back to the car. I have no plan and I'll just wind up tipping them off.* Before she could turn around, someone grabbed her from behind, knocking the breath out of her.

Chapter 33

She kicked and struggled like in her nightmare, past the point of fatigue. She fought as she felt him pulling her kicking and squirming body toward the parking lot. She tried to scream, but his hand was clenched tightly over her mouth. So tight that she felt her jaw squeezing together. *I can barely breathe. If I had enough slack, I'd take a bite out of his hand. But I don't.*

When he dragged her into the parking lot, she dug her heels in and felt the back of her ankles scrape against the gravel. He hadn't uttered a word, but the vague smell of woodsy cologne gave him away.

She went limp, figuring dead weight would be harder to drag. Still facing the factory, she had no idea where he was taking her. Then, he stopped. He lifted her and pushed her into the front of a truck. A truck she'd ridden in before.

I knew it was him. How could I have been stupid enough to get into this situation? Scott warned me. Travis had her captive in the front cab of his truck.

"Shush! If you calm down, I'll take my hand away. It's not what you think."

She'd heard those words recently enough from Preston Montague. She forced herself to hold still. She nodded, and felt her numb cheeks come to life as he released his grip. "Why are you doing this? I know you killed Ellie and I suppose I'm next. I trusted you. You're in on this whole recall scandal. Do you get a cut for each patient you send for surgery?"

"You've got it all wrong. I'm not going to hurt you."

"Then why did you abduct me and throw me into your truck against my will? Why did you lie about being close to Ellie and being at her house the night she was murdered? You didn't have the courtesy to tell me your real name. Where have you been sneaking off to, Cameron?"

He seemed taken off guard. "So you know. How did you find out?"

"I saw the prescription in your bathroom. Then I found the orange ski cap in your parka lining. Scott works intelligence and it didn't take him long to figure you out."

"You have to keep my identity a secret. My life depends on it; I'll explain later. Hear me out. I was about to get a tour of this factory. I have a spy camera in my pocket, see? I found it on Amazon. I was planning on getting evidence that Medivision hadn't destroyed the recalled joints after all. You were about to ruin it for me. That's why I grabbed you before anyone discovered you."

"If you're on my side and didn't murder Ellie, you have a lot of explaining to do. Did you get the spy camera from the same site you bought the tracker you put on Ellie's car?"

"Tracker? On Ellie's car? What are you talking about?"

"You know what I'm talking about. Scott found it."

"Look, brace yourself. I didn't kill Ellie. I'm...you have to swear you'll keep this to yourself or my life will be at risk...I'm in the witness protection program. Yes, my real name is Cameron Stokes, but the agents faked my death and gave me a new identity here in New York."

"I've known a few pathological liars in my lifetime but this takes the cake."

"Please, just hear me out."

"You aren't from Chicago, either."

"No. Seattle."

"Seattle. Scott was right."

"Your brother knows who I am? Great. I stopped at a convenience store late one night after a long day of surgery. I didn't think I'd make it home without coffee. Two armed robbers burst in and started shooting. They shot the owner and all the customers in the store. They shot at me and by some miracle, missed. I played dead, then ran out the back as soon as I had the chance. I saw both men clearly. I was the only witness left alive that night."

"You helped the police identify them. That doesn't explain the witness protection overkill."

"I was the only witness left alive. This wasn't their only crime. When I described them to the police, they knew right away who the men were. Members of a dangerous gang responsible for dozens of deaths."

"Seriously? Do you hear yourself?"

"They'd been after them for years but could never get enough evidence or a witness to hold up in court. I agreed to testify, but the police said the gang would kill me if I did. They have far reaching connections, even from prison. The only way to testify and stay alive was to enter the witness protection program."

"You left your family behind?"

"My parents. Breaks my heart every time I think of them. They think I died in a car crash. I had to leave behind any evidence of my previous life and start over. Couldn't even continue orthopedic surgery in case they realize I'm alive and look for me through professional channels."

"And the disappearing act you pulled the other night? My mother made extra food just because you were coming. And being a no show at Grandpa's birthday party? That party was a big deal to all of us."

"I had to go back and forth to court whenever they needed me. Never knew when the marshal was going to pick me up. It's not like they allowed me to tell you."

"I saw you arguing with a man outside your front door before one of your little disappearing acts."

"Yes, the Marshall assigned to my case. I was asking if I could delay the trip, and, of course, he said no."

"You had nothing to do with Ellie's murder? Why were you at her house that night?"

"She confided in me that she suspected Medivision was still using the recalled joints. I'd been helping her compare data."

"That's why I found the notebook with her handwriting in your coffee table."

"You found...never mind. The night she was murdered, she called and asked me if I'd go to my office and bring back copies of patient files—physical therapy patients who had previously undergone hip replacement surgery. I was bringing them to her when I ran into you on the road that night."

"No way. Why didn't you tell the police?"

"I didn't want them to know my identity either. The Marshall said to tell no one."

"You'd been working with Ellie. What about Jailyn?"

"We suspected she was involved. She was using Medivision products and there was a connection between her and the CEO of the company. Ellie caught them whispering."

"And I saw them together at the restaurant. When was Ellie going to tell the police?"

"She said that with my files, she thought she'd have the proof she needed."

"What proof?"

"She said she'd explain when I got there. She was working as a whistleblower, gathering evidence against Medivision. When I went over, she was already dead."

"You're the second man Brayden saw that night. The one wearing the parka and orange ski cap."

"Yes, but I wish I knew who the first man was. The older man in the dress coat and baseball cap. He must be Ellie's killer."

"Where are those files?"

"I brought them back to the office. I didn't see anything useful in there."

"If you found her before I arrived, why didn't you call the police? You saw a dead body and just went back home to watch TV?"

"I couldn't have my picture splashed all over the national news for finding a dead body. I had to, *have to*, stay beneath the radar. I was heading back out to pick up an untraceable burner phone, but when I opened the door, I heard the sirens and knew it was too late."

"So, what are you doing here at the Medivision plant? What did you mean when you said I was going to blow it?"

"I have a tour scheduled. I'm already late. As a physical therapist, I'm a potential customer. I was hoping to find some physical evidence they haven't complied with the recall."

"Is it too late?"

"I'm late, but it's the middle of the day. I'll bet they're still willing to accommodate me."

"Let's go."

"You can't come with me. That would be totally suspicious."

"Say I'm your nurse or assistant."

"I'm not sure they'd buy it. You've been to Ellie's office, right?"

"Yeah, but the only rep who'd recognize me is Camaya and she wouldn't say anything. Besides, why would the reps be hanging out at the factory anyway? While you distract the guide with questions, I can be snapping pictures with your little spy cam."

"I don't know."

"Think how many lives we may be saving if we expose this sham."

"Okay, but just nod and smile." He grabbed a legal pad from the glove compartment. "Pretend you're taking notes." He tucked a strand of hair behind her ear. "Ready?"

"Yes, sir. Let's go."

At the front desk, Travis made up a story about having car trouble and hoping he could still get a tour. Sara looked at the wall and saw a picture of the CEO, Craig Danalchek. He was wearing a captain's hat and standing in front of a yacht!

The receptionist picked up the phone. "Okay, I'll send them back."

Within minutes, they had their very own tour guide. His speech began like a late night infomercial.

"Most medical supply companies import premade parts from China and India. Here at Medivision, we make our own. Saves the consumer money, and insures quality control. Look through the window on the right. That's where the metal and screws are unpacked."

It reminded Sara of the oboe shop, only on a larger scale. Not the physical surroundings, of course. This wasn't a homey family business, but rather a sterile factory. The basic process, assembling parts, crafting the product...that she was familiar with.

The guide walked them down the corridor. "The parts come out on a conveyor belt, here, after the preliminary assembly is finished. Then they're separated into specific parts. See how the conveyor belt divides? Hip joints are made from the belt on the left, while knee joints are assembled on the right. We have a separate feeder system for assembling plates and pins."

Sara pretended to take notes, drawing a sketch of the building's interior and the conveyor belt system.

Travis said, "These parts are assembled by hand?"

"Not completely, but the finishing measurements and adjustments are. Then we stamp on a serial number and ship them out."

"Our hospital must give you lots of business."

"It does, though we have competition from foreign factories. Labor is cheaper over-seas."

"What happens when there's a recall? Wasn't there a big recall back a year or so ago?"

"Expensive, but we ate it. We destroyed the faulty joints and started over. Safety is paramount." He led them into an elevator. "Down here is our shipping department. The trucks pick up over there."

Sara saw floor to ceiling boxes plastered with shipping labels. *This is overwhelming. How do we know what's in those boxes?* "Excuse me, is there a restroom here?"

The guide said, "Nothing fancy. If you go through that door, take a left and you'll see it. I'm warning you, it's a factory bathroom and mostly men work here."

"Right now I'd settle for a porta-potty. I'll be right back." She slipped through the door and found the restroom, but stopped when she heard the sound of machinery. The guide told them all the manufacturing was done upstairs and this basement was storage and shipping. She followed the sound, which got louder as she walked further down the hallway. The hair on her arms stood up and her gut told her she was coming close to something big.

Now the machinery made a loud, regular rhythm, like a metronome on steroids. She put her ear to the door. For a moment, she couldn't decide whether to turn back or try the door. *It's now or never. I won't get this close again.*

She opened the door slowly. She didn't see anyone in the room, just another conveyor belt with parts. She went for a closer look. *This machine is removing the serial numbers.* She grabbed the spy-cam and took pictures. *I'll bet these are the recalled parts. Even if they are manufacturing new devices, surely these are being sent out as well.* Satisfied that she now had proof, she gently shut the door and returned to the shipping area.

The guide said, "We were worried you'd gotten lost. I was telling your boss we'd be happy to send over trial parts. The ortho-surgeon over there, Jailyn Peters, uses our inventory exclusively."

Travis shook his hand. "Appreciate the tour, and we'll be doing business."

They headed into the elevator. *Oh, no. Ellie's boss! What if he recognizes me from the funeral or from when I went by to pick up Ellie's things at the office?* Her heart thumped and she felt a panic attack brewing.

Craig Danalchek said, "I hope our tour answered any questions you may have. We have a superior product. If my own mother had to have a hip replacement, I'd only agree if we'd be using a Medivision artificial joint." He didn't seem to remember meeting her. He was wearing a tweed coat. And a captain's hat that looked an awful lot like a baseball cap! And a gold pin on his shirt!

Travis said, "I was quite impressed."

Sara thought Travis was slick, giving the impression his job actually involved doing surgery. Craig Danalchek looked at her.

"Have we met before?"

Her mouth went dry. "I don't think so."

Travis said, "She runs around the hospital helping not only me but other ortho surgeons as well. Chances are if you spent any time at the hospital you'd have run into her."

Sara held her breath.

"Hmmm. I guess that's it."

Sara sighed with relief when the elevator door opened and they parted ways. She and Travis scurried to the truck. She almost slipped more than once thanks to the freezing rain pelting the parking lot.

"I got it. Pictures. Lots of them. There's a machine in back that smooths over the serial numbers, and another that stamps on new ones. Want to bet those are the recalled joints?"

"We're going straight to the police station with this."

Sara's phone vibrated. She noticed half a dozen missed calls when she took it out of her pocket. She played the voicemails. "Oh, my God. It's from Scott." She called him back.

"Scott, what's wrong?"

"Grandpa took a bad spill. The ambulance brought him to the hospital. They're prepping him for surgery." The last sentence of the message resounded in her head. "Scott said they might need to replace his hip!"

"Guess we're taking a detour." He floored the truck, spinning into a skid. "Call your detective buddy right now." He straightened out the truck. This was the same curve of the road where Sara had skidded the first time she met him.

She grabbed her phone. "Now it's dead! I'm so stupid! I forgot to charge it last night. Where's yours?"

"On my kitchen counter. I took the spy camera— didn't have room for both in my pocket." He again floored the truck, steering into another skid.

"Be careful." She clutched the seat.

Sara heard a siren and watched the flashing lights of an ambulance as it passed the truck.

"Do you think that's him?"

"Your brother said they were already there, right? So he's probably at the hospital by now. The slick roads are prime for accidents."

"Jailyn Peters is Grandpa's doctor. At this very moment she might be putting a metal leaching, recalled hip joint into my grandfather!"

"We're almost there."

Sara saw the bright hospital lights ahead. As soon as Travis pulled into the parking lot, they made a run for the entrance. Travis grabbed her by the hand, helping her keep her balance on the ice as they ran for the door.

Once inside, they flew up the steps to the surgical floor. Sara's family, and Gail Capelli, were gathered in the hallway.

"Dad, where's Grandpa?"

"They're wheeling him into surgery. You just missed him. What's wrong?"

"Wait here," said Travis. Sara ignored him.

They ran down the corridor in time to see the door to the surgical suite open. Travis yelled, "Stop right there! Step back. No one is operating on this man." Jailyn Peters, in dark blue scrubs, ready to operate, was waiting on the other side of the door.

Detective Lambert appeared and ran to the doorway. "Dr. Peters, you're coming with me. Sara, are you okay?"

"I am now. How did you piece this together?"

"Your brother told me you'd gone to Medivision and I figured it meant trouble. He'd contacted a federal agent who'd been working with Ellie Rossi. Your friend was a whistleblower."

"Then do you know who killed her?" She was quite sure she'd figured it out.

"Brace yourself. The unidentified print on Ellie's nightstand belongs to Craig Danalchek."

"Ellie's boss?"

"Yeah. He figured out what she was doing and killed her. We got a warrant and found the murder weapon in his bedroom closet. The tire iron we found earlier had to have been planted. The real murder weapon was a golf club. Dumb move, keeping the evidence in his own home. At that point, he confessed. He's locked up in a cell."

"Can you prove he knew Medivison was using recalled parts?" asked Sara.

"Yes, thanks to Ellie." He pointed to Jailyn Peters. "This one was aware of what was going on but chose to keep quiet and kept using the recalled parts."

"What about the boating accident? Did he plant the prints, too?"

"The night of the boating accident, Ellie was delivering a key piece of evidence to her contact. She realized her car was being tracked and decided to go by boat. Craig Danalchek overheard her asking her co-worker, Camaya, to borrow her boat so he followed her. He was chasing her in the third boat. That's why she sped. But Hunter Griffith's other son was driving and was quite intoxicated as it turns out. The accident wasn't Ellie's fault."

"Why frame Ellie for the boating accident?"

Jailyn said, "You have to ask? It was a perfect way to keep her out of our hair. If she had been arrested and safely tucked in a jail cell, we wouldn't have had to kill her."

"Was it worth it? Worth murdering for?"

"Craig made it worth my while. I own shares in Medivision." Jailyn looked almost smug, disgusting Sara.

"Danalchek made regular deposits into her bank account," said Phil.

"That was interest from the stocks I own. I earned that money fair and square," whined Jailyn.

"Do the Montagues know? They own shares, too." asked Sara.

"They have a lot invested in Medivision, but they were unaware of this whole nonsense. They were horrified to find out people had died and said they would find a way to pay back society, whatever that means. Preston found out not long ago."

Jailyn said, "I told him to keep his mouth shut. We had no choice but to stop him. He was meeting to spill the beans to you, Sara. If only you'd have keep your nose out of our business."

"The night Ellie was murdered, Preston was coming to rescue her, wasn't he?" said Sara.

Jailyn said, "She'd finally gotten to him. When she found out he knew about the scheme she gave him an ultimatum. Come clean, or the engagement was off. Obviously, he chose to keep quiet."

"But he couldn't live with the guilt, could he?" said Sara.

"The fool was in love with her. After Craig shut her up, Preston panicked. When he reached out to you with that note on your door? Of course he had to be stopped."

Detective Lambert nudged Jailyn toward the exit. "I'll need statements from both of you. Right now this one is going to join her boss."

He led Jailyn Peters away in handcuffs. She flicked her hair over her shoulder and grinned at Sara.

"Take Mr. Baron back to pre-op while we settle this," said Travis.

Sara kissed her grandfather. He whispered to her, "Tell Barack he..."

"Grandpa, what are you saying?" He was slurring his words as the sedative began to work.

He squeezed her hand. "Tell Barack he's okay in my book."

Sara smiled and kissed his forehead. "I love you, Grandpa."

Travis said, "He's going to be okay. They're paging the other orthopedic surgeon on staff. He doesn't use Medivision products. Let's find your family."

Down the hall, Sara saw her father pacing in circles. As soon as she was within earshot he said, "Sara, what's going on? Scott called the police but didn't explain anything."

"It's a long story. Grandpa's going to be okay, thanks to Travis."

Travis said, "Thanks to Ellie Rossi and your daughter. Sara wasn't going to stop until her friend's killer was caught."

Chapter 34

Winter, while certainly not over, was giving way to occasional hints of spring. It was a sunny, February day and the dirty snow melted like 7-Eleven Icees along the sides of the road. Sara parked in front of ShopRite. *It's about time I learned how to make Mom's cheesecake.*

She and Travis had started seeing each other and tonight, Heaven help her, she was cooking him dinner. They'd agreed to take things slowly, but she felt cautiously optimistic about where this relationship might lead.

She grabbed a wagon and headed to the dairy aisle. *Cream cheese, butter, eggs…*

"So you have time to cook now that you're not chasing clues." Phil Lambert had snuck up behind her.

"I'm thinking catching a killer might seem like a snap after looking over Mom's cheesecake recipe." She looked in his wagon. "Wine? Oysters? Cooking dinner for someone special yourself?"

"I started dating the daughter of your mother's book club friend. Turns out we have a lot in common."

Sara laughed. "I think she's got a brother. Mom tried to set me up with him when I first came back."

"I'm glad you stayed. I hear the music shop is kicking butt."

"My great grandfather's design turned out to be a winner. Word is getting out and already orders have doubled. Thank goodness Scott got the shop into the age of technology so we can keep up with the orders and billing. He's been marketing through social media as well."

"I'm sure they appreciate the extra hands. How's your Grandfather?"

"Better than ever. Travis has been working with him on physical therapy since the new hip was put in. He's walking without his cane. Pain free. He's talking about taking Gail hiking at the Grand Canyon this spring."

"I hear the senior center is opening up in a few weeks," said Phil. "The Montagues came through on their promise to repay society."

"I can't believe they donated the building and all the furnishings. They even purchased books, games, and computers."

"Best of all, they bought a brand new van and are going to employ a full time driver to pick up and deliver seniors who are unable to get there on their own."

"Yes, and the transportation will extend to doctor appointments and errands as well."

"*The Ellie Rossi Senior Haven*. What a good way to keep your friend's memory alive."

"Are you here to stay?"

"I'm on leave for a few more months. My dystonia seems to be improving with the medication Travis recommended, so with any luck, I'll be able to resume my job."

"We'd miss you, but I know San Francisco is your home and from what I hear, that band you play in is pretty famous."

"You could say that." She looked at her watch. "I've got to go if I want to avoid relying on take-out tonight."

"Me too. It was good seeing you. Give my best to Travis."

As she drove home through Hudsonville, Sara felt at peace. If worse came to worst and she couldn't continue her job, maybe she's find a way to cope, surrounded by her family, friends, and Travis.

She unpacked the groceries and set to work on the cheesecake. She wasn't sure she'd left enough time for it to chill. *Guess he'll have to stay until it does.* She assembled the lasagna and popped it in the oven right before the doorbell rang.

Travis stood there with a bouquet of roses. "For you. Do I smell lasagna?"

"Where did you find roses in the middle of winter?"

"Like I told your mother, I know a guy who knows a guy. May I come in?"

"Of course. It's freezing out. Why don't you start a fire? Alexa, play mood music."

"I taught you a trick! *Bolero*? That's a little cheesy, don't you think?"

"Gotcha. Alexa, play *Gabriel's Oboe*."

"Better." Travis had a fire going in no time. "Did your brother get off okay?"

"Yes. He has a decision to make. In a few months he'll be eligible to retire from the military. With his training, he could easily find work as a civilian. Wouldn't it be great if he came back home?"

"Are you saying this is home?"

"It'll always be home. As to whether or not I live here permanently, that remains to be seen." *I can't imagine giving up playing. Then again, I can't imagine not seeing where this relationship with Travis might go.* "Travis, if I do go back to San Francisco, is it even possible for you to relocate? I mean, if things get serious and if I'm well enough to resume my job."

"I'd have to talk to the federal marshals. Remember, I'm not out of danger. You can't tell anyone, not..."

"Not even my family. I know. Your secret is safe with me."

"At least we'll be neighbors while you're here."

"Ellie's family is so generous. They said I may stay in the house as long as I want. They won't even accept rent. And who knew I'd ever be a pet parent to a black cat!"

"You found their daughter's killer. That's big."

"Want some wine? I have a cork screw handy." She poured the wine and sat down in front of the fire next to Travis.

"Sara, you look especially beautiful tonight. Can I tell you something?"

"Of course."

"I think we might…Maybe…."

She soaked in the delicious smell of his woodsy cologne and moved in closer. She held his face and pulled him into her. When she felt his warm lips against hers, her heart fluttered like a metronome on steroids. She wanted to kiss him forever.

He pulled away. "Sara, what's that?"

She jumped up. "It's the fire alarm. My lasagna!" they ran into the kitchen.

"You're right. You really can't cook."

"Shut up! You try making lasagna from scratch while whipping up a cheesecake."

"Your mother manages it quite easily. I'm just saying…" He grabbed the fire extinguisher.

"I think you got it all."

"Yeah. No more flames. So you can't drive *and* you can't cook."

"I…You can…"

He pulled her close. "Just kidding. But I'm not sure about there being no more flames."

She looked into his chestnut eyes and melted right into his arms.

The End

PATTY'S LASAGNA
Contributed by reader Deanna Yearsly

<u>Ingredients</u>

1 box lasagna noodles
1 lb. shredded mozzarella cheese or a cheddar/mozzarella mix
2 large jars of red sauce
2 cans tomato paste
1 can tomato sauce
3 – 5 cloves of garlic, pressed
2 T oregano
2 T parsley flakes
1/2 cup onion, finely chopped, or grated for more flavor
1 T basil, rosemary & onion salt, blended (or mixed Italian spices)

<u>Steps</u>

1. In large pot, blend red sauce, tomato sauce, tomato paste, garlic, onion and spices and slow cook over low-medium heat for 2 – 3 hours, stirring frequently, until flavors are blended (for this you MUST taste test!)

2. In another large pot, bring salted water to a boil...add lasagna noodles and cook only until the noodles are pliable (overcooking will cause them to tear when assembling the lasagna)

3. Prepare a large baking dish by lightly spraying sides and bottom with olive oil spray.

Assembly

1. Begin by spooning a layer of sauce over the bottom of the baking dish

2. Follow that by spreading a layer of the shredded cheese over the sauce.

3. Drain and cool the lasagna noodles, until you can handle them without burning your fingers.

4. Lay noodles over the cheese (you may need to cut some of the noodles to fit the dish)

5. Cover the noodles with a liberal layer of sauce, then cheese, then more noodles; ending with the final layers of sauce and cheese.

6. Bake at 350 degrees for 45 – 70 minutes (ovens vary) until the sauce is bubbly and the top layer of cheese begins to brown.

Serve with a crisp salad and toasted garlic bread.

Variation

Spread ricotta cheese over the noodles before adding the sauce and shredded cheese. This is a little more time-consuming, but it is good that way, too.

SARA'S PLAY LIST

1. Bach, Johann Sebastian, *Oboe D'Amore Concerto in A Major BMV 1055*

2. Beethoven, Ludwig Van, *Symphony No. 3 in E flat Major, Op. 55*

3. Brahms, Johannes, *Symphony No. 2 in D Major, Op. 73*

4. Brahms, Johannes, *Symphony No. 4 in E minor, Op. 98*

5. Mahler, Gustav, *Symphony No. 4 in G Major*

6. Morricone, Ennio, *Gabriel's Oboe* from *The Mission*

7. Mozart, Wolfgang Amadeus, *Oboe Concerto in C Major*

8. Mozart, Wolfgang Amadeus, *The Marriage of Figaro: Overture, K492*

9. Prokofiev, Sergei, *Peter and the Wolf, Op. 67*

10. Rachmaninoff, Sergei, *Piano Concerto No. 2 in C Minor, Op. 18*

11. Ravel, Maurice, *Bolero*

12. Ravel, Maurice, *Daphnis and Chloe, Suite No. 2*

ABOUT THE AUTHOR

Award winning author Diane Weiner is a veteran public school teacher and mother of four grown children. Fond memories of reading mysteries by Nancy Drew and Mary Higgins Clark on snowy weekends in upstate New York inspired her to write books that would bring that kind of joy to others. Being an animal lover, she is a vegetarian and shares her home with two precious cats—Chelsea and Callie. In her free time, she enjoys running, shopping, attending theater productions, and spending time with her family.

Visit dianeweinerauthor.com to find out more about the author.

www.ingramcontent.com/pod-product-compliance
Lightning Source LLC
Chambersburg PA
CBHW020236260626
47156CB00002B/698